PR

The

'A strikingly assured and wonderfully original performance . . . the fascination with obsession and identity, doubling and impostors, acquires real charge, provoking larger questions about the nature of literary identity, fiction and fictionality, and finally—and most satisfyingly—the fictionality of authorship itself.' *The Australian*

'An audacious fictional memoir [that] moves flexibly between pathos, humour and suspense . . . there is always enough to drive the reader on to two shattering and unexpected denouements.' *SA Advertiser*

'Farcical, surreal and utterly unique.' *Readings Monthly*

'A richly imagined story of the friendship, fraud jealousy and betrayal within an extraordinary literary rivalry.' *West Australian*

'*The Lost Pages*' creative approach to the historical record is both disorienting and refreshing.' *Sydney Morning Herald*

Marija Peričić lives in Melbourne, where she teaches English as a foreign language. *The Lost Pages* is her first novel.

The Lost Pages

Marija Peričić

ALLEN&UNWIN
SYDNEY • MELBOURNE • AUCKLAND • LONDON

This edition published in 2018
First published in 2017

Allen & Unwin
83 Alexander Street
Crows Nest NSW 2065
Australia
Phone: (61 2) 8425 0100
Email: info@allenandunwin.com
Web: www.allenandunwin.com

 A catalogue record for this
book is available from the
National Library of Australia

ISBN 978 1 76063 335 6

Set in Garamond Premier Pro by Bookhouse, Sydney
Printed and bound in Australia by Griffin Press

10 9 8 7 6 5 4 3

The paper in this book is FSC® certified.
FSC® promotes environmentally responsible,
socially beneficial and economically viable
management of the world's forests.

For James R. Fleming

Foreword

FOR SCHOLARS OF KAFKA, THE NEWS OF THE FORTHCOMING release of the Kafka papers raised the tantalising prospect, however unlikely, of an undiscovered novel by the great author. The trial leading to the release of the papers was initiated principally by the Israeli National Library, whom I assisted, against the Hoffe/ Wiesler sisters. The sisters' possession of the papers has kept them from public view since Max Brod supposedly handed the papers to the mother of the Hoffe/Wiesler sisters in the 1960s, and the trial has once again focused the international spotlight on the legacy of Kafka. Hopes of a lost work were dashed, however, by the release of a documents list during the discovery stage of proceedings: the Kafka papers consist only of short notes, drawings and a memoir— the latter not by Kafka but by Brod. Yet this memoir of Brod's was for me a more exciting prospect still.

Franz Kafka is undoubtedly the most important figure in modern German-language literature, but the survival of his work is only due to the lesser-known Brod. As the story goes, when Kafka lay in bed dying of tuberculosis, his friend Brod at his bedside, his last words were, 'Burn all my work—everything—and spare none of it.' Thankfully, Brod defied the instruction. At that time, only a few of Kafka's short stories, including 'The Metamorphosis', had been published and this only with Brod's help.

Brod did much to establish Kafka's place in the literary firmament, promoting his young protégé as he sought out publishers, and editing his work, especially after Kafka's death. Kafka's posthumously published work includes such literary marvels as *The Trial*, *The Castle* and *Amerika*. Many of these works were finished by Brod's own hand, and certainly none escaped his influence.

If Brod was so central to the emergence of the towering literary heavyweight that Kafka would become, then the nature of the man to whom this great task fell is naturally of some curiosity. Those tempted to associate Kafka with his characters—the self-loathing, insect-like figure of 'The Metamorphosis' or the tortured soul in 'A Hunger Artist'—might be surprised by his contemporaries' description of a confident, charming, cheerful and handsome young man. In reality, Brod was the one who struggled with crippling anxieties, and chronic psychological and physical difficulties.

While Brod's novels and, to a lesser extent, his musical compositions achieved popularity and acclaim in his lifetime, they are of comparatively little interest today. And this is one of many reasons that the public release of Brod's memoirs from the contested Kafka papers should be tantalising. The question on my mind as I await the prospect of reading them is not so much what more they reveal of Kafka, for we already know much about him, but what they will tell us about the man behind him; the man striving to cultivate the talent he must have known would one day completely eclipse his own.

Professor Wendell Persson
University of Kent

Editor's note

THE PAGES THAT APPEAR HERE HAVE BEEN TRANSLATED FROM THE German. They come from a series of notes handwritten in exercise books, which also contain a number of loose sheets of notepaper, photographs and other documents, which together, make up Max Brod's memoirs. The material is in fair condition, considering its age, although there are some areas of illegibility due to water damage and ageing of the paper. Some sections of the papers are also presented in nearly illegible handwriting. Areas where approximations have been made are indicated in the text.

The translation and verification process of these papers has been a slow one to date, partly due to the poor quality of some of the documents in the archive and their disorganisation. This section represents the first coherent manuscript from the collection that has been translated, and will shortly be available for online access—as will, in time, the rest of the Kafka papers.

I.

I STILL REMEMBER THE FIRST TIME I SAW FRANZ; A DAY THAT seems now either the beginning of or the beginning of the end of my life's misfortune. It was October, when the days are still bright and sharp, and Prague was just beginning to fall into the quiet embrace of autumn. At that time I was writing a book about Schopenhauer, and I was to give a lecture on the subject. I had studied Schopenhauer since my university days and, although I am no authority on the man and his theories, I certainly know more about him than most. The lecture room where the talk was to take place was small but crowded, and the shuffling of bodies and the scratching of pens on paper formed a constant accompaniment to my voice.

I had hardly been speaking ten minutes when a voice sang out from somewhere at the back of the crowd.

'You idiot!'

The outburst caused me to pause momentarily. I had just mentioned in passing Schopenhauer's assertion that this world was the worst of all possible worlds, since a worse world could not continue to exist—an idea with which I happen to agree, its flaws notwithstanding. I decided to ignore the man and push on with my lecture. Perhaps I had misheard.

But I had not. After a moment he called out again.

'What a load of shit. Any fool can argue against that.'

The heckler was blocked from my view, but his voice was young and self-important. People began shifting in their seats and craning their necks to look at him. I had given many lectures and talks, but this had never happened to me before and I did not know what to do. Was it better to ignore the heckler and continue, or to answer him? I stood, hesitating. By now the heckler had taken the attention of a good part of the room, which from my perspective had transformed from rows of faces to rows of head-backs and collars.

His voice came once more.

'You are a fool if you truly believe that. There is an infinite number of possible worlds that are worse than this.'

I cleared my throat. 'Well,' I began, 'problems do exist with—'

'Consider yourself personally,' he interrupted.

He stood up and I saw him for the first time. He was of a slight build, dark and handsome in a somewhat delicate way. His handsomeness surprised and angered me.

He went on, 'I could name a thousand things that could be changed about the world that would make the world worse for you, and it would still continue to exist. You could lose your voice, for example.'

There were a few scattered laughs from the audience. I ignored them.

'But of course Schopenhauer is not referring to individuals; greater human existence is his theme,' I said.

'It is merely an example,' he said. 'There could be incremental changes in any condition in the world—choose any one!—and still we would go on. Things can always be a little worse.'

He sat down again, seeming to be satisfied with having voiced his disagreement. I struggled to appear composed, and wavered between countering him, which I felt compelled to do, or ignoring him, which I knew was the more dignified approach. His face peered out from the crowd, goading me, but I resolutely turned my eyes back to my page of notes. For the rest of the lecture, the heckler limited himself to snorts and noisy sighs, but I had nevertheless lost the attention of most of the room. Each of the heckler's percussive snorts would trigger a chorus of smiles and whispers in the crowd, and by the time I had reached the end of my talk I felt that he had certainly made the world of my evening worse than it could have been.

I was expecting a volley of questions from him during the question time at the end, and braced myself, but he remained silent; indeed, he seemed to have disappeared. Now I could see only a gap in the crowd where his dark head had been. As soon as I left the lecture hall, however, there he was again. He lunged out from the shadows of the corridor and tried to block my way, but I was able to dodge around him. I heard him scurrying after me, calling out my name and then an apology. I walked on. He followed me outside, where he fell into step beside me on the footpath and began to talk about my novel, which had had some success the year before. He flattered me in an ingratiating tone that I hated, but he piled his

3

pretty words up and up, and soon I had fallen into his trap. I am as vain as the next man and, because I have no grounds for pride on any other front in my life, my writing is my weak spot. Later, when everything lay ruined around me, I thought often about how my life would have been different had I not spoken to Franz* that night, had I been able to resist him.

He walked with me all the way to my house, and when we were at the door he thrust a sheaf of papers at me—his short stories, he said. He asked me to look over them, perhaps show them to my publisher. This had happened to me a good deal since the success of my novel; I admit that I always felt a bloom of pleasure at the request, especially with the inevitable realisation that the stories or poems or novels that were pressed on me were no good—or at least nowhere near as good as my own writing. I acceded to Franz's request in an offhand way, and then promptly lost the stories among the drifts of paper that covered my desk.

A few weeks later, I found his short stories again and read them, not remembering at first what they were. As my eyes passed over the pages a slow horror grew in me, sending my body cold. The stories were not merely good; they were exceptional. I read them again, and then sat for a long time with the papers in my hands. I turned to the title page and stared at the name printed there: *Franz Kafka*. How that name would come to haunt me.

I could tell you that I was moved and instantly sent the works to Theodor, my publisher; that I hastened to have Kafka's work

---

* In the manuscripts Franz Kafka appears as 'F.K.' or 'F-'; we have replaced this with his first name in the interest of consistency.

4

brought out into the world; that I eagerly welcomed what was to become such an important addition to the modern German canon. I could tell you that I felt pleased and proud to bring his work to light, but it would be a lie. All I felt was the sick poison of jealousy, the panic of self-preservation, and a determination to stop Franz at all costs. To show these stories to Theodor would have meant certain death for my literary career, which was at a critical stage. I had had one success, it was true, but now I faced the enormous pressure of cementing my literary reputation with an equally brilliant second work. I began to have nightmares about Franz: of him meeting Theodor, and the two of them conspiring to thwart me; of Theodor telling me that he was no longer interested in me; of Franz taking my place. I would wake from these dreams breathless and rigid. A terrifying abyss seemed to open in front of me; if I lost my status as a writer, what did I have left?

I wanted to destroy Franz's stories, and I thought often about it, but I had not yet sunk quite so low. Instead I stuffed them into the drawer of my writing table and locked it. I can say nothing much in my own defence, only that I have not been a fortunate man, nor a happy one, and I was fixed on defending to the death what little I had wrested from the world.

It turned out that even if I had burned the stories, as I had wanted to, it would not have made the slightest difference. Even without my help, they found their way into print. Some months later, I was invited to the launch of the new edition of *Hyperion*, to which I had contributed, and in which I saw Franz had published his first story. I had been reluctant to attend the party, knowing there was a strong likelihood that both Franz and Theodor would be there. The thought of being present as Theodor and Franz met, watching them smiling at one another and shaking hands, made me suffer with the hot jealousy of spurned love. But the alternative was to stay away from the party, which would mean that this meeting would take place out of my view, leaving my imagination free to adorn and amplify, as I knew it would, to the point of madness. I decided that, no matter now distasteful the occasion might be, it was better to be present. It was also prudent, I knew, to appear pleased at the coming union, and to keep Franz close—to make a friend of him, in fact. I braced myself, and on that Thursday evening I set out, a sick feeling in my stomach.

The party was being held at the Café Slavia. I had arrived on foot, walking for part of the way along the Moldau, the slide of its black water keeping pace with my step. It was a clear night, and cold, and the slick river was like a sheet of moving glass, the surface so smooth that the orbs of lamplight mirrored in it were no less solid and steady than the light of the real lamps high on the bank.

Couples and small groups hustled along either bank on their way to the theatre or the opera, and the swinging skirts of the women corresponded in some musical way with the swaying of the trees above their heads. Ahead of me, I could see the bright lights spilling from the café windows, making orange tongues on the footpath. When I arrived at the Slavia, my legs were already aching from the walk, and I longed for a chair, but still I stood, composing myself, on the corner of the street. I could feel the compact bulk

6

of the National Theatre rearing up into the empty sky behind me, compressing the air around it. The dark awnings above the café windows swayed like flags. The windows were uncurtained, and I saw the little tableau of a party scene. A woman held a small glass poised at her lips, her pale wrist an elegant curve against her dark-clad breast. A man leaned over her shoulder in the act of whispering something to her. Behind her, two men embraced and clapped each other on the back in a syncopated pattern.

Bursts of laughter and music trickled out of the café onto the street. Then the doors swung open, letting out a blast of heat and noise, and two men came out onto the footpath. I saw them look at me and felt immediately ashamed of my solitary watching. I caught the doors as they were swinging closed and plunged inside.

I had not even managed to find a drink for myself before I was set upon by a small group, eager to claim me. They clustered around and gave me their opinions of my novel and quizzed me on what I was writing now. While I spoke, I was the whole time surreptitiously looking around for Franz, but I could not see him. The room was very crowded and I felt an urgent need to find him. With difficulty, I extricated myself from the group around me and slowly struggled through the crush in search of him, impeded every few steps by someone wanting to congratulate me on my book or ask my opinion on their story in the magazine.

Stacks of *Hyperion* stood on tables. The idea of Franz's story printed there beside mine roused a gnawing resentment that was hard to ignore. I tried to imagine how Franz must feel about his first publication. I remembered that, when I had first seen my own book in print, I had thought it to be the best moment of my life, and, looking back now, perhaps it was. The smooth and solid surface of the book, my book, had seemed to give off a radiant energy that was absorbed by the skin on my hands and fingers, and travelled up my arm into my chest, where it expanded to warm and relax me, as though it were a narcotic. I had taken up a copy, and gripped it first in one hand and then both, feeling its weight, the texture of the cover. I opened it and ran my fingertips and palms over the pages like a blind man. I held the book up to my face and fanned the pages and breathed in the smell of paper and ink. And it was not a question of just one book; the boxes on the floor of the publisher's office were full of copies, the cover-pages and spines made unreal by their repetition. Theodor had laughed.

'I often feel I should leave the room when first-time authors see their work in print. I feel like I'm intruding on a lovers' tryst,' he had said. His polished face, egg-like, had shone with good humour.

There seemed to be no sign of Franz, or Theodor either, for that matter. I would have been quite happy not to have to see Theodor at all: he would certainly be keen to remind me of my approaching deadline. Lately, the process of writing had become mysterious to me, and at times it felt fraudulent to call myself a writer at all. Most of the time I could not quite believe that I had produced the book that had brought me such success, and I could not understand how I had done it. Looking at the book now was like looking at some complicated mechanical object and being told that I had built it, when I understood not the first thing about its inner workings or how it was put together.

I stood there and scanned the room. Suddenly the crowd shifted and I could make out a plump figure on the far side of the room.

It was Uta. She was struggling along, her elbows protruding at awkward angles to shelter the two glasses of schnapps that she was ferrying towards me. The sight of her immediately caused a small knot of muscles in my neck and shoulders to contract in an unpleasant spasm, and I had the impulse to duck behind someone or run from the room. I turned my back to her, hoping, uselessly, to make myself invisible. My body tensed in anticipation of her approach.

Once, at some long-ago point in my life, I might have found Uta attractive, in desperate circumstances with limited light. She was blonde and round with sticky, pinkish skin and a penetrating voice of calculated vivaciousness. I had first come across her at one of the earlier public readings I had given from my novel. At that stage, I was still overwhelmed by the amount of attention I was receiving, particularly female attention, and had, I now saw, responded to her far too warmly. She began to shadow me and attend every reading I gave, besieging me with questions and coy turns of her head. Soon she was appearing regularly on my street at just the moment I was leaving the house to go to work. I would see her everywhere: on the tram, walking on the Laurenziberg, in cafés I frequented. When these tactics of hers brought no return of her affection she managed to befriend my sister Sophie, using her to gain access to my home. Sophie is a girl of infinite kindness and, through her, Uta rapidly won the acceptance of the rest of my family, who were soon loudly proclaiming her charms. To me she seemed like a pestilent cloud that blew through the city, to be avoided at all costs.

I sensed a commotion in the crowd behind me and braced myself for the inevitable tap, which soon came. I made an effort to affix an expression of friendly politeness to my face and turned, groaning inwardly and already planning my escape, but my eyes fell not upon Uta's frizzed blonde hair and pouting lips but on another face altogether. It was shaped like a heart, with wide cheeks slanting to a little pointed chin, and eyes that were dark and warm: black, with flecks of gold. The eyebrows flew out over them in two straight wings, grave and intense, but the pink lips twitched up at the corners, parted, with two white tooth tips visible within.

'Excuse me,' the woman said to me, 'but are you Herr Kafka?'

I was stunned, able only to look at her.* The beauty of her face burned into me like a flame, and I wondered that people did not collapse in the street at the sight of it. She was like a woman in a Philipp Veit painting: gentle, and with an air of such sweet melancholy that I wanted to reach out and touch her.

She spoke to me, and for a moment I simply stood and listened to the sound of her voice as though it were music, without understanding the words she uttered. The timbre of her voice was unusually low, with a pleasant burring undertone. If it were the voice of an instrument, it would be a cello, slow and quiet. When the meaning of her words reached me, I realised she was praising Franz's story.

'I'm sorry,' I said, interrupting her. 'I am Brod. Max Brod. But Kafka is a very good friend of mine.' I extended my hand, which until then had hung paralysed by my side. She shook it, and

---

* This sentence is crossed out in the manuscript.

introduced herself as Fräulein Anja Železný, but I thought I caught a flash of disappointment in her eyes.

While I still held her hand clasped in mine, I felt another tap on my shoulder, and this time when I turned I was greeted with the face that I had been expecting earlier. The closeness of the room had deposited a shining film over Uta's pink complexion and small beads of perspiration studded the down that grew on the upper corners of her mouth. She stood very close to me and handed me one of the glasses of schnapps, inserting her body at an angle that blocked me from Fräulein Železný.

She gave a pouting smile that left her eyes unmoved and began in a loud voice to talk some familiar nonsense of my family, seeking to display a closeness between us that was pure fiction. Uta's voice droned on and on, with the high-pitched cadences of an unpleasant insect trapped in a summer room, beating its head against the hot glass of the windows. After a while I gave up trying to interject and fell silent, hoping for rescue.

With relief, I spotted Theodor fighting his way through the crowd towards me. Though I was keen to avoid Theodor's questions about my work in progress, this feeling was now outweighed by my desperation to get away from Uta. I was also quite anxious to learn if he had met Franz yet. There still seemed to be no sign of Franz at the party, but the room was far too packed for me to be certain. Of course, by this stage it was inevitable that Theodor had read Franz's work. I could even see a rolled copy of *Hyperion* in his hand. I greeted him with excessive warmth, grasping his hand with both of mine, and soon Uta drifted off sulkily. As I had expected, Theodor's main objective was to reprimand me for my failure to produce a finished manuscript, but I smoothed over my difficulties with a slick of lies. I waved my hands about and made much of how well it was proceeding, and, surprising myself, was even able to improvise some ideas that sounded moderately plausible.

When it seemed that I had satisfied him, I asked, 'So, have you had the fortune to meet with the great prodigy? Kafka, I mean.'

'Ha! The great prodigy is a hard man to pin down, it happens. I have not yet had the pleasure. I try and try, but he strings me along like a heartbreaker.' He shook his head in a sorrow that was not entirely false. Franz's evasiveness clearly bewildered Theodor, who was used to being courted by would-be writers to the point of harassment. From time to time I noticed his eyes darting through the crowd behind me in a vain search, his eyebrows tensed and lips pursed.

'I've been trying to get hold of the fellow for weeks,' he went on. 'I write letters and invite him for lunch, I go to every party, but nothing. The man's like a ghost.'

'Perhaps someone else has got to him first,' I said, voicing my own fears.

Theodor shook his head. 'Impossible. I'm keeping a close eye on this one. I hope that he's so hard to catch because he's locked in a room somewhere, pumping out some more of these.' He waved his copy of *Hyperion*. 'Anyway,' he continued, 'you should be happy that he's not here: less competition.' He looked at his watch. 'But I must go. Will you tell him, if you see him, that I would very much like to meet him?'

He laughed when he saw my expression. 'Don't worry, my friend,' he said. 'I still love your work the most.'

My face darkened with shame.

Theodor began to make for the door, but he was too slow, and soon he was corralled against the window by a little half-moon of hopeful writers, vying with each other for his attention, while he struggled to get away.

I should have been relieved that the meeting I had dreaded was not to take place that evening, but in fact I felt worse. Franz's shunning of the party was as incomprehensible to me as it seemed to be to Theodor, and fed into my raging jealousy. I imagined Franz sitting high above me like some king, lofty and unconcerned, as he was courted from all sides, while I, below him, toiled along in the dusty wastes, labouring over every line, craving acknowledgment.

Standing alone in the crowd made me feel vulnerable to a renewed offensive from Uta; she was sure to be watching me from some hidden vantage point. I remembered Fräulein Železný, and looked around, but I am not a tall man and was rewarded only with maddening glimpses of slim arms or knots of dark hair. I noticed my legs beginning to ache again from the prolonged standing and considered leaving, but at that moment a movement in the crowd gave me a clear glimpse of Fräulein Železný: she was standing at one of the windows, looking out. She was as brightly lit as though she were on a stage,* but an instant later the bodies surged together again and she was lost from my view. I fixed on the direction of the windows and began to squeeze my way through, murmuring apologies as I pushed people aside with increasing urgency. It

---

* In the space below the text there are several small pencil sketches of a woman's head in profile.

seemed to take hours to cross the room, and when I arrived at the window, instead of Fräulein Železný, I found only a little group of actors from the theatre, drunkenly toasting each other and spilling their schnapps on the floor. I saw the café doors swinging closed on the other side of the room as someone left the party. Was it Fräulein Železný? I felt sure it had been. The room seemed dulled and flattened somehow with her absence, as though someone had turned off a bright light, and people's voices now seemed shrill and echoing.

I stood with my back against the wall, watching the undulating crowd, their heads and mouths animated in conversation, and hands lifting and lowering glasses to their mouths. I could see no one who I knew. I felt completely drained of energy. My legs and the right side of my body now radiated with a pain that would not be ignored. I quietly collected my coat and left, without bothering to take my leave of anyone.

Outside the damp air of the river blew in my face and a dirty fog had rolled in. The Franzensbrücke rose up indistinctly, like a fairy-tale bridge that would melt under your feet when you tried to cross it, and its lamps hung like tired moons. I walked slowly up Postgasse, steadying myself against the walls as I went.

My body was tight with anxiety on the walk home and my mind ran over and over the problem of Franz. Although Franz and Theodor had not met, and thus I should be glad, I was not. I saw that the encounter between the two men had merely been delayed, pulled out into the future, where it lay in wait for me once more.

Where could he have been that night? If I were him, I would certainly have wanted to celebrate my first publication, to bask in the attentions of Theodor and the others at the party. I remembered Franz's insistence when he had thrust those stories upon me all those months ago; surely this slow unfurling of recognition was what he had been aiming for? It was both puzzling and rankling. I could still see the look of naked longing on Theodor's face as he scanned the room for Franz; he had certainly never looked for me in that way, even in the beginning—not that I had ever given him the opportunity to seek me out. I had always been the more eager one, the one doing the chasing. Franz's absence began to seem like a personal insult to my own fierce ambition.

By now I had arrived home. Everyone was asleep. Even Elsa, the housemaid, had retired for the night, and the only sound was the uneven ticking of the loud clock that stood in the parlour. I creaked my way slowly up the stairs to my bedroom. As soon as I opened the door, my eyes fell on a glowing white object that lay in the middle of the floor. Without even turning on the lamp, I could see that it was a parcel, and when I picked it up I saw that it was from Franz. It was a thick bundle of papers—more stories—and the letter enclosed made no mention of the party he had missed. Why he would bother to send these stories to me after my lack of response to the previous ones was a mystery. Why court me at all when he had no difficulty getting published without my assistance? It was nonsensical. It seemed almost threatening. His persistence made me wary, but, contrary to my instinct to run, I decided that befriending him might be the best course of action.

2.

SEEING THEODOR AT THE PARTY HAD MADE ME ANXIOUS[*] TO continue again with my own writing, which I had neglected for some weeks. At that time I had put down some ideas that I had thought were quite promising, and had filled several notebooks with pages of notes and plans, but I was still having difficulty fitting everything together. My first book had been a work of fiction of the most conventional sort, but I had, in the interim, written some essays on different philosophical subjects, particularly on Schopenhauer, and I wanted my second work to be a grand avant-garde novel that would blend philosophy and fiction into a totally new form. I was especially interested in Schopenhauer's ideas of representation and reality, and felt that incorporating these into the inner life of a fictional character was the perfect way to examine them.

But no—when I read back over the paragraph I have just written I realise that it is misleading. It is true that my first novel

---

[*] This word is unclear: it has been crossed out and written over.

was conventional, and it is true that I had grand ideas about Schopenhauer and fiction, and had been excited and interested in the idea for this second novel, but the fact was that I had by this time become bored; bored and also desperate. The success of my first novel, *Schloß Nornepygge*, had completely transformed my existence; I could almost say that I had barely been alive before it, when I was only Max Brod: postal official. And, as Theodor was constantly reminding me, my name as a novelist was slowly fading, by the day, by the minute, and I dreaded being relegated to obscurity as one dreads poverty or illness.

When I returned home from work the day after the party, I told Elsa that I was not to be disturbed and locked myself in my study. I am a habitual worker when it comes to writing and most of my work has been completed in that study, at the old writing table that had been my grandfather's. The table was of such a size that it seemed to possess a personality of its own, like a large and docile animal crouched in the centre of the room, waiting for me to arrive. I occasionally felt the urge to pat its leather top as one would pat a faithful old horse or dog.

I sat down and took out my notes, hopeful and ready to begin. But when I looked at them I found that what had seemed a few weeks ago to be coherent and promising plans were now nothing but pages of vague scribblings of unconnected ideas. I could no longer trace my old thoughts, and the threads that had seemed so clear to me earlier now wandered directionless and I could not follow their logic. Even my own handwriting was suddenly difficult to decipher. I tried to focus. I sat up straight in my chair and grasped the pages firmly. I bent my head over my notes and forced myself to read again from the beginning, but my mind kept switching off, and soon I was staring at the paper without seeing the words upon it.

My gaze drifted to the wall in front of me, my mind as blank as if it were sedated. I took in the minute details of the wallpaper's topography. My eyes, outside of my control, travelled up and down the light stripes of the wallpaper's design, shifting them in and out of focus. I became aware of the tick of the clock in the parlour, which slowly grew louder and then became syncopated with the scrabble and gnaw of some insect's jaws at work on the inner beams of the house.

Schopenhauer. I conjured up the image of the man, the photograph that was etched on the frontispiece of my copy of *The World as Will and Representation*. He looked sternly out from under the great cliffs of his eyebrows, undisturbed by the clouds of fluffy white hair that shot wildly out from either side of his head. His mouth was a grim line of concentration.

'Max,' his voice boomed out at me, 'concentrate. Will. Will to live. Will to write.'

At that moment I had no will. Only perhaps the will to sleep. I felt the profound exhaustion of one who has been working for hours.

I began to tidy the papers on my desk, telling myself that when it was all straight and neat, then I would be able to begin. I felt quite virtuous as I sat sorting out papers and exercise books, creating a little ordered pile and making more of the surface of the table free. I pulled out a fat bundle and saw that it was Franz's manuscript. The thickness of the pages between my fingers made my jaw clench tight with a spasm of raw envy. Cautiously, in the manner of one examining a wound, I took the papers out of their wrapping and began to read. The story was too good. When I had finished, I put it down on the table. I could hear the blood roaring in my ears. I watched my hand steal out and take hold of the pen and lower it to the page. A line emerged from the pen, a line of shining blue ink that intersected with the dried black shapes on the paper. A word was crossed out. I crossed it out again. Then another. The blood was pounding through my head, but my hand moved with precision. A curving blue line now ran across the page, making small tears in the paper. Then the next page lay before me, dry and black and white at first, but soon covered with glossy blue, unreadable. Page after page came faster and faster, and the rustle of the papers had soon drowned out the roaring in my head.

I must have fallen asleep or lost consciousness, for I heard a voice saying my name close in my ear. The next moment I was looking upon an arid desert landscape that was spread out below me, over which I seemed to be flying. I became absorbed in its features, boulders and mountain ranges, but after a moment the perspective shifted and the landscape resolved itself into the underside of the chair upon which I had been sitting, and I found that I was lying curled on the floor with my head underneath it. I lay for a moment, looking at the unfinished wood and dusty canvas of the underside of the seat. My mind and body retained the dim ghost of some euphoria, of a dream that had fled from me but left its evasive imprint. Lying in its warm glow I felt completely relaxed and relieved of all burdens. This feeling gradually faded and soon my body began to feel cold and stiff, host to a catalogue of familiar pains and discomforts. I rolled awkwardly out and straightened myself up into a sitting position.

Paper was scattered across the desk and formed tessellated patterns on the carpet. I began to gather up the torn pages of Franz's story. Some had fallen face down beside the writing table, and when I lifted them up I saw that the carpet beneath them was stained with ink. The writing that covered the pages, dense blue lines of it, was now smudged, but still legible.

I began to read it with difficulty, and, as I read, I felt a sensation of lightness and expansion in my head. My body became unreal to me, my hands, my fingers, blue-tipped holding the papers, were foreign, no longer belonging to me. The phrases that I read, though they were plainly before me in my own handwriting, were new to me. I had never seen them before.*

The story was completely unlike anything I had ever written, crystallising private sides of myself that were barely conscious to me and that I would never dare commit to paper. An uneasy sensation grew in me, one of being watched by an observer hidden in the dim and silent room. My skin contracted and I began to shiver. Phantom shadows danced in the gloomy corners of the room and I turned up the lamp, feeling ridiculous. I forced my movements into deliberate slowness, trying to reassure myself, but my breath and heartbeats were ragged. A loud bang came suddenly from the fastened window. It was only the night-time wind, I knew, pushing at the glass that was loose in the frame, but I jumped as though I were under fire. My hands shook as I tried to collect the fallen pages from all around me. My ears began to ring and I soon abandoned my measured

---

* This sentence is followed by several others that have been heavily crossed out and are illegible.

pace and hastily grabbed at the pages of Franz's ruined manuscript. I bundled them up roughly and crumpled them into an untidy pile on the writing table. They hissed at me for my rough treatment of them. I took the pages covered in my writing and shoved them in the drawer and locked it, as though I feared some contagion that dwelled in their pages might leak out and poison the air.

3.

THE NEXT DAY I SAT AT MY DESK AT THE POST OFFICE COMPLETELY
exhausted. After my fainting fit, I had gone straight to bed but I had
not been able to sleep. I had felt hot and cold by turns. Indistinct
pains travelled up one side of my restless body and then the other.
The skin of my feet became so excessively sensitive that the weight
and movement of the bedclothes upon it was almost intolerable.
Every position that I adopted quickly became unbearable, and the
night was endlessly long, each minute stretched out by discomfort.
My mind ran over and over the story that had appeared to me
and I tried to consider it rationally, but my mind ran stupidly in
circles. I drifted along loosely connected lines of thought, picked
out in bright strings on a black background; not quite dreams but
not quite thoughts either.

Elsa woke me when it was already quite late, and in the light
of day the story seemed a product of my long, restless night. I no
longer believed that it had happened. Before breakfast I went into
the study, expecting the locked drawer to be empty, but the pages

covered with dense lines of blue ink were exactly where I had left them. I read a few lines, and the feeling of reading my own writing still unsettled me, even in the brightness of day.

At the post office, I sat and dozed the whole morning through, unable to concentrate. Once again I was thankful for the mercies of having my own office. I had been in my position at the post office for more than four years and had settled into an easy work life there. At that time I considered it imperative to keep my writing separate from the need to earn money, rather than using it as a means to do so. There were many benefits of my position at the post office that were well suited to my writing vocation. I found the work easy and could complete the allotted workload in less than the time expected without any difficulty. I kept my quickness a secret and used the time that I had won to write undetected in my office during the workday.

As I sat there that morning I was aware of my briefcase propped up under the desk. It contained my story from the night before, and I pictured the white pages making a pale ghost in the dark leather cavern of the briefcase pocket. The air around the briefcase seemed to prickle with contained energy. The thought of the pages by my feet gave me a sinister feeling, and I had the impression that they were emitting a malignant energy that was being absorbed by my body. I felt an absurd reluctance to open my briefcase.

'Don't be an idiot,' I muttered aloud to myself and picked up the briefcase. I could not help but attribute some strange magic or sentience to those pages, and I would not have been surprised to look at them again now and find them blank or covered with a completely different writing altogether, perhaps even in a language unknown to me. I undid the clasp with a beating heart and pulled out the loose bundle of pages.

There came a knock at the door. I knew by the characteristic percussive sequence that it was Stephanie, the stenographer from the adjacent office, a vapid girl whose skin strained to contain her plumpness. I straightened myself and adopted a serious expression, the briefcase and papers hidden from view in my lap. But instead of Stephanie's blonde head at the door, I was surprised to see Franz enter.

He seemed to flow around the door like an eddy of water around a stone. His lean, flat body moved with a fluidity that made me conscious of the smooth muscles surging under his skin, effortlessly controlling the levers of his bones. He seated himself opposite me with the nonchalance of a regular visitor.

'So, did you get the story I sent you?' he asked, not even bothering to greet me. 'Is that it in there?' He pointed at the papers in my lap.

Blood flowed to my face. 'No, ah . . . these are something else,' I said as I stuffed the pages back into my briefcase, fumbling with the clasp.

Franz's appearance in my office disoriented me. How had he discovered my place of work? And he spoke to me with such casual familiarity, even using the informal mode of address. It was almost as though he had mistaken me for someone else.

'Oh well,' he said, 'never mind about the stories now. I've come to impart a fantastic piece of news.'

I sat with the briefcase still on my lap and tried to compose myself. Although I was by no measure happy to see him, I remembered my resolve to make a friend of him. I forced my face into a smile.

He took an envelope from his jacket pocket. 'Yesterday, I got this—' he paused and held it up in the air—'from your old friend Theodor. He wants some of my stories for a collection, an actual book.'

He leaned back in the chair, radiating satisfaction, and the leather squeaked to accommodate him. He slid the envelope back into his pocket.

Even though I could not say that I was surprised, Franz's news gave me an unpleasant shock, and it was an effort to keep my face fixed into the friendly expression of encouragement that I had conjured. I felt betrayed by Theodor. Franz, harmless though he looked, loomed large and threatening; it appeared that he could, with a flick of his finger, destroy everything that I had taken years to build up. My impulse was to order him from the room or to leave the room myself, slamming the door. But this would be unwise.

Questions swarmed up in my mind. How much of Franz's work had Theodor seen? The fact that Theodor would go to such efforts to hunt Franz down and secure him seemed to indicate that he must also have read the stories that Franz had given me. What would this mean in regards to my own position? Had Theodor and Franz already met? The fact that the proposal had come in a letter allowed me the hope that they had not. And had a contract been included; was it already signed? I was desperate to know, but I was aware I had to be careful not to betray my anxiety. I breathed out slowly and clenched my fingers into two tight knots in my lap. I felt the muscles in my forearms straining with pressure.

Franz sat there like a snake in the chair, his unblinking eyes on mine, waiting. I had to keep him close, I knew, either to destroy him or to save myself somehow. I stood up and offered him my hand, and we shook hands across my desk.

'Let me invite you for a drink to celebrate,' I said.

We made for the beer hall in the cellar of the Gemeindehaus. As we walked along Wenzelsplatz to the Konigshof, Franz shared his ideas for the stories he was planning for the proposed collection. Listening to him, there was a numbed, hard feeling in my breast—fear, I suppose—which emerged and was then smoothed over again, like a jagged stone lying below the surface of the sea, covered and uncovered by waves.

As he talked, his plans became more and more ambitious, and he mentioned that he was also working on a longer piece, of a kind never seen before, which would forever change the face of literature. I listened with half an ear while I thought of ways to casually question him about the nature of Theodor's offer. Perhaps it was only an offhand politeness of Theodor's. If only I could take a look at the letter. Surely I could ask him to show it to me if I framed my request as friendly interest. After a few beers, perhaps. Or else, if he removed his jacket when we were inside, I could quickly take a look while he was in the bathroom.

The beer hall was packed and noisy. Everywhere men sat crammed against one another on the bench seats, the tables in front of them covered with empty glasses. We ordered our beers and squeezed in side-by-side at a crowded table in the middle of the room. Franz had removed his coat, but kept his jacket on. He drank steadily and, wishing to keep a clear head, I allowed him to outpace me. Franz was relaxed and voluble, and talked as though we two were old friends. I kept waiting for a gap in his monologue so I might steer the talk to the letter, but he never paused.

It was hot in the cellar, the humid heat of a roomful of drinking men, and I took off my jacket, hoping that Franz would follow suit—which, to my joy, he soon did. He laid it between us on the bench, beside mine. The breast of his jacket was folded back on itself, and I could see the tantalising edge of the envelope inside. I tried not to stare at it as he talked on. After some hours of speaking, he excused himself to use the bathroom. Now was my chance.

As soon I saw that he had left the room I grabbed for the jacket, but in my haste I pushed it to the floor, right under the table. I had to bend awkwardly into the tight space between the bench and the table to retrieve it and when I rose was met by a shout.

'Hey! You!' A red-faced man sitting on the opposite side of the table was pointing a fat finger in my direction. 'Gimme back my jacket! Are you trying to rob me?'

'This isn't yours,' I said, holding Franz's jacket up for him to see.

'I think I know my own clothes!' he shouted. He stood up and made a grab for the jacket, knocking over my empty beer glass as he pulled it towards himself over the table. I wanted to protest, but the man was a huge, hulking creature, apparently formed solely of overlapping layers of muscle.

'Sir,' I said, 'I do assure you, that jacket belongs to my friend,' but my voice was just a thin little quiver in the noise of the hall. The man ignored me. I was conscious that I had only a little time before Franz returned, and I could hear the loud ticking of every precious second as it slipped past.

The man's fleshy face was like a pink cabbage, contracted in concentration as he bundled the jacket this way and that, searching the lining for identifiable markers. His fussing had attracted the attention of his two friends, who sat on either side of him, and they both scowled at me across the table. I could not help risking a few nervous glances towards the door to see if Franz was coming back.

'What are you looking so antsy for then?' the friend on the left, a raw-skinned redhead, asked me.

But the fleshy-faced man gave a roar of laughter. 'It's alright, Karl. The gentleman's right.' He stood up and bowed, handing me the screwed-up jacket along with many apologies, but it was too late. Before I could sit down again, Franz was there beside me once more. He saw his jacket in my hands and absent-mindedly took it from me and put it on. I could have cried with frustration.

'So,' Franz asked, 'how was the *Hyperion* party?' His mouth was set in a smug line: he need not even make an appearance to have half of Prague chasing after him with publishing offers.

'It was fine,' I said. I breathed slowly in and out. 'We all wondered where you were. Especially Theodor.'

'I gathered as much.'

This could be my chance. 'Hence the letter,' I said, prompting him to go on, but he was silent. I continued, 'Have you had the pleasure of meeting Theodor yet?' I tried to sound casual and uninterested, but even I could hear the anxiety straining at every syllable. I wished I had not spoken.

Franz ignored my question. 'I heard that Uta was lavishing you with attention,' he said. He looked amused, and I felt the prickle of irritation that Uta always brought with her. I wondered how Franz had come to hear about her.

'Uta is a nice girl, but unfortunately I am allergic to her. She causes me to suffer from a terrible nausea when I am exposed to her for any length of time.'

Franz laughed at my joke, but it was true. I found there to be something viscerally repulsive about her; her flesh, or what I had seen of it, was too soft, too pliant, and gave off the fetid odour of overripe fruit.

I was at that time in the—for me—unfamiliar and privileged position of being able to reject women's advances, which, since I had become well known in literary circles, suddenly seemed to come from all around. This had the perplexing and wholly unexpected effect of making women far less attractive to me than before. A few years earlier I would never have dreamed that I would be plagued by such a lack of attraction to women.

In the days of my obscurity I was like a sensitive machine built to detect the attractive aspects that lay in all women, no matter how faint or tarnished, and then magnify them until the woman had become absolutely irresistible to me. No woman was spared— housemaids, flower sellers, the aged wives of my father's friends; it did not matter who they were, I would feel drawn to them for some minute characteristic that was so distilled, so rarefied that it barely existed.

I would happen to stand behind a woman on the tram, for example, and become captivated by the mobile curve of her neck, which ran from the lobe of her ear to her shoulder, and this curve would become the foundation of a whole lustful sequence of imagining. This sequence would grow and grow, and when the woman stepped down from the tram a few stops before my own destination I would feel a blind impulse to run after her, as though I would certainly die if I lost sight of her. Sometimes I actually would follow her, leaping from the tram at the last moment. My eyes would be riveted to her as I followed her through the crowd as if my gaze were a fine wire that was attached to her, and with which she pulled me along in her wake. Everything else around me—the streets, the crowds—would fade and disappear, until she suddenly turned into the doorway of some apartment building or office, and the connection would be broken. I would be left standing on the footpath, unmoored, with no idea where I was. This woman would linger in my memory until the next one took her place in an unending procession of unattainable objects of attraction, an unbreakable chain of frustration and thwarted desire.

After I became well known, though, women would approach me and I would feel nothing. I would desperately try to seek out things in them that would attract me, little hooks on which I hoped to snare myself, but I was invariably disappointed. Occasionally I would feel a hopeful stirring of interest but, at the sound of a too-shrill voice or a down-covered cheek, the interest would die away again.

The desire I felt at the party for Anja Železný was like a return to my old mode, and I welcomed it with a sense of relief. But with it, too, came attendant worries and anxieties. Would she return my affection? Might she already have a lover, or prefer someone else—Franz for instance. His handsomeness blazed out at me again, and I remembered the look on her face as she had searched the crowd for him.

I had no idea if Franz had a lover. Up until that night I had never thought of Franz in relation to anything other than writing. That he had emotions and relationships had never occurred to me, as if he did not exist in the world. It struck me that I would not like to have him for a sexual rival as well as a literary one. The possibility of him attracting the attention of Fräulein Železný the way that he had attracted Theodor made me forget all about the letter. My mind filled with paranoid thoughts of Franz and Anja together.

Though I knew it was unlikely, I had to ask Franz if he knew Fräulein Železný. I began to feel almost superstitious about the question: as though the only way to avert certain disaster was by asking, but I found that I did not know how to formulate the question. 'The nausea is a problem,' I said, and then added clumsily, 'but from Anja Železný I get not a hint of it.' I gulped at my beer to hide my embarrassment.

'Anja Železný,' he repeated, and began nodding slowly. I waited for him to continue, but he just reached for his beer, silently drank the dregs of it and then placed his glass down again. It made a hollow sound on the wooden table.

'Do you know her?' I hated myself for pressing him.

He picked up his empty glass and examined the sediment that lay at the bottom as if I had not spoken. My body was hot with embarrassment at having exposed my obvious interest.

'Uta, Anja,' he said. 'It looks as though you have too many women in your life. Too many is as bad as not enough.'

'I know which I would prefer.'

'In that case, shall we go now and find ourselves some more women?'

'Go? Where?'

'Corpse Lane. Don't tell me you've never passed through there on a midnight walk.'

Corpse Lane was the common name given to Der Hohler Weg, a narrow laneway that intersects the Little Quarter. It got its nickname long ago when it had been the thoroughfare to the local graveyard, now disused, and funeral processions used to pass along it. Corpse Lane's main traffic now was quite the opposite of bygone days; mostly young men, alone or in small groups, looking in the many windows of the houses there and examining the girls on display, girls that could be bought. Franz's assumption was correct: I had passed along Corpse Lane on several occasions. To make this journey was something of a rite of passage for the young men of my city, although for me undertaking that journey was always a source of shame.*

---

* This last paragraph was written in different ink, which has been verified as dating from the 1960s at the earliest. This suggests that Brod reviewed the material shortly before his death.

4.

WE LEFT THE BEER HALL AND CROSSED THE RIVER AT THE Karlsbrücke, which was almost deserted at that time of night. The statues of the saints that squatted along the walls raised their dark heads against the clouds and I felt uneasy passing under their stone gaze. On the other side of the river we climbed up the steep streets of the Little Quarter. There were no lights here, and hulks of broken buildings crowded the narrow and twisting lanes. It began to rain very gently. On my previous visits I had always come alone and furtively, with my coat collar pulled up and my hat pulled down and my heart shuddering as I hurried along, terrified of discovery. But Franz amazed me; his demeanour was of such calmness that he could have been walking anywhere, for any purpose. He sauntered along, loose-limbed, and nodded to passers-by as though he were taking a turn in the city park on a Sunday afternoon.

When we had entered the steep canyon of Corpse Lane, lighted windows began to appear above us, orange and pink squares on the black walls that framed here one pretty girl plaiting her dark hair, and there an older girl, less pretty, her elbows resting on the windowsill as she looked out into the dark. Some of them called down to us, and Franz would respond with a little joke, evading them.

After we had passed what seemed to me a hundred lighted windows and heard a hundred voices calling to us, Franz stopped outside a corner house. He looked up at it.

'This is the place,' he said. 'The girls here . . .' He made an appreciative gesture with his lips and fingers.

He stepped up to the door and knocked, and then took off his hat and beat it against his leg to shake it free of raindrops. The madam of the house opened the door. She was a thin woman whose extremely small stature was apparent despite her high-heeled boots and the mountain of hair piled onto the top of her head. She greeted Franz as though she recognised him and they started chatting like old friends.

I had remained standing in the lane, looking up at the dark old house. It too held a lighted window that framed a girl. This one was very young. Her face was gentle and her body was a collection of flowing arcs and curves enclosed in polished skin. She was absorbed in fastening a ribbon around her slender neck, her head bent and her hair falling over one shoulder. She must have been around the same age as my sister Sophie. It pained my heart to think of Sophie and to know that this girl in the window once, and perhaps still, had a mother and father and perhaps brothers somewhere who worried about her and wanted to protect her. It pained me that I could know this yet still desire her all the same.

Her animal sense felt my eyes on her and she turned and looked down at us. I saw her look first at Franz and take in his upright bearing and the cut of his clothes. Then she looked at me. Revulsion flashed across her face. I instinctively readjusted my position to make myself appear more unobtrusive, hating myself for doing it. I saw myself through the girl's eyes as I stood there beside Franz. I saw how she must be anticipating with disgust the moment that she would be obliged to touch me and feel my body pressed against hers, how she must be hoping to be chosen by Franz and not by me.

Franz called my name, and the madam held the door wider and motioned for me to come in, but the image of the girl's face was in my mind, and my shame at myself had obliterated any feeling of desire I had had. Franz made a show of trying to entice me in, but I could see now that the girls were more important to him than spending the remainder of the evening with me.

I walked the long distance home, allowing my tired body to relax into its natural misshapen form. My gait collapsed into its usual pitching roll and my uneven footfalls on the cobblestones broadcast my affliction out into the night. I met no other walker on my way.

When I arrived home, the house was dark, but I could hear my father moving around in his room next to mine. I turned up the lamp in my bedroom and removed my hat and coat, my jacket, trousers and collar, my undershirt and socks, and went and stood in front of the mirror. The mirror was large, as tall as myself, and beautifully framed in a mottled red wood. I surveyed myself.

My dark hair, already receding slightly at the temples, had been flattened to the contours of my head by my damp hat and looked as if it were painted on. My face, an echo of my body, had a slight twist to it; the cleft in my chin was not quite in line with the tip of my nose, and the whole lower half of my face was crooked, as if it had been wiped to one side. My left shoulder rose much higher than my right, and I had my jackets and coats made up with extra padding on the right side in an effort to disguise this. My whole right side appeared shrunken and hollow and my body collapsed over to this side while above it my head struggled for equilibrium. My right leg, a ruined thing, twisted inwards and its toes curled pathetically into the instep of my left foot as if they were seeking shelter there.

I turned my crooked side to the mirror to examine it more closely. In profile I was a question mark, with my straight legs and curved back, my head at the top poking forward like the head of a tortoise.* I had learned over the years to control my body to a degree, to make it appear more like other bodies, but it cost me much discomfort and required a great deal of concentration.

No one ever spoke a word to me about my deformity. Out of all the people I passed every day around Prague—the tram drivers, the maids, the whores, Stephanie in the next office, my mother, Sophie, the postman—not one ever said a word. The tongues of all those who inhabited my world were silent, but their eyes were not.

---

* Pencil sketches in a spare, cartoonish style appear in the margins of the manuscript here. They depict a male human figure and have been partially erased.

Their eyes spoke, that sea of eyes through which I moved each day. They glanced and looked in secret and averted their gazes, and this looking and not-looking spoke louder than any voice of disgust, curiosity or, worst of all, pity. I offended them. I frightened them. I showed them what they had, and what they had to lose.

I could still see the eyes of the girl in the window as she looked from Franz to me, her face twisting unknowingly as if to mirror mine. I felt no malice towards the girl; her reaction was justified and even warranted. I was able to observe myself objectively from the outside just as easily as I could observe Franz or any other person, and even I—especially I—would have preferred Franz to myself.

I often imagined how life would be if lived in a normal body. I obsessively watched people in the street and chose features that I would like to have for myself, composing a vast catalogue of them. A strong neck like a pillar, a back that spread outwards from the spine in two even wings, square shoulders that hung balanced from the neck, legs straight and muscular, moving like pistons. All of these were like fabulous riches to me, wonders I would never possess. Franz did possess them, together with a supple elegance, like that of a dancer. His body appeared weightless, borne upwards from the soles of his feet as though he were moving in water, or he were composed not of flesh but vapour. What a fool I was to think that Fräulein Železný, who could have anyone she chose, would be interested in me. I, who disgusted a cheap whore on Corpse Lane.

5.

SOME WEEKS LATER A CITY BOOKSHOP ORGANISED FOR BOTH
Franz and me to attend a literary evening where authors were to
read from their work. I had managed to salvage enough from my
notes to give an overview of the Schopenhauer book, and Franz
was to read an unpublished story. The event was to be held at
the Charles University, where I had studied some years ago. As I
walked through the grounds, I found the old buildings unchanged
and instantly familiar, and I was surprised to find that I still knew
my way around the echoing corridors. The students I passed also
seemed unchanged as they hurried past, singly, with clutches of
books, heads ducked, or strolled together in small clusters, arguing
in loud voices.

Speaking to a large group of people about my work still brought
with it the sharp bite of anxiety. Whenever I had to read my own
work in public, my body, which had already failed me so much,
added to its crimes with bouts of nausea and headaches for days
beforehand, and tremors and sweating as I stood facing the crowd.

This had originated with my first public-speaking engagement. It was the year before, in summer; a season that I have always disliked because the fewer clothes one wears, the more difficult it is to disguise a hunchback. That summer, though, was the only one that I remember ever having felt at ease with myself. I was the happiest I had ever been at having my work published—and not only published, but praised. I would wake in the morning and the thought of my book gave me the same feeling of lightness that one feels when one wakes and remembers that it is a holiday. For the first time, something in my life eclipsed the reality of living in my crooked body.

Theodor had arranged for me to speak to a group of literature students and professors about my work. To me, this event was an even more coveted marker of my success as a writer than the high rate of sales that my book was enjoying. To engage with my readers, inspire them and hear their ideas about the world and about my work was for me the real prize at the end of my long toil.

When I proudly told my friends about the speech, I detected in those closest to me a hesitation, a reticence, which had at first confused me and which I then attributed to jealousy on their part and then, later, paranoia on mine.

I also told my mother, hoping to be at least a small source of happiness to her. There was always a dissonance between memories and thoughts of my mother and the reality of her. When I was a child my mother had been kind and sharp-witted, her gestures sure and swift, and even now this is how I most often remember her. But in fact she had declined rapidly throughout the years of my childhood. Her mind had scattered and her body had faded and

39

curled in on itself. I never allowed myself to calculate how much I might be responsible for her deterioration.

That afternoon she was in her room, as she was most days, crouching small and shrunken in her chair near the window. I felt the tug of pain that I always felt at the sight of her. Elsa was sitting in the corner, watching over my mother while she busied her hands with some sewing. I had to explain the situation to my mother as though she were a child and I her mother.

'Mama, they have asked me to speak next week about *Nornepygge*, at the university.'

She just stared at me uncomprehendingly. '*Nornepygge*?' She began to look frightened, as she did more and more often at each unknown thing she encountered. Her hands started patting around her lap and knees, looking for something, as though her understanding was an object she had lost in the folds of the blanket that covered her.

'*Nornepygge*? *Nornepygge*?' she kept repeating with increasing alarm and volume.

I knelt beside her chair and took her fleshless hand in mine. I tried to anchor her shying eyes with my gaze.

From the corner of my eye I could see Elsa deciding whether to intervene, and my mother's gaze skittered away uncertainly in Elsa's direction for reassurance.

'His book, Frau Brod: *Nornepygge* is the name of the book. He has been asked to read from his book at the university.' Elsa nodded encouragingly at me and returned her eyes to her sewing.

My mother's face turned back to me and seemed to wince with pain. 'My poor child. And will you go?'

'Of course! It is a wonderful thing. I had hoped you would come too.' Although I knew that she couldn't.

'If you have already written it, why must you show yourself? All those people looking at you. Just send them the book if they want to read it.'

I could see Elsa ducking her head further into her neck, trying to make herself invisible.

'Why not ask your brother to read for you?' My mother was looking at me eagerly, pleadingly, wanting to help.

I felt a great, weary sadness then. My brother had been dead for more than twenty years. I had never even known him. I patted my mother's hand. 'Yes, Mama,' I said. 'What a good idea.'

Although she did not intend it, her words awoke in me the habitual dread that had been lying dormant under my unfamiliar happiness, a dread that was so connected with my broken body it was as though it formed its central organ, its dark pulsing heart.

That night I began to think of the reality of giving the speech. I had always disliked speaking to groups of people. Being called to the front of the classroom at school to give an answer or recite a poem had been painful for me. I would feel the eyes of the audience watching me, burning on my skin like little points of flame.

I began to wonder if people were only interested in me because I was an object of curiosity, a marvel such as one might find at a carnival sideshow; a two-headed man, or a dog that could sing. I remembered the hesitant faces of my friends when I had told them the news, and at last I understood the reason.

As the days passed I became more and more self-conscious, and at night I dreamed I was giving the speech, but instead of words coming from my mouth clouds of vermin spewed forth. Mice, bats, spiders and fleas crawled over the faces of the audience, no matter how much they tried to beat them off with their hands. I dreamed this dream so many times that it began to seem like it could really happen, and it spilled over into my waking life with bouts of nervous vomiting.

I found myself once again back in my old place, facing my old enemy, and now everything seemed to be against me. It was midsummer and over the next days the temperature rose. I began to obsessively check the weather forecast for the appointed night and deliberated over what I would wear—could I get away with my padded jacket? I stood for hours in front of the mirror, trying to straighten my poor body in preparation for the eventuality of having to appear without the jacket and expose it to view.

The night of the speech came, hot and close even after the sun had set. I had walked to the university and arrived with my face beaded with sweat and my shirt sticking transparently to my skin. Theodor met me outside, totally unaware of my distress. He was excited because there was a better turnout than he had hoped.

'It's quite a crowd! They can't wait to see you.'

I knew he was trying to reassure me, but at that moment I was wishing for the opposite, for a shamefully empty room, a sea of vacant chairs. I went to the bathroom and splashed water on my face. In the mirror I could see my hollow chest tremble with the beating of my heart. I felt a spasm in my gut and tried to vomit into the sink to relieve myself, but couldn't.

I still remember entering the lecture hall, feeling as though I were entering the scene of my own death. It was very crowded, with people standing around the door and up along the back wall. As I made my way through the crush towards Theodor, whom I could see standing at the front, I heard, or imagined I could hear, a hissing wave of shuffles and gasps as the bodies parted to let me through. I felt faint and hot. Sweat prickled on my back. My pounding heart filled all the space inside my chest, leaving no room for air, which I had to take in shallow sips.

Theodor introduced me and I mechanically read through a section of my novel and elaborated on its themes, but I was aware the whole time of all the eyes in that room. Even as I spoke, my brain was perversely trying to calculate the exact number of those eyes, and what percentage of the surface area of my body was taken up by their gaze. 'Each eye,' a voice said in my head, 'is the size of a five-heller piece.' Two hundred people in the room equalled four hundred eyes, which was approximately twelve hundred centimetres square, thus covering at least the whole of my upper body.

I fought a rising tide of nausea and struggled to keep my voice level, which I managed to do until the time came for the audience to ask questions. An old professor was the first to speak, giving a long-winded opinion about a seemingly unrelated theme, and I quickly lost the thread. By this time I was almost blinded by the sick feeling in my stomach and the room was swaying before me. I could no longer control my body and I was propelled, stumbling, off the podium. I limped through the audience, awkwardly steadying myself against their seated bodies with my hands. I could no longer suppress the spasms of retching, which echoed down the stone hallway like peals of thunder when I reached the door.

43

I ran down the hallway towards the bathroom, but I made it only a short distance, and vomited instead into a flowerbed. I stood for a long time afterwards, bent over and looking at the tips of my shoes. Sweat dripped from my face. I could sense someone, probably Theodor, standing a short distance away. Out of shame I didn't turn my head to look at him.

Even now, more than a year later, the thought of a crowd of faces all turned towards me, with their silent, waiting eyes, unnerved me enough to raise my blood pressure. It was no longer the display of my ruined body to those appraising faces that was the source of my anxiety; to this act of exposure I had become resigned. Regardless of what a poor specimen it was, my body had still honoured its function of acting as an external barrier that protected my internal self from scrutiny and trespass.

To me now there was something about the act of reading my own words out loud that stripped me bare. I had a horror of speaking my words with my own voice, because I feared, as though it were some magic incantation, that this combination would enable the innermost part of myself to be exposed, recognised and, like my body, deemed monstrous, reprehensible.

That night, the fact that Fräulein Železný might be in the audience was making me more nervous than usual. I felt ill at the thought of her seeing me standing there, exposed, but at the same time I longed to see her again. The thought of meeting Franz also added to my unease; I could see again the young whore's eyes sliding from him to me as we stood at the door, and I did not want to witness Fräulein Železný's eyes making that same journey. My last encounter with Franz had changed my apprehension of him and

I felt a panicky urge to keep him away from Fräulein Železný if possible. For this reason I had planned to arrive early, determined to get to Fräulein Železný before Franz had the chance. There was also the problem of Theodor. Once again I had found myself in the position of being forced to witness his first meeting with Franz. I could not hope for the possibility of Franz's absence that evening. And now there was also the matter of Theodor's offer of the book, the details of which were still unknown to me.

Despite my anxieties about Franz and Theodor, my nervousness about seeing Fräulein Železný again was dominant as I climbed the stairs to the room in which the reading was to be held. With each step, my heart tightened and my eyes began darting about, searching for her. The room was still quite empty and Fräulein Železný was not there. I could see Theodor and my friends Kurt and Felix, who would also be reading from their new works. Avoiding Theodor, I made my way over to talk to my friends. I could not see Franz anywhere. For some reason Kurt and Felix did not cause the same sense of threat and rivalry that Franz provoked, but rather exuded a sense of solidarity and camaraderie. In fact, I had been the one to enable both of them to make their names as writers, and I was happy to have been able to use my own success to help them.

After a short time Theodor rushed over, his face stretched tight with concern. He interrupted our conversation with neither greeting nor apology.

'Franz,' he said, spreading out his hands. 'Where is Franz?'

He looked around the room, which was fast becoming crowded, and then at me, accusingly, as if Franz were an article of furniture that he believed I had stolen. I did not see why I should be held responsible for Franz's behaviour and simply shrugged at Theodor and turned back to my conversation. As he grunted and hurried off again, I smiled to myself. My satisfaction was twofold; first, there was Theodor's obvious distress, and second, the dawning possibility that Franz might miss the reading altogether, just as he had missed the party. This possibility, slender though it seemed, was like a gift handed down from the angels. Without Franz, the field would be clear for me to approach Fräulein Železný. Equally pleasing was the idea that Theodor's estimation of Franz, however high it might now be, would also be certain to fall if he failed to attend the reading. I began to eye the door with a vigour to rival Theodor's as I watched now for both Franz and Fräulein Železný. The hands of the large clock on the wall slid around the dial to the appointed time of the reading, and then past it, but neither of the two appeared.

Theodor sent someone to Franz's house to hunt him out and he himself began pacing outside the door like a guard. I, for my part, was quite tired out from the anxious waiting. My eyes scanned the faces behind Kurt's and Felix's heads as I listened to them talk, my heart leaping in my chest every time my gaze lighted on someone resembling Fräulein Železný. After quite a long time I saw Theodor's messenger return alone, shaking his head, and Theodor had no choice but to start without Franz. I could hardly believe it: luck so rarely smiles on me. If only now Fräulein Železný would come.

I was the first to read, and up on the podium I took a last look around the room for Fräulein Železný, in vain. Theodor sat at the very edge of the crowd, not listening to me at all, but looking alternately down at his watch and up at the door. He was no longer interested in me. Now he had eyes only for Franz. I was surprised at how wounded this made me feel. When I finished my reading, Theodor was still so absorbed with keeping watch that he did not even bother to applaud along with the others.

I gathered up my papers and was stepping off the podium when I glanced up and at last saw Fräulein Železný. She was at the back of the room, standing beside the entrance as if she might have just arrived. The sight of her gave me a physical shock, like a current of electricity passing through me, and in an instant I had forgotten all about Theodor's indifference. I sat down and pretended to listen to Felix's reading while I rehearsed things I might say to Fräulein Železný in my head. But every sentence I could think of seemed trite and stagey, and I considered and rejected topic after topic.

I imagined I could sense her presence in the room, which had manifested as an electromagnetic field that pulled the muscles over my ears pleasantly tight. The desire to turn and look at her was almost irresistible. I still had no idea what I could say to her. I had thought so much about her since our last meeting, and attributed so much importance to it, that the idea that she might not have done the same, and indeed might even have forgotten who I was, caused a pang that was almost physical.

Suddenly I became aware of a murmuring unrest in the room around me and realised that Felix had left the podium, which now stood empty. Theodor had announced an intermission, no doubt in order to allow Franz more time to appear. People were shuffling around, clustered in small groups discussing the readings or calling to one another across the room.

I stood up and could see that Fräulein Železný was still standing in the same place. She was alone. I made my way through the milling crowd, managing to dodge those bearing down on me to claim me for conversation. As I went, I desperately rehearsed conversational gambits in my head. But when at last she was there in front of me all of my rehearsed phrases fell away like dead things, useless. When I looked at her, my body floated away from me and I became only my eyes, outward-looking.

The reality of her was so different from my flimsy memories that they almost insulted her in their inadequacy, like a picture postcard of the seaside insults the real living sea, with all its complexity. To take all of her in at once was impossible; it overwhelmed me, and I was able to apprehend only small slices of her with each glance, like a series of photographs that focused on only one tiny detail—a curl escaping from her chignon, the corner of her mouth turned up in a smile, the painful grace with which her wrist turned in on itself.

I think neither of us spoke, but our eyes held a secret conversation. I must have said, *Let's go outside* or *Let's go for a walk*, or she must have, because then we were outside. The outside scene followed the inside scene with no bridge between them, as in dreams where one is suddenly transported somewhere else without explanation, but one accepts it all the same.

She took my arm and we walked along and my entire being seemed to be concentrated in that one spot, in the crook of my left elbow, under the light pressure of her hand. I let her steer me and then we were in the botanical gardens of the university. All the thick heat of the day lay caught among the trees, and the thousand lilac and azalea blossoms breathed out their clouds of scent, and the air, or my head, became filled with a pressurised, musical humming. The sky arched overhead like a glass dome, full of stars and the restless call of insects and night birds.

We walked slowly up and down the twisting paths, talking, and after a while sat upon a bench under the ginkgo tree. I looked down at our feet, resting on the gravel. Hers, tiny in their shoes, seemed to me such precious things, but absurd; it was unthinkable that they could be made for walking on. My own shoes beside them were like shipwrecked boats. I tucked them under the shadow of the bench, out of sight.

She told me about herself and I hoarded away each detail as if it were a morsel of food and I a starving man. Her father was a professor, and she was studying philosophy at the university. She lived close to me in the Old Town, with her mother and father; she was an only child. We spoke about literature, of which I found she had a deep appreciation. She had read my novel, and told me that she had felt quite shy meeting me at the party the week before, and naturally I did not admit to her how overwhelmed I had been on that occasion.

We talked and talked for I do not know how long, nor do I know which other topics we discussed; I knew only my feelings for her and how her face looked framed by leaves and flowers and lit by the benevolent moon. The surface of her skin and the character of her eyes shifted and changed with the flow of expressions and emotions that animated her as she spoke and listened. It occurred to me that each expression of hers was like the flowers of some African plants that bloom only once, for a short time, and then die away. Smile again she certainly would, but for her to smile that particular smile, with that quality, about that subject would only happen at

49

that moment, and then never again. My body grew cold as a great sadness seeped into it at the thought, as though I could hear the ticking of a great clock that marked all time running on, inexorably.

I looked up and saw that there was a man standing before us, holding, inexplicably, my hat. I recognised first the hat, and then after a moment that it was Franz who was holding it, balanced on his palm like a tray. I was so absorbed with Fräulein Železný that at first I wasn't shocked to see him; I simply thought that the interval must have finished and he was calling us to go back inside to see his reading.

'Herr Brod, Fräulein Železný, may I accompany you home? I believe we all go in the same direction.'

When I took out my watch, I saw that the whole evening had passed.

Fräulein Železný had come on her bicycle, and we all three walked together to where she had left it. Franz's appearance had broken the evening's spell, and as we walked along I began inwardly to rage against him. Of course he had appeared at the worst possible moment. I had been intending to ask if I might call on Fräulein Železný but now, with Franz standing on her other side, holding her other arm, this suddenly became infinitely more difficult.

Fräulein Železný was turned towards him, eagerly questioning him about his new story. She was very familiar with him, so much so that it seemed clear that the two must have met since the *Hyperion* party. I heard her say that she had been looking forward to hearing his new story, and then he recited some lines from it that he knew by heart. He was so handsome and elegant as he strode along, his eyes on her. I felt like some fairy-tale monster beside them.

I wished Franz to the devil. Why could he have not come five minutes later? Or left us in peace? All I needed was a few minutes more alone with her. I desperately tried to telegraph this need to Franz over Fräulein Železný's head, but he never even glanced in my direction. He was so engrossed now in relaying to her the plot of a longer story he was writing that he did not notice the anxious motions of my head and my eyes only a few centimetres from him.

I spied the bicycle perhaps ten metres ahead of us, and I had never felt so much despair at the sight of such a machine. Franz had still not paused his monologue by the time Fräulein Železný was mounted on her bicycle and ready to leave. She gave me her hand to say goodbye; the first words she had addressed to me since Franz had interrupted us. The nervousness I had felt earlier in the evening returned, and I mumbled my question to her in the worst possible style, painfully aware of Franz nearby, noting every hesitation.

She said that she would be happy for me to call, and my humour was slightly restored. She then took her leave of Franz, who asked with stagey hesitance and excessively flowery language if he too might call. She simply laughed, which signified I had no idea what, and cycled away.

Franz resumed our homeward walk as though nothing untoward had occurred, while I fumed beside him. His inconsiderateness on this occasion bewildered me; surely he must have seen the intimate nature of the talk we were having before he interrupted us.

'Do you intend to call on Fräulein Železný?' I asked after we had walked in silence for some distance. After the words were out of my mouth, I heard the petulance of my tone and instantly regretted them.

Franz laughed, and I didn't recognise him. 'I may, if I have the leisure.'

I was unsure now of our position in relation to each other in that never-ending struggle of position that men love to engage in. I wanted to be able to claim Fräulein Železný for myself, but there was no way I could do this, there was nothing I could say that would not make me appear ridiculous. We walked on and the air between us was tightly compressed with my unsaid words.

'I was reading *Nornepygge* the other day,' Franz said after a while, 'and I think I've solved some of the problems that you had with it.'

At first I couldn't understand what he was talking about. Besides, I wasn't aware of having any problems, and if I did have any, I certainly did not feel disposed to discuss them with him on that walk, but he talked on about the motivations of the character seeming empty, about a confusion with the setting.

I let him talk while my mind drifted back over my evening. Walking along now with Franz, with the clatter of our feet on the cobblestones echoing in my ears, the time I had spent with Fräulein Železný almost seemed unreal to me. In comparison with the garden, the scene around me now seemed stretched thin, without substance: the call of voices, the slamming of doors, seemed to fall flat onto the street and the buildings with no resonance, with the dull slap of a wet rag on a stone.

Franz's appearance had soured the whole evening, and I felt a great emptiness; everything was lost. I remembered my awkwardness with Fräulein Železný as she was leaving, and Theodor's disregard. Franz was to blame for both of those. He was still enumerating the problems that he saw in *Nornepygge*—evidently the list was long—and it occurred to me only then to wonder what had happened to make him so late to his own reading. I interrupted his demolition of my writing to ask him how his story had been received, even though I already knew the answer. I imagined how Theodor's face must have lit up at the sight of him coming through the door at last.

'Oh, the reading,' he said carelessly. 'I didn't make it.'

'Didn't make it?' Had he really said that? 'But why?' I asked. I could never imagine behaving like this.

Franz shrugged. 'Oh, something happened. Things get in the way—you know how it is.'

I didn't know, but I didn't say anything. Theodor must be furious, I thought with glee. I pictured his shiny face, boiled red with rage from watching the empty doorway and the hands of his watch creep around and around.

The sour weight that Franz had brought with him suddenly lifted. Surely, Theodor would not allow himself to be treated with such scorn. In a few weeks he would have forgotten all about Franz, and by then I would have made great progress on my Schopenhauer book. And even if I had been nervous at the end with Fräulein Železný, it did not matter: she had still encouraged me to call on her. She had said yes. To me she had said yes, but she had only laughed at Franz. Perhaps Franz was nothing to worry about after all. He was only a little fly, an insect buzzing around the room: annoying, perhaps, but soon gone.

'Yes, I know how things get in the way,' I said, 'but don't worry. Theodor is a very understanding man. I'm sure he won't mind at all.'

6.

ANJA, ANOUŠKA, ANJALEIN: IN THE NEXT DAYS AND WEEKS, SHE
was all I could think about, and I remember nothing of that time
but her. I think those weeks were the happiest of my life. I found
a contentment and joy that went far beyond mere attraction.

When I went to call on her for the first time my nerves were
so great that I had to walk past her house twice before I could
bring myself even to knock at the door. Her house was on the
Martinsgasse, a street that was familiar to me; I had passed along it
many times on my way to or from work, though I had never really
noticed it before. Now it had become the centre of Prague; the
most beautiful street in the city. The sunlight was brighter there,
the air fresher and the birds more musical. A hush fell around me
as I approached her house, as though behind its curtained windows
invisible watchers stood, holding their breath. I rang the bell and
automatically began to count in my head as I waited, a nervous
habit of mine. My sweating palms were beginning to leave damp

stains on the wrapper of the bouquet that I held out in front of me like a sword.

The maid let me in and showed me to the living room, where Frau Železný greeted me. She was tall and thin, a faded version of her daughter, with the same long hands and graceful neck. I handed her the bouquet and immediately felt purposeless and naked without it. Frau Železný busied herself with the flowers, which allowed her to surreptitiously observe me with little darts of her sympathetic eyes; I wondered if Anja had forewarned her family about my deformity. Frau Železný talked inconsequentially about varieties of flowers and the difficulty of raising this or that strain in the climate of Prague. I perched on a tightly upholstered chair opposite her and worried about what to do with my hands now that the bouquet had been taken from me. I folded them in my lap, and they lay heavy there, sweating like bony hams.

Herr Železný now entered the room together with the maid, who was pushing a trolley on which the afternoon coffee was arranged. In her father I could see nothing of Anja. He was dark and stern, with a bald spot on the very top of his head that was wreathed around by wiry hair. He shook my hand, keeping his eyes trained on mine as though he had been told not to stare, but at the same time not to avoid looking at me. My eyes were the first to fall. He lowered himself into a large armchair by the fire and seemed to get straight down to business, asking me about my position at the post office and my writing, some of which, to my surprise, he had read.

I balanced as upright as I could in my hard chair. I had to concentrate very hard on holding my cup and plate balanced so as not to disgrace myself by dropping anything on the carpet. I managed to get my coffee down, but the cake crumbs stuck unpleasantly to the walls of my dry throat. Eating and drinking and then also talking at the same time suddenly seemed an immensely complicated task, requiring great dexterity and skill. Sweat prickled under my collar.

After a short while, Anja appeared, wearing a blue dress that rustled like tissue paper. I stopped talking and looked at her as she stood, framed in the dark doorway, light falling on her hair, her fingers resting lightly on the door handle. It was like when one sees a deer step out of a wooded area into a clearing and time stops for a moment. We looked at each other. Then she came into the room and sat down on the little sofa next to her mother. Herr Železný was now explaining the content of my first novel to Frau Železný as though I were not in the room, so I was free to let Anja take my attention. She reminded me of a bird with her quick, darting movements, her head turning from side to side. Her slender hands were like fluttering leaves and the shapes they described in the air awakened a tinkling tune in my head.

I must have satisfied Herr Železný, because after he had finished his coffee and risen from his chair to leave the room he turned first to me and then to Anja, with a little bow, and asked us if we might like to go out on a walk together. Then he gave one sharp nod and left the room.

Walking down the stairs, I was finally able to relax. The soft sounds of Anja walking behind me—the rustle of her dress, her gentle footfalls and the hiss of her palm over the bannister—caused a pleasant tingling in my scalp and ears.

Out in the street she took my arm. I let my fingers brush the back of her hand as it nestled in the crook of my elbow, and it was so soft and yielding that when I brushed my fingers over it they seemed to pass through the skin.

Walking with Anja was a completely difference experience to walking alone. Over the years I had become used to people looking at me wherever I went and I had learned to ignore their rigid faces and round eyes. With Anja beside me I was surprised to find that people looked at us even more, but with a completely different gaze. At first it was as though my happiness had transformed either myself or the world, and I was met by only smiling faces, but then I slowly realised that the eyes that would usually be hooked by my outlandish form now slid past me, without taking me in, to light instead on Anja. Women, especially older ones, smiled at her with a kind of nostalgia, men's eyes snapped over to her apparently of their own volition, and children looked with upturned faces as though they were watching a fireworks display. I walked like a ghost beside her, invisible but happy, seeing my joy reflected in the faces of those we passed.

We went to the Laurenziberg and wandered for a long time through the gardens that covered the eastern slopes. I was aware of the beauty of the gardens and the views of Prague without really seeing them. But the sky I took notice of. I can still recall precisely how it looked that day as we stood and gazed down on the city. It ranged over us in a broad sweep, the blue deep and full directly over our heads but stretched thin and pale at the horizon. There were some insignificant clouds, like wreaths of smoke, and Prague too was nestled in a hazy smudge of dust and sun, shot through with flecks of white as light glinted from the windowpanes and the surface of the river. Faint sounds of the city drifted up to us, the shouts of children and the whistle of a distant train. Looking back now, this afternoon seemed to have been suspended in a golden mist, held out of time like a leaf in amber.

We wandered to a seat and sat together. Anja looked around at the view, and exclaimed at the sun and the colour of the leaves and grass. I could only see these things in relation to her: how the sun gilded the skin of her face with a layer of iridescence, or how the greenery saturated the colour of her hair and eyes.

And Anja talked, or chattered rather, telling me tales about her parents and friends, her teachers at the university. She began on a long and complicated story about a Herr Liška, a lawyer that Herr Železný was acquainted with through his work. It seemed that Herr Železný thought this Liška would be a good match for her; it appeared that he was to her what Uta was to me.

I was relieved to be able to explain to her about Uta in such a natural way. From our very first meeting I had been worried that Anja would come to hear about Uta, perhaps even from Uta herself, and form the idea that I was romantically involved with her. Now I was able to explain the truth of my feelings for Uta. I even managed to be kind about the poor girl; sitting there on a bench with Anja, I could afford to be generous.

'Oh, Max,' Anja said, 'it's so good to have you to talk to.'

To hear her speak my name was the most exquisite pleasure. She took my hand in hers and I thought that I might die.

Only when it was getting dark did we make our way back to the Old Town, and only after I returned Anja to her door did I become aware of the tiredness of my body. I gave in to the aching and took the tram home, instead of walking.*

It was not until I had reached my house that Liška occurred to me again, and now he appeared in a more sinister light. I knew that Uta's advances had no effect on me, even with echoing chorus provided by my family, however the eligible Herr Liška's powers of attraction were unknown to me. I sat in my study a long time that evening, writing the day's experiences in my diary and then, later in the night, brooding over Herr Liška. I tortured myself with images of wealthy, muscular, straight-backed men with faces like stone carvings and voices like booming drums. I tried to reassure myself that Anja would not spend her afternoons with me if she did not wish to; she was perfectly free to take Herr Liška to the Laurenziberg instead of me. Still my doubts raged. I enumerated my strengths to myself, counting them on my fingers and then even going so far as to write them down in my diary.† It occurred to me then that she must have shared her story about him to awaken my jealousy and spur me to pursue her. Tired and relieved, I seized on this explanation and went to bed.

§

Anja and I began to see each other frequently, and when I look back at this period it is at a succession of days of savage happiness,

---

* These facing pages are stained with the imprint of a pressed flower. The flower has not been retained.

† This diary has not been recovered among the Kafka papers.

each bleeding into the other, an unfamiliar world full of burning light and painful beauty bursting out at me from every object in space. I soon became obsessed with her. I was like a collector with a mania for finding new things and cataloguing them; facts about her, minute alterations in her appearance, her moods shifting from day to day, how her skin looked against fabrics of different colours, her eyes in different lights, how she would look in the snow, or swimming in a lake, or ill with a fever.

My thoughts were full of her, and even when I was away from her I would see the world through her eyes, or look forward to the time I would next see her, or remember the last time that I did. Time changed its function, lost its objectivity, and was reduced to a measure of her proximity. I was like the addict who can think only of the drug, anxious and unseeing of the world before he imbibes it, but afterwards imbued with light, floating in the beauty of the world.

On most days I would collect Anja from the university after work and walk home with her, or meet her during the day if I could get away from the office. She would call on me, collecting me from my home or my workplace. Her appearance in my life did much to raise my status. I noticed that my father beheld me with a new respect, as did my colleagues at the post office. On Anja's first visit to my workplace, it was Kröner, the head clerk, who greeted her in the central hall of the post office building, the part that was open to the public. He escorted her upstairs to my office and showed her inside. I was gratified by the look that he flashed at me when he opened the door and held it wide for her to walk through. Before this day he had never greeted me if I happened to pass him in the street, but now he would give me a slow nod and a quizzical stare, as if I kept some secret that he would have liked to know. At the post office he began to ask my advice on work matters and invite me to have lunch with him. Stephanie too changed her behaviour towards me. She became much friendlier, almost sisterly, and would loudly proclaim Anja's loveliness whenever she had been in the office to visit me.

The kinds of things Anja and I would do together on our outings were quite ordinary; visits to parks and museums, attending concerts and theatrical performances, sitting in coffee houses and talking. Anja recounted all kinds of stories to me, speaking without reservation or calculation. She related stories of her childhood, told me of problems with her university subjects, and described the friends she had made among her fellow students.

When taking leave of her, usually at her front door, I would delay and delay the final moment of separation. I would stare at her face and use the whole of my concentration to try to fix it in my mind like a photograph. She would be smiling at me, perhaps she would blink, perhaps some strands of her hair would blow in the breeze, but the image of her would become like an object that I could carry away with me, to take out when I was alone and immerse myself in. I would leave Anja's house already looking at the latest portrait I had taken, remembering the hours we had spent, not seeing the streets I passed along, sated and happy.

She occasionally mentioned Liška, but as week followed week the terror he had at first inspired faded into the background. After all, I was the one who was with her every day, and the way she spoke of him made it clear that the two knew each other only slightly. But as my worries about Liška dissipated, I found that their place was taken by worries about Franz. Before long I could not rid myself of the image of Franz's face as he gazed at her that evening of the reading in the botanical gardens. The expression of his face that night spoke of a mastery and a longing with which I could never compete. His face began to appear to me at all times of the day, disturbing my hours of work and sleep. I obsessively replayed his conversation with Anja that evening, trying hopelessly to gauge their level of closeness. I would occasionally mention Franz in a casual way in my conversations with Anja, my eyes fixed sharply on her to detect the smallest sign of affection, but I could never discover anything. Many times I resolved to ask her how well she knew him, but I could never bring myself to do so, partly out of an unwillingness to have my worst fears proven, and partly out of a fear of exposing my own insecurity.

7.

DURING THIS TIME I NEGLECTED EVERYTHING BUT ANJA; MY friends, my writing, all of these fell into the background. I gave Schopenhauer not a single thought, and when Theodor wrote to reprimand me for missing a deadline, I just laughed and threw his letter into the fire. Theodor also sent other letters. He was clearly having great difficulty pinning Franz down, a situation which, I admit, gave me great pleasure. He had still never even met Franz. Though he scheduled appointment after appointment, Franz failed to attend. Theodor's tenacity in this matter surprised me. I would have expected him to give up in the face of such rejection. At any other time I would have been prostrated with jealousy by Theodor's pursuit of Franz, but Anja had made me feel so serene that the whole situation seemed only amusing. As the weeks passed, my frenzied determination to destroy Franz had faded and been replaced with a calm assurance that the problem he presented would resolve itself without any intervention on my part.

Another thing that failed to perturb me at that time was Theodor's misapprehension of my relationship with Franz. Theodor appeared to be under the impression that Franz and I were particular friends, and that I had some great influence over him. I never replied to Theodor's letters; not out of ill will, but only because with Anja in my life I hardly had time to give them a thought. In light of this I was not greatly surprised to receive a visit from Theodor at the post office one morning. To my relief, he seemed to have completely forgotten about Schopenhauer and my deadline. Instead, almost as soon as he had sat down, he asked me about Franz, talking as if the two of us were intimates. But I had not heard from Franz since the long-ago evening of the reading, and I told Theodor as much.

'He's probably left Prague for a holiday,' I said. 'Or perhaps he's ill.' Really, I did not care. I wondered whether Theodor would start pressing me about Schopenhauer.

'No, no. That's not it.' Theodor shook his head. 'I've sent messages to his work. I know he's there; they just refuse to let me in.'

He sounded so much like a jilted lover that I almost felt sorry for him.

'I'd like to invite you to dinner,' Theodor said. 'And Franz, of course. Actually, the dinner is for Franz. Your role would be to persuade him to attend.'

This was a ludicrous suggestion.

'But I haven't seen the man for weeks,' I protested. 'He could be dead for all we know.'

Theodor looked stricken at this suggestion.

'I'm relying on you,' he said.

64

A dinner with Theodor and Franz was the last thing I wanted.

'I think you will find that, if you see to it that he is there, I might be inclined to extend the deadline on Schopenhauer—the one that you have repeatedly missed.'

The sly fox. Of course I had to agree.

I tried to contact Franz, but, predictably, I could not reach him. I did not feel particularly worried. I could only do so much after all. I put a note in my calendar to remind myself of the dinner, and then forgot all about it.

The following week, I came home from work one day, my head full of thoughts of Anja as usual, and found another letter from Theodor. I knew without opening it what it would contain: a reminder about the dinner, now only a few days away, along with some insults about my own laziness perhaps. I absent-mindedly put the letter in my pocket, where it remained until the next evening, when it tumbled out as I was looking for a handkerchief. I tore the envelope open and gave its contents a desultory glance.* The letter began as I had expected, with a reminder about the dinner followed by another reminder that the deadline for my book was long past. But what came next made my eyes widen in surprise. Theodor then threatened to drop my Schopenhauer book if I did not produce Franz at the dinner.

At first I thought that it must be a joke, but the signature at the bottom was without a doubt Theodor's. I read the letter again with shaking hands. Theodor must have lost his mind. All the serenity

---

* The letter has been located among the papers, but water damage has rendered it illegible.

of the past weeks melted away in an instant. Without my writing, what was left to me? I had Anja, it was true, but how long could I expect to keep her with nothing to recommend myself? I would be no one, my broken body the only notable thing about me. I grew numb inside when I saw how easily Theodor would cast me aside in favour of Franz.

The dinner was still two days away, but it was already past nine o'clock in the evening. I knew that it was probably too late to call on Franz, but I put on my hat anyway and went in search of him. I had only a vague idea of his address, but there were one or two places where I thought it might be possible to find him. First I went to the Europa café, which was crowded and smoky, but Franz was not there. Next I tried the beer cellar at the Gemeindehaus where we had drunk together those long weeks ago. Franz was not there either. I looked in at the Café Slavia and at the Arco, but no Franz. I knew he worked at the Workers' Accident and Insurance Institute in the Old Town, but of course that would be closed at this hour. I toyed with the idea of going there and leaving a note for him to find the next day, but in the end my tiredness won out. In the morning, I told myself, and went home to bed.

I had expected to have a sleepless night of worry, but instead I slipped off immediately into a quiet, dreamless darkness. I became conscious again because of a persistent warmth on my face. It was the sun, burning through the window; I had neglected to draw the curtain the night before. I was lying awkwardly splayed across the bed, and had a raging thirst and a throbbing head, as though I had spent the previous night drinking. I rolled out of bed, and when I looked at my watch I saw that I had overslept, something that had never happened before. It was past ten o'clock. I cursed Elsa, who invariably woke me if I had not emerged by eight.

I pulled on my clothes hastily and hurried out of the house. I had planned to stop at Franz's workplace on my way to the post office. Franz worked in Poříčer Strasse, and to pass by there would add perhaps twenty minutes to my journey, not counting the time I would spend talking to him. I was already so late that I supposed another half an hour would be of no consequence. Luck, however, was not on my side that morning, for almost the first person I encountered in the street was my boss, Herr Jelen. When I saw him I froze in shock, wondering whether I should try to explain myself. I decided it would be more prudent to remain silent to make it appear that everything was in order.

I had little to do directly with Jelen, but Kröner and Stephanie lived in awe of him, and a mere glimpse of him walking past the office was enough to send them scurrying about their tasks twice as quickly as was usual. Jelen was a very large man, with every part of his body seeming to have been scaled up. Each one of his thighs was the size of a small man's torso, and his pink fingers were surmounted by monstrous nails like coins. His head was at least double the size of mine and his meaty neck seemed to strain under the weight of it. I had always privately thought that his large stature was the chief reason for his effectiveness as a leader. Proximity to his bulk produced a visceral subservience in the most intractable of workers.

He looked mildly surprised to see me out at that hour, but did not question me, and instead fell into step beside me and remarked politely on the weather. He was clearly on his way to the post office, but the way to Poříčer Strasse lay in a different direction. Up ahead I could see the Königshofergasse, which I would need to take to get to Poříčer Strasse. Could I risk simply taking leave of him? I wildly thought up different excuses I might make for parting ways, but Jelen's great mass was looming over me, blocking out the sun and seeming to pull me gravitationally in his wake; at the crucial moment my courage failed me and the necessary street sailed past without me turning into it. I glanced down it longingly. The early afternoons in the office were often quiet in any case, I reassured myself. Surely I could escape for an hour unnoticed then.

What was left of the morning passed quickly, and in my lunch hour I slipped out of the building and took the tram to Poříčer Strasse.

My journey, however, was in vain. Just as Theodor had said, the head clerk at the insurance office refused to confirm whether Franz was there, let alone allow me in. Frustrated, I stood outside the street door for a while, watching the crowds in case I might spot Franz coming back from his lunch hour, but I had no luck. I hastily scribbled a note and left it with the silent head clerk with a request that he pass it on to Franz, and then I made my way back to the post office.

Back in my office, I could not concentrate on my work. I pulled my chair to the window and sat looking out, brooding over the situation. Life on the street continued, indifferent to my plight. I watched the people hurrying along the footpath, each of them absorbed in their own joys, their own sorrows. The dinner was the following evening. Although I was fairly certain that Theodor's letter was not a joke, I was not at all certain about his state of mind or how serious his threat was. It was true that his patience with me had been waning of late, and that I had violated our agreement. But I had always believed that he and I enjoyed a special relationship that went beyond the terms of a mere contract; we had, at any rate, before Franz came on the scene. Franz had destroyed all that. Now it seemed that I was nothing more to Theodor than a means to secure Franz, like a piece of bait for a prize fish. I resolved to slip out of the office early that evening and return to Poříčer Strasse to try to ambush Franz as he left his office at the end of the day.

I arrived at Poříčer Strasse just before five o'clock and took up a position directly opposite the insurance office. I kept my eyes trained on the street door of the building, tensed and watching for Franz. Five o'clock came and a few workers left the building, but Franz was not among them. My eyes burned into the wood of the door. It was a heavy double door, painted green, of which the left wing swung back into the dark entrance hall. I stared intensely, willing the door to open and reveal Franz, but it did not obey me. The sun was setting and it grew cold as the buildings began casting their damp shadows. At half-past five a regular trickle of workers began to issue from the doors, and I crossed the street to be closer, but Franz still did not appear. By six o'clock the trickle had slowed and only the occasional person came through the door. Most of the lights in the building had been switched off. It was time to go.

I was tired and hungry. With the last of my energy I made a rapid tour of the cafés I had visited the previous evening, again with no result. My last stop was at the Café Slavia, where I stopped for a beer and a quick meal. It seemed that there was nothing to do but wait and hope that if Franz did not appear at the dinner

Theodor would understand that it had nothing to do with me. I was sitting beside the window that looks out at the National Theatre. The statues along the roof were all illuminated and my eyes could pick out every detail of their faces against the black of the night sky. Down on the theatre steps a small crowd stood laughing and calling to one another—actors, by the look of their clothes.

I reflected on the irony of my plight. Now it seemed likely that my fervent wish of Franz and Theodor never meeting might come to pass, but the very thing I had desired for my own self-preservation would be the cause of my downfall. Looking into my beer, I considered the problem as I might a difficulty in a narrative plot. It was very simple: Theodor wanted to meet Franz, but Franz apparently did not want to meet Theodor. I did not want the two to meet, but if Theodor did not meet Franz, I would be sacrificed, thus I was forced to facilitate the meeting against my will. What Franz wanted, or why, did not remotely concern me. I finished my beer and ordered another. If only, I thought to myself, Franz really were dead, this whole situation could easily be resolved in my favour. This would be the ending that I would choose if this were a story and I the author. It was not even really necessary that he be dead; emigration would suffice, or serious illness.

Theodor, I mused, had never met Franz and was relying on me to introduce him. He did not know who Franz was. If Franz really were dead or otherwise safely out of the way—and, as I had suggested to Theodor, we did not know for certain that he was not—I could simply present some other person to Theodor as Franz. No one would ever know the difference, provided that the 'Franz' I introduced was credible. Perhaps it was not even necessary that

Franz be out of the way for my plan to be feasible: to the real Franz it would simply appear that Theodor had finally lost interest and given up.

I was now on to my third beer and the potential benefits of this solution seemed limitless. It was perfect. I would regain Theodor's favour by giving him what he was unable to get for himself; Theodor would get his precious contract signed; I would have time to find my feet again with Schopenhauer. The problem of Franz would be neatly solved without the need for any drama or confrontation. He would simply fade away as if he had never been. Granted, the book of stories would possibly go ahead, but I could certainly contend with one book. The more I thought about it, the better the idea seemed. The relief of having Franz out of the way was immense. I even began to feel grateful to him for being so evasive; what had been an irritating problem, a cocky affectation, began to seem like a rare gift from him to me.

Somewhere along the line I had begun thinking of the whole enterprise as a fixed plan rather than a mere hypothetical possibility. The only question was, who could I use to play Franz? Obviously it would have to be someone unconnected with literary circles, preferably someone from outside Prague. Someone I could trust. I ran through my host of cousins and in-laws, a cohort of whom lived in Brünn. But what explanation could I possibly give them? And how could I arrange it all within twenty-four hours? It was impossible. I would have to look closer to home. I half-heartedly scanned the room for likely candidates. There was no one who really resembled Franz, but perhaps this was not a necessary requirement. I looked out of the window and my eye fell on the theatre opposite, still wreathed in its yellow glow. Of course: an actor. There could be nothing better than having a professional undertake the task.

The group of actors who had been standing on the theatre steps had left; it was by now very late. I had also drunk rather more than I was accustomed to, so I resolved to consider the plan afresh the next day. I made my way home, feeling warm and sleepy, with my belly full of beer and the satisfaction of having conquered adversity.

The next morning the idea had not lost its piquancy. I did not feel the slightest bit apprehensive; on the contrary, I felt a self-congratulatory thrill at my own inventiveness. I dressed, humming to myself, and went downstairs to eat a leisurely breakfast and read the *Prager Tagblatt*. I decided to take the morning off work to organise the matter. The dinner was that evening, but this did not worry me in the least. Surely the whole thing could be arranged in less than two hours. I turned my mind to the question of where to find an actor. There were of course the national and municipal theatres, but I thought that it might be more prudent to look at one of the smaller dramatic societies, where the actors were more likely to be unknown. As I drank another cup of coffee, I looked at the entertainment notices at the back of the newspaper and copied down the names and addresses of some of the smaller dramatic societies into my notebook.

I decided to make my first call the Bohemian Company, a students' acting group. They had a theatre close by, near the opera building. Outside in the street the day was bright and clear and I made my unhurried way through the morning crowds. The prospect of having solved the niggling problem of Franz had me smiling broadly as I walked along. The sun warmed my skin and

I had the benign feeling of a man on holiday. The only thing that remained now was what to tell the actor who I would engage. The true story was out of the question, naturally. I considered my options. I could pose as a director, an eccentric director, and present the thing as a kind of audition. But word of that might get out and I needed to keep this as quiet as possible. Ideally I would tell as few people as possible, but approaching a theatre troupe meant that of course the whole group would come to hear of it. It would be much better simply to approach an actor individually. I ran through those of my acquaintances who acted, but of course those known to me might also be known to Theodor.

Perhaps if I offered a large enough cash incentive, I could limit the amount of questions that would be asked. But how much should I offer? Too much and people would certainly start talking. Perhaps I could offer the amount equivalent to a day's wage, or slightly more. Would eighty crowns do? I had my chequebook with me, but I decided it would be a good idea to have a sum of cash also at the ready. I stopped at the bank and withdrew two hundred crowns, which would certainly more than suffice.

I found myself at the address that I had written in my notebook. It was a small corner building, damp and dirty and overshadowed by the opera. A rusted tin plate announced that the Bohemian Company had their rooms in the cellar. Suddenly all my good humour deserted me. What exactly should I say? The clock struck, making me jump. It was already ten. I felt conspicuous, hovering there in the doorway, so I went in. I would improvise.

I went down the stone staircase and into the cellar. The underground room was very dark, with only one feeble lamp and a row of narrow windows high on the wall, just beneath the low ceiling. At first I thought that the room was empty, but after a moment my eyes adjusted and I could see a circle of people sitting on cushions on the floor, their heads all turned in my direction. We looked at each other for a stunned moment before a very tall young man got up to greet me. The rest of the troupe remained sitting on the floor, where they murmured to each other in low voices.

I decided that an indirect approach would be best. The young man came over with an outstretched hand, introduced himself as Jan, and asked what he could do for me. I had not thought of preparing an alias, but I gave my name as Schmidt. I tried for a bold and worldly demeanour and told Jan that I had some work to offer one of them.

'What kind of work?'

'Well, acting, of course.'

The room had grown silent and I could see the rest of the Bohemian Company watching us from their corner.

'Fine, but what kind of show do you have in mind? Our current focus is work in the style of Meiningen.' Jan stretched himself a little taller as he spoke the name of his heroes.

'Well, it isn't so much a show as, ah, a single-night performance.'

Jan frowned and waited for me to go on. I desperately searched for a way to explain my request. My eyes wandered from Jan's face and stared out through the narrow strip of window through which the feet of passers-by were visible.

'Ah, realism certainly is the style,' I said after a moment. 'Authentic realism.'

I glanced at Jan. He was still frowning and his eyes had narrowed. He folded his arms across his chest. I decided to just tell him.

'Look,' I said, 'there's this man who I'm looking for and can't find. I just want someone to play him for one night.'

It was only after the words were out of my mouth that I realised how shameful they sounded. As I spoke, Jan had taken a step backwards, away from me.

'At a dinner I mean,' I went on. I could feel my cheeks reddening. 'For a few hours only. At a public café. I can offer you eighty crowns.'

Jan's lips had curled in disgust. 'Herr Schmidt,' he spat out the spurious name, 'we here are serious artists. Perhaps you would have more success at some other establishment. Good day.'

He turned his back and stalked back to rest of his company. I tried to keep my head up as I slunk to the stairs and left the room. Out on the street I hurried from the scene with my head buried deep in my collar. I let the crowds carry me along, my only concern to put as much distance as possible between myself and the Bohemian Company.

When I had walked enough to be out of breath, I looked at my watch. It was half-past eleven. I had thought that by this time I would have had the whole thing organised and I would be sitting comfortably at the desk in my office, drinking a cup of tea. My confidence began to falter and my heart started up a panicky rhythm: there were not more than seven or eight hours remaining until the dinner. I pictured how Theodor's face would look—stony, one eyebrow cocked—if I dared to appear without Franz. I forced my mind away from this scenario.

I realised that I was quite close to the insurance office and considered calling there again in case I could produce the real Franz at the dinner. I had somehow forgotten in the hours of that morning that there was in fact a real Franz. But by now my plan had taken root in my mind, and the idea of sitting alongside the real Franz while Theodor got what he wanted filled me with disgust. Besides, given that Franz seemed not to actually want to meet Theodor, by producing a substitute Franz I was actually doing the real Franz a favour. I decided to forgo another visit to the insurance office and instead I took out my notebook to look up the address of the other theatre group that I wanted to try: the Black Cat Ensemble in the Ziegengasse. I estimated that I could go there and still be back at the post office within an hour.

As I walked, I considered the plan anew. Now I could see two possible problems. The first and most significant was if Franz had received Theodor's and my messages and did appear at the dinner that night. But I considered his past behaviour and concluded that the chance of this was rather low. Besides, if I arrived at the café with the impostor Franz Kafka first, then should the real Kafka arrive later he would be the one to appear as the impostor if I labelled him as such. It would be his word against mine. I merely had to ensure that the imposter and I arrived at the café early. The second potential problem was that the person I presented as Franz might be known to Theodor. But this could be explained away if Franz Kafka was a pseudonymous creation. In fact, that might even help to explain Franz's reluctance to meet with Theodor in the first place.

There still remained the question of what to say when I arrived at the Black Cat theatre company. Clearly, I needed a different approach to the one I had used with the Bohemians. Perhaps saying that the evening was an audition was a better plan. Or I could say that I was playing a practical joke on a friend. Of course! This seemed like a winning idea to me: innocuous, amusing. It was perfect.

Obviously I also needed to think of a more plausible name than Schmidt. Czerny? Cervenka? Karel Czerny. He sounded like a practical joker. I could surely pass as Karel Czerny. *The name is Czerny*, I mouthed to myself as I walked along.

I soon arrived at my destination. This group had a little wooden sign with a painted image of a black cat, hissing, with an arched back and bared fangs. Its long tail was raised in a question mark that curled around the top of the sign. The cat's green eyes bored into mine, daring me to go in. *Karel Czerny*. I went inside.

Despite my preparation this time, my experience with the Black Cat Ensemble strongly resembled the one I had had at the Bohemian Company, and once again I found myself scurrying away down the street, shamefaced. There must have been something shifty in my countenance, for I am usually a highly credible liar, my body having schooled me in the arts of deception from a most tender age.

Now I was at a loss. It was past midday. I let myself drift through the streets at random. My mind was numb and empty, and I concentrated only on negotiating the uneven stones of the street. What with my slow progress and keeping my eyes trained on the ground, now and then people cannoned into me. After one of these collisions I looked up directly into the eyes of Franz. He was walking towards me, still a few metres away. He seemed not to have seen me. I felt dizzy and a kind of violent mist rose up before my eyes. I felt the urge to kill him on the spot. I reached out for the wall to steady myself, but when I looked again I saw that it was not Franz after all, only a man so like him that he could have been Franz's twin.

I was still standing with my hand on the wall, and I remained there while the man walked past me, coming so close that I could smell his dusty odour of tobacco. I turned to watch his receding back. Without thinking, I began to follow him. The man walked quickly, deftly threading his way through the traffic, stepping sometimes onto the street to move around some slower walker. It was a strain to keep pace with him. My intractable feet slipped and twisted on the difficult stones, and I clutched, uncaring, onto anything near me to keep my balance: windows, walls, other people. My heart was hammering with exertion and the fear that I would lose him. The man was perfect. He was the one I wanted. But how to approach him? I would say that I had a proposition for him, a way to earn some money, I decided. I would invite him for a drink to discuss it. I would keep to my story of the practical joke.

The man was slowing down and seeming to hesitate at a cross-street. I caught up with him and then I was standing beside him. The base of my throat throbbed with my laboured breathing. Now was the moment.

'Excuse me,' I said, touching the fabric of his suit lightly with my fingertips.

He turned slowly towards me. I was standing very close to him and I inspected the side of his face. Even at such close range, every detail of his appearance was like Franz's. I saw his eyes widen questioningly as he focused on my face, but very quickly this expression was overlaid with one that I quickly recognised as disgust. I saw his eyes flick down the length of my crooked body and he immediately took a step away from me, his features disfigured in a sneer. He shook his head slightly, a small flick to the right and the left, and then plunged across the street. He gave one glance back over his shoulder, probably to make certain that I was not following him, still with that look of revulsion.

The old shame at my body crept over my skin and my scalp contracted with it. I could feel the sweat beading on my forehead and plastering my shirt to my back. My breath wheezed in and out. I reached up to remove my hat and noticed that it had been perched crookedly on my head. No doubt I would present a frightening prospect to a stranger in the street. I leaned back against the wall for a moment to rest, but I was too conscious of the glances of passers-by to gain any comfort, so I forced myself to shuffle onwards. Pain radiated up through my feet and stiffened my right side. I desperately needed to rest. I looked around and saw that I was on the Karlshofergasse, in an area of the city I rarely visited. There was a small pub on the corner. Normally I would not enter such a down-at-heel place, but my body was crying out in exhaustion, so I went inside.

The walls were panelled with dark wood, which made the place into a well of gloomy damp, stinking of sour beer and unwashed flesh. There were few patrons at this hour and I found a table away from the others, close to the window. A pale serving girl in a dirty blouse came up immediately, and I ordered a beer. I sat looking out of the window, the glass of which was so encrusted with dirt that the street outside was distorted into a hazy landscape that resembled a grey ocean scene, with rolling dunes and striped waves. The girl came back with my beer, which was slopping down the sides of a grubby mug. I didn't want to touch it, let alone bring it to my lips. I sat watching the bubbles slowly deflate. It was a huge relief just to be sitting down, and my tired body was beginning to relax. I let my head lean back against the wall and I closed my eyes.

'Good day, sir.'

My eyes snapped open. There was a man sitting opposite me at the small table. He was about the same age as me, handsome in a rugged way, dark and unshaven. He was wearing the light blue uniform of the mountain infantry, though it was hardly recognisable for its shabbiness. The limp collar was worn thin and marked with a greenish stain of sweat around the neck. His cap was ragged and pushed far back on his head to allow room for the rakish black curl that fell almost to one eye.

'You looked lonely sitting here all on your own,' he said. 'I thought you might like a little company.'

His voice was deep and musical. He bent forward and slid his loosely clasped hands towards me across the surface of the dirty table. His knowing eyes sought mine and he smiled, full-lipped.

I had no doubt as to his intentions, but I was surprised to be propositioned so boldly in the middle of the day, even here in the Karlshofergasse. Also, the fact that he wore his uniform was shocking to me. But perhaps he had no other clothing. I wondered what awful punishment would await him were his superiors to discover his attempts to sell himself, no doubt out of the need to supplement his insufficient army income. I am not a homosexual, though homosexuality has often been attributed to me. I know that this comes from my monstrous appearance, which at a glance aligns me with that dark shadow world where forbidden love lives.

But I have no horror of these men, and rather feel sympathy for and a kinship with them.

The soldier looked thin, with burning eyes glaring from sunken hollows. He was certain to be unknown to Theodor. Perhaps this was better than a theatre actor; arguably the practice of his trade also called for the adoption of roles, one might even say to a far more convincing degree than that demanded by genteel theatre audiences.

'Karel,' I said, stretching my hand across the table. He took it almost tenderly. I realised then that, if he was going to meet Theodor, he would have to know my name. 'But call me Max,' I said.

He did not blink an eye. 'Alexandr,' he said.

I told my story of the practical joke, and he heard it with a bland expression. He asked no questions, outside of what he would be required to do. Then he told me his fee. The whole thing was arranged in a matter of minutes and at a far lower price than I had expected. He asked for half of the sum now and half afterwards. 'Seeing as it's an advance booking,' he explained. I was glad that I had thought of withdrawing the cash that morning.

The only difficulty was Alexandr's uniform. It seemed altogether too unlikely that the author of the works of genius that Theodor had read was an infantryman. As I had suspected, Alexandr said when I asked that he had no other clothes, at least none that would be suitable to wear at a dinner. My budget did not run to a new suit of clothes and Alexandr would not fit into my other suit. We haggled a while before Alexandr agreed to find a suit before this evening, for an extra twenty-five crowns. We agreed to meet at the café where Theodor's dinner was to be held. Completely irrationally, I instinctively trusted Alexandr. There was something reassuring and honest about him—no doubt one of the tricks of his trade.

We shook hands, and I left the pub and went to the post office. I had thought I might feel nervous, but in fact I felt relaxed and freed of responsibility. I had tossed the whole problem into the lap of the fates to decide; now I would simply await the outcome.

§

I was the first to arrive at the café that evening. I sat watching the door with a complete absence of anxiety, merely interest as to who would come through it. Would it be Theodor? 'Franz'? Franz? I did not have to wait long before Theodor arrived, and his expression on seeing me alone made me glad of the labours I had undertaken that day.

'And where is your friend?' he asked me, before he had even taken his seat. His voice came out at a higher pitch than usual.

'You are early,' I said. 'He will be here.'

Neither of us spoke as we waited. I could feel the tension rising off Theodor like waves of heat. He had his eyes trained on the door with the intensity of a gun dog.

At exactly the appointed time, a figure appeared at the door. I could make out a black hat through the glass panel, and my heart tightened for a moment, but when the door swung open Alexandr came in. He had certainly kept his word. He was scrubbed and shaven, wearing an elegant suit of light grey.

'Here he is,' I said.

Alexandr moved with grace and precision. Theodor's face as he watched Alexandr thread his way through the tables was as beatific as if he were in the grip of religious ecstasy.

I introduced the two men. Alexandr played his part perfectly; I doubted whether one of the actors from the National Theatre could have pulled it off so well. In ten minutes he had charmed Theodor, and even I had almost forgotten that he was not the real Franz.

It had occurred to me that Theodor would ask Alexandr something about the stories, about which he would know nothing, and the deception would be revealed, so I sat ready to intervene at any moment. But I needn't have worried. While we ordered the food and waited for it to come, Theodor kept the talk about general topics before he gradually steered the discussion around to his main objective: the terms of his contract with 'Franz'. I could see that Theodor was uncomfortable discussing this with me sitting by, and before long I began to feel the same way. I was resentful, though not surprised, to find that the terms he was offering Franz were much more generous than those under which I laboured. I felt like a child whose father favoured his sibling over him. I had to keep reminding myself that the man sitting in front of me, who now had the pen in his hand and was signing the contract, was not Franz, and that I had in fact averted a crisis.

As soon as the contract was signed, Theodor slipped it into his briefcase and stood up to go, leaving most of his meal uneaten. No doubt he was afraid that the precious contract that had for so long eluded him would somehow be snatched from his grasp at the last moment.

'I do apologise,' he said. 'Tomorrow morning I go to Vienna for a conference. I must bid you goodnight.'

He directed a small bow in Alexandr's direction and then in mine.

'Max, you are a good man,' he said. 'I am in your debt.'

I watched him walk out the door, then I sat back with a sigh. I knew that I had done the right thing.

8.

IN THE FOLLOWING WEEKS I HEARD NOTHING FROM EITHER
Theodor or Franz, and the problem of Franz appeared to have
been solved. I was happy to be able to forget the whole thing, as I
was more preoccupied than ever with Anja. Her university examination period was about to begin and, in much the same way that
I had been neglecting my work on Schopenhauer, Anja had been
neglecting her studies. I felt no guilt whatsoever about this; to me
the neglect was solely a validation of the strength of her feelings
for me.

I began helping her to prepare for her exams. She was particularly nervous about the oral examination, and in order to better
assist her I had learned her subjects with such vigour that it was
as though I were taking the exam myself. I set her difficult questions and interrogated her—once, I recall with shame, until she
started to cry. I enjoyed my role of tutor. I enjoyed watching her
strain to express herself concisely and synthesise ideas. She had a
quick intelligence and I had no doubt that she would impress her

examiners. Of course, at that time beautiful young female students were more of a rarity than they are now, and I felt that this would put her at no disadvantage with her professors.

I was walking back to my house from one of our many hours of study together, my head deep in the planning of the next lesson, when I heard my name being called. I looked up and there was Franz, the real Franz, standing in front of me in the street. At first I could not believe that it was really him. Seeing him gave me a morbid jolt, like seeing a man whom one had thought was dead. Indeed, the whole episode with Alexandr had almost convinced me that he was. But there he was, alive as ever. His nose sliced the air in front of him, underlining his presence, and the outline his body made against the street scene was as sharp as though he had been cut from a page and superimposed onto it.

Without preamble he proceeded to describe a new work that he had been writing. He told me that it was almost finished, and then he produced a sheaf of papers—his manuscript—which he handed to me as though we had agreed to meet by appointment for this purpose. He did not mention the many messages I had sent, and although I was bewildered by this, of course I did not probe him.

'You'll look over the manuscript,' he said to me. It was more of an order than a request. Once again I was baffled as to why he would bother to press his writing on me when it was clear that he did not need my help.

I had automatically taken the manuscript, and the weight and thickness of the pages in my hand reminded me that my own writing had gone neglected and forgotten, the pages lying crumpled and senseless in the dark of desk drawers and briefcase pockets.

The extra time that I had bought for myself had made me lazier rather than spurring me on. It was true that at odd times I had sat down at my writing table with my notes arranged before me, ready to work, but all it ever amounted to was me discovering anew that the material I had was depressingly impenetrable. After a short time I would give up and instead take out my journal and write about Anja.

But even the pages of my journal were strikingly blank for all the time I devoted to them. In truth, most of the minutes and hours when I should have been writing were spent sitting and staring out of the window in a reverie. Thinking about Anja induced in my body a feeling of floating warmth, which cocooned me from the passing minutes and hours. In a way, I preferred this time of remembrance and musing to the time I spent with her. When I was with her, her presence was too overwhelming, too beautiful for me to fully take in.

As I held the pages of Franz's manuscript in my hand, the bile rose in me. How foolish I had been to think that the problem of Franz would simply fade away. I had never even considered the obvious fact that he would continue to write. For the first time I did not agree to look over his work as he had asked. Instead I told him about Anja, about how close we had become over the last weeks and months. I felt the unfamiliar thrill of sexual victory in the telling, something I rarely experienced; the thrill of having won a prize, of having beaten an opponent. Thrill, and a kind of pity. After all, what worth was some manuscript, even one that might prove a masterpiece, compared with the discovery of love?

I had expected Franz to be surprised by my revelation, even openly upset or bitter, but he just nodded and said that he had heard about it.

'Congratulations.' He said it with the most correct politeness and gave a crisp little bow. 'Tell Anja that I wish her well for her exams.'

We parted, and for the remainder of my way home there was a heavy stone of uneasiness in my chest. I carried the papers in my hand, and they hissed at my side, rebuking me for my laziness. Of course the manuscript had upset me, but there was also the shock of seeing Franz again. Now it dawned on me that my deception of Theodor was brazen and irresponsible in the extreme. Surely the affair would come to light and then I would be completely ruined. It was only a matter of time. Franz's parting words came back to me and I took them in for the first time. How could he know about Anja's exams? I had not mentioned them to him. Had she been in contact with him? On the one hand it seemed unlikely. When would she have had the time to meet with him? During the day he was barricaded in his office, seeing no visitors, and in the evenings I had been with her. It was impossible that they could have met. But then how else could he have known?

When I arrived home I stuffed Franz's manuscript into one of the drawers of my writing table and tried to put him out of my mind. I went back to revising my notes for Anja's study.

The exam about which she was the most anxious was her final one. It was in a few days' time, and I was planning to feign illness on that day so I would be free to accompany her. I had also bought her a small gift for the occasion: a jewelled comb for her hair. I took it from the box in which the jeweller had packed it and held it in my hand. It had three tortoiseshell prongs, which were surmounted by a little crown of red and silver stones: garnet, the jeweller had told me, and marcasite. It gave off a gentle warmth and the stones shot darts of light up at me. My heart raced at the idea of giving it to her and a host of doubts crowded into my mind. Was it the right style? Was it too serious to give such a gift? Too overblown? I had deliberated over the gift for hours, touring all the jewellery shops of the city and changing my mind a thousand times. I had never before had the occasion to purchase anything of this nature.

When the day of the exam arrived, the thought of giving Anja the gift reduced me to a state of nerves that must have rivalled Anja's own. I was acutely aware of the little box with the comb sitting in my breast pocket, where it exerted a uniquely painful weight and pressure on my chest.

I could feel it there in my pocket when I collected Anja from her house and during the whole walk with her to the examination room. I spent the hour of her exam wandering the university grounds and the botanical gardens. The summer had faded since I had last been there and the gardens had assumed their autumn colours. There were several people walking the paths and admiring the red and gold foliage of the trees, but I found the dying leaves repellent; the yellow ones like ghosts, the few remaining green ones with their living edges being eaten away by a rusty decay that would slowly engulf them before they silently fell to be crushed underfoot or swept away by a gardener. The people's exclamations at their beauty seemed inconsiderate, even gruesome, as if they were admiring the hue of the bruises on a dying man.

I went and sat on the bench beneath the ginkgo tree where I had first sat with Anja. We had returned here several times to sit and talk, but I had never really seen the garden; when I was with her she filled all of my gaze. I looked up at the yellow leaves quivering against the sky, echoing my heart with their nervous motion. I took out the comb for the hundredth time and looked at it, rehearsing again in my mind what I would say when I presented it to her.

I became aware of a rustling hiss and felt something brush softly against my face. I pocketed the comb and looked up once more and a ginkgo leaf drifted past, and then another. The rustling became louder and soon the ginkgo leaves were fluttering down all around me, though there was no wind. I sat perfectly still, now staring straight ahead, and let myself be covered by their fall. People walking the paths stopped in front of the tree to exclaim, and to catch the leaves as they fell, for luck. Soon there was a small crowd standing around the tree.

'You're going to be the luckiest man alive!' a man said to me as he caught a leaf and then discarded it in the hope of a more perfect specimen.

The leaves fell over me and filled up the brim of my hat and the cup of my palm lying open in my lap. I turned my face up and closed my eyes and the leaves rained down around me in a curtain of crisp sighs, brushing over my face like dry butterfly wings.

I remained sitting there until Anja's exam had finished, but before I left I selected two of the most perfect leaves from my palm—one for her and one for me—to keep as good-luck charms.

It was a good omen: for Anja's exam, for our love, for my own writing. I put Anja's into the jeweller's box. The ginkgo rain had dissolved the tension I had been feeling and I felt strong and happy, chiming at one with the pulse of the world. It was just like the man had said: I was the luckiest man alive.

When I met Anja, she was flushed and talkative, and was swaggering along like a little sailor after a few glasses of rum. My heart ached with love for her. We walked aimlessly about the corridors while she unleashed a torrent of words: the questions she was asked, the answers she had given, and effusive gratitude for the hours I had spent practising with her.

Now was the perfect moment to give her the gift. I kept putting my hand into my breast pocket to take out the box but she always had something more to say and I was unwilling to interrupt her. My fingers nervously ran up and down one of the sharp edges of the box inside my pocket while I waited. At last there came a pause and I steered her to a low balustrade where we both sat down.

I took out the box and gave it to her with a trembling hand. My prepared words failed me and all I could manage was a broken, 'Congratulations.' My hands were clammy and I had to look away while she opened the box and took out the comb. When I looked back again she had taken out the ginkgo leaf and was holding it up with a questioning look.

I told her then about the ginkgo rain, and being the luckiest man alive, and her the luckiest woman. Later I realised how arrogant this sounded. She did not say anything, but looked into the distance and twirled the leaf against her lips. Her soft breath fluted over its edges. The comb lay still in its nest of cotton.

'Won't you try the comb?' I tried to keep my voice steady.

She looked down at the comb and then closed the lid and gave me back the box, the ginkgo leaf held now between her ring and small finger. She shook her head. 'I can't take it, Max. I'm sorry.'

For all my nerves and worry I had somehow not prepared myself for this, yet at that moment I felt no emotion. Mechanically, I pocketed the box again.

'But this leaf,' she said, 'I will keep forever.'

She suggested that we take a stroll through the gardens. We climbed up and down the stone steps and she talked and exclaimed and hung onto my arm as though the incident with the comb had never occurred. At her touch my feelings began rushing back, all my love for her, together now with a desperate and crushing panic.

How could she have rejected my gift and yet still promenade with me now, whispering in my ear and collecting pretty leaves to show me? I could not understand it, and yet a part of me knew. Franz. It had to be. The idea clicked into place with all the inexorable finality of a lock snapping shut. Clearly, I saw now, he had mentioned her exams to me in order to demonstrate that he, too, was close to her, but I had not been willing to look this fact in the face. But perhaps, I told myself in a moment of optimism, it was Herr Liška. It could equally well be him. Losing Anja to Liška would be terrible, but it could be borne. But Franz . . . I could not live with that ending to my and Anja's story.

Of course I could have saved myself the inner torment of this guessing game simply by asking her. I could know the truth in seconds. But somehow I could not bring myself to do it. The question was too shaming. Instead I walked mutely along beside her, through the gardens and then back to her house, my mind sick with whirling suspicions. I imagined her meeting with Franz and his thin, elegant hands pawing at her, his slick smile inches from her face. I imagined the two of them laughing together, perhaps about me, and Franz mocking me. For a few moments I began to hate her.

After I had returned her to her house, I automatically made my way home, but when I arrived at the door I was unable to go inside. The house seemed suddenly as small as a coffin. Instead of going in I turned away from the door and began to walk at random. I walked up the darkened Karpfengasse and crossed the Moldau over the little Kettensteg bridge. I stood for a long time on the bridge, watching the surface of the water slide away beneath my feet.

I took the little box from my pocket, the comb still inside, and dropped it into the dark river. I felt no emotion. I did not even hear it hit the surface. I found the ginkgo leaf in my trouser pocket and dropped it in too. It fell to the water in a series of swoops like broken sobs, then it sailed away down the river, a little yellow boat on a sea of black.

9.

FOR SOME DAYS AFTER THIS I STAYED IN MY ROOM, SUFFERING with a fever that made a truth of the illness I had feigned at the post office. I drifted in and out of sleep, slipping between the world of the familiar room, and Elsa and Sophie, and another world of a continuous dream that was just as real as the world of my bedroom.

In the dream I was running after Anja and Franz was running after me across the whole city. My body was as heavy as a lump of stone and wouldn't obey me. I strained to catch up with Anja, who was reduced to the hem of a skirt or a sweep of hair that was always just disappearing around a corner, out of reach. My chest burned with exertion and I let out mute cries, and the terror that I would lose sight of her was the terror of death. Meanwhile, Franz pursued me with a giant's strides, brandishing a sheaf of papers like a club. I would wake gasping from these dreams, my sweat chilling my skin.

When I was awake the anxiety about my writing and Franz returned and competed with the anxiety I felt about Anja's rejection. After some days, when I had recovered slightly, I began to write her letters, but I did not know what tone to take, who to be in the letter. Letter after letter I wrote and then discarded, throwing them into the fire when my wastepaper basket had overflowed.   .

I lay in bed and analysed her behaviour, every look, every word, every gesture that I could remember, in a futile round that always ended with everything slipping away from me. The only conclusion I could reach was that I was uncertain as to what was between us and what might be between her and Franz.

Postcards and letters began to arrive for me: from Kröner at the post office, from Felix and Kurt, and of course several from Uta. I received none from Anja.

Uta's were the first to arrive: she must have heard from Sophie about my illness. They were written, of course, on pastel-shaded, scented paper, Uta's looping hand scrawling inferior epigrams and clichéd wishes across the page. I opened the first one by accident and was overcome with nausea as the perfume with which the paper was infused reached my nostrils. Uta also visited several times and my ears were constantly on alert for her shrill voice raised in greeting at the front door. As soon as I heard it I feigned sleep, so that when Sophie brought her to my bedroom the door only opened a small way and then quietly closed again. I would lie motionless until I heard their whispered voices recede down the hallway.

A postcard also came from Theodor, ostensibly to wish me well in my illness but really to remind me of my looming deadline. It seemed that he was not as much in my debt from my procurement of 'Franz' as I'd hoped. To give myself the courage to examine my shambolic notes, I took out a copy of my novel and leafed through the pages. But the printed words I saw there were so foreign to me that I felt my eyebrows travel up my forehead in surprise at my own cleverness. I could not recognise myself in the words I read.

Perhaps, I thought, the problem was that it was written too long ago. I went through my papers to find something more recent, but after some searching I realised that there was nothing, apart from the few scratchings of notes that I was steeling myself to read. Then I remembered the story that I had written a few months before when I had fallen asleep at my writing table. I searched through my desk without finding it, before remembering that I had taken it to work with me. But when I looked in my briefcase it was not to be found there either. I must have left it in my office.

My desk and the floor around it was now littered with papers and books. My eyes fell on Franz's manuscript. The weight of all of that paper, the thought of his hand making all those minute motions of the pen across the page, dismayed me. I felt drawn to read it, compelled by a sick desire to measure myself against him. I took the manuscript back to bed with me and looked for the first time at the title page: *Die Verwandlung.* I disregarded the pages with plans that preceded the text and began to read.

Even the first lines caused the skin over my skull and the back of my neck to contract with horror. When I read the description of Gregor, the vermin, getting out of the bed, his body monstrous and uncontrollable, I had the impression that I was reading a story about

---

* *The Metamorphosis*

myself. It was like looking in a mirror. Gregor's experience on that first morning is my own on every morning of my life. In the realm of sleep I am not hampered by palsied limbs and misshapen bones. There, I glide through the world without obstacles. Waking every day is waking to a cage that must be carried around at all times, without exception.

When I was five years old my childhood ended. My body had grown enough to reveal the broken form that it would take and my poor foot trailed behind me as I walked. I listed like a ship, as I had not yet learned how to negotiate the distribution of my weight. My mother took me to the house of a healer she had heard of—a shoemaker and man of miracles who lived in the forest to the south. It was winter, and a long journey, first by a series of trains and then the final part by carriage over the icy roads. I remember pressing my face against the cold sheet of the carriage window and seeing the forest advancing darkly upon us like a storm cloud.

I did not really know where we were going, only that we were going to make me better, make me like the other boys. As a child I was desperate to please my mother. I was aware that somehow I was always disappointing her but I did not know the reason for it. I strained for her affection, hungered to make her proud of me. But whenever she looked at me there was always in her eyes a wall of sadness, a regret that she would quickly hide behind some other emotion. No matter how well behaved I was or how many things I learned, this look was always hovering close by, ready to emerge at an unguarded moment.

The shoemaker's house was far from the nearest village, on the very edge of the forest. It was a small cottage, cosy and neat, with smoke drifting from the chimney, but behind it a dense wall of trees surged up like a black wave about to engulf it. There was a little kitchen garden, covered in snow, which was surrounded by a wooden fence. Beside the front door was a kind of trellis, and when we came closer I saw that upon it hung a range of rusted tools. My eyes fell on the blades of all kinds of jagged saws and monstrous scissors and metal implements that I could not name. At the sight of these I began to cry and pull on my mother's hand, refusing to go any closer. I had visions of the man hanging me up somewhere and slicing pieces of flesh from my side with the rusty tools, the way a butcher slices sides of meat from a hanging carcass.

The interior of the shoemaker's house was filled with an even greater range of nightmarish tools and machines. Of the man himself I had seen only his large and muddy boots, which sprouted from the ground like huge brown mushrooms. I was too afraid to raise my eyes, so the current of his conversation with my mother took place over my head, against the background of my jagged inhalations and snuffling breaths. Eventually, the man crouched down before me and raised my head with his hand under my chin. His hand was rough and hard but I was surprised at the kindness of his eyes. He looked at me for a moment and smiled, and then straight away got down to the business of measuring me. He stood me on a raised block, like a little pedestal in the middle of the room, and I swayed unsteadily there, crying for my mother. He produced a series of callipers and measuring tapes. I had never seen callipers before and I imagined them to be some kind of device for torture that would compress parts of me in their jaws. I could see them crunching down on my bones. I screamed and cried when he approached and my mother came to my side and held my hand, stroking the back of it and speaking to me in a low monotone to soothe me. She told me that the man was only measuring me and not to be afraid, and that it was just like being measured by the tailor for my clothes. Measuring took a long time, and the man laboriously wrote the numbers on a scrap of paper.

My mother and I stayed in the nearest village for some days, but the details of the place have been lost from my memory. I only remember that my mother's sadness seemed to intensify during this time. She was also excessively gentle and permissive with me. She allowed me to choose the food I would eat, and did not insist that I rise from bed at a particular hour. Although this pleased me at first—normally I only received these privileges when it was my birthday, or some special occasion—as day followed day, these unaccustomed freedoms began to make me uneasy.

I remember clearly our second visit to the house of the shoemaker. My mother was very agitated on the journey and told me that the man had built something very special for me to make me well. Since she had mentioned tailors to me before I imagined that this would be some item of clothing, like one of the magic cloaks that I had read about in my books of fairy tales at home. The shoemaker's house seemed less sinister to me as we approached it, now that I could associate him with the wise men and women of the stories. I became quite excited and forgot my apprehension of recent days.

The man stood me once again on the pedestal and I eagerly looked around the room for my magic garment, but there were no bolts of cloth to be seen. Neither were there any rows of coloured cotton on long stands as there were at the tailor's shop.

The shoemaker left the room and I imagined the moment that I would be dressed in the cloak. I wondered what magic powers the cloak would give me, and worked myself up into quite a state of nervous expectation.

At last the shoemaker returned. In his hands he held not a cloak, but a kind of skeleton made of wood and metal with leather straps hanging off it and a canvas middle section. It looked a bit like the harnesses used for horses, but much smaller. He approached me with it and, like a young untrained horse, I shied away when he tried to place it on me. Even my mother's words could not soothe me this time and I dodged the shoemaker and tried to run out of the room, but he caught me in his arms and lifted me back onto the pedestal—patiently at first, but after a few attempted escapes he grasped hold of me roughly and shoved me onto the hard ground, holding me down and forcing the harness over my head. I struggled and tried to fight him with my fists, but it was like hurling myself against a great tree. I was soon totally exhausted and lay back, limp, on the dirty stone floor. The shoemaker picked me up again and placed me on the pedestal, and this time I did not resist and just stood slack and still. He adjusted straps here and there and turned me about.

The harness had two curved pieces of wood that hooked under my armpits, and from which two flat metal bars ran in a vertical line down my ribs to my hips on either side. A further two rods reinforced the back of the harness. Two leather straps like stirrup leathers on a saddle were fastened in a crossed fashion over my shoulders onto the front of the two wooden hooks. This wood and metal structure was lined with canvas in the shape of a tight vest. It was uncomfortable enough with the straps unfastened, heavy and thick. When the straps were tightened, it was almost unbearable. My crooked torso did not fit the shape of the straight metal reinforcing rods and, although they were slightly flexible, they strained against my flesh and threw me off balance. I looked at my mother and saw that she was crying. The shoemaker lifted me down from the platform and I waited for him to undo the straps again, but he did not. I wore that harness for the next year of my life for every hour of the day, except when washing. It was impossible to sleep the first few weeks. I would lie in every position I could think of and secretly loosen the shoulder straps, but to little effect; for that whole year I felt I was living in the grip of a vice, where I had to strain to take every breath.

Each time I had a bath my mother would come and examine me to try to find signs of my body straightening, but even after some months had passed the only visible effect the harness had on my body were several permanent open sores under my arms and on various points of my torso, where the metal bands pushed against my soft skin, and two deep grooves on the tops of my shoulders from the straps, which I still carry on my body today.

Lying there in my bed, I could feel again the leather straps and metal rods tighten around me, cutting into my flesh. I touched the deep runnels on my shoulders. Reading about Gregor was about as unnerving as hearing another person speak with my voice. I read and reread the opening sequence and felt a sense of vertigo, as though my fever had returned.

It occurred to me that I was Gregor; I was the model for him. I must be. That Franz, all the time we had been together, had been silently observing me as though I were some rare specimen, storing up impressions and noting them down to imprison me in his story like pinning an insect to a card. The more I read, the more convinced I became that this was the case, and that Gregor was a thinly veiled version of me.

I felt terribly ashamed, as if I had been paraded naked down the Wenzelsplatz in the middle of the day, with every one of my flaws and faults visible to all. I quite literally felt that I wanted to die. I threw the manuscript into the corner of the room and it landed with its pages splayed out, flower-like, over the carpet. I fell back onto the bed. I felt too ill to get up and go out, but too well to sleep in the middle of the day. I expected to lie there in agony for hours but instead I immediately fell into a deep sleep.

I dreamed that I had woken in my own bed. Everything in the room looked exactly the same as it had earlier, except now it was night-time, which made it difficult to tell if I dreamed or was awake. I looked over to where I had thrown the manuscript, but it was gone. I heard a shuffling sound and a white shape like an enormous flat spider scuttled out from under the bed and ran underneath the sofa. Its many-legged, jerky gait made me nauseous and light-headed. I got out of bed and picked up one of my shoes. Silently in my bare feet, with my knees bent for stealth, I tiptoed very slowly across the room. I brought the shoe up over my head, ready to strike.

Holding my breath, I bent down to look under the sofa. The creature was huddled there against the wall. It looked like it was made of paper. I reached my hand with the shoe under the sofa to chase it out, but it flattened itself onto the floor and the shoe passed harmlessly over the top of it. As I withdrew the shoe and was standing up again, considering what to do next, the creature dashed out from under the sofa straight at my bare ankles. It flew against me with angry rustles, the edges of the paper cutting and cutting my flesh. It wrapped its pages around my ankles like the tentacles of an octopus, hobbling my legs together.

I screamed and began swiping at my legs and jumping from foot to foot, trying to dislodge it. The touch of the thing against my skin disgusted me and worried me much more than the streaks of blood that were running over my feet and onto the carpet. I raised the shoe over my head and brought it down on the creature with a crunch, dislodging a few pages. I beat and beat at it until it was a torn lump of pulpy pages scattered on the floor.

I awoke with a sense of triumph. It was night-time and I could see the whitish glow of the manuscript in the corner where I had thrown it. It was only a manuscript: perhaps it was the only manuscript, the only copy. Was this likely? I did not know if Franz made carbon copies or had arranged for the novel to be copied before passing it to me.

I revisited the satisfaction of my dream, the feeling of beating the bundle of papers to a pulp, then began to fantasise about different ways I could destroy the manuscript. I could throw it in the fire, using the poker to break up the last remnants of paper into the finest powder. I could shred it into pieces as small as snowflakes and cast them over the Moldau. Or I could drown it in water and then mash the pages into a papier-mâché ball, which I would then mould into the shape of a man's head and display on a shelf.

As pleasant as my thoughts were, these actions were unlikely to have any effect. Franz, I mused, was a lawyer who worked for an insurance company. If anyone were likely to keep copies, an insurance lawyer was sure to. And where would those copies be? Would he go so far as to stow them away in a safe somewhere? I imagined myself creeping into his house or his office at night and rifling through the papers in his writing desk by torchlight.*

But it was useless. I knew that even if I did any of these things it was unlikely to make any difference. The best I could hope for was a short delay in having the thing brought out. Franz would have no difficulty in having the book published, with or without my help, and I had no doubt that it would be a success. It was a work of genius. I imagined my friends reading the novel and recognising me in Gregor. They would meet and excitedly discuss the novel, each wondering whether it would be indiscreet to speculate on whether Gregor had originated with me. They would slyly eye one another, gauging whether the others were thinking the same. After a while someone would hesitantly raise the subject.

'Did the descriptions of Gregor's . . . condition . . . remind you of anyone?'

The others would feign confusion for a moment and then someone else would offer timidly, 'Well, you know, Max did come to mind.' Then would follow a chorus of loud and eager sympathy to

---

* The preceding three paragraphs were uncovered from beneath a scrap of lined paper, on which the following three paragraphs appear. The scrap has been fixed over the notebook paper with adhesive. The glue has partially dissolved the ink in some areas, and the meaning has been approximated from the context.

cover their greedy curiosity: 'Poor Max, so brave, he manages very well I've always thought.' And then: 'Has he read it, do you think?'

And of course I would see my friends soon, I would encounter them at a party, or a café, or walking down the street, and they would be thinking all of these things and watching me for some reaction. I had to put a stop to it.

The manuscript was still lying in the corner where I had thrown it. I rolled out of bed and retrieved it. I took the papers to my writing table and smoothed them on the surface of the desk with my palms. The black ink burned against the white page. I saw my hands drift to the top of the pages, and it was like watching the hands of another person. The hands picked up the manuscript and tried to tear it, but it was too thick. I watched them tear off the first page, slowly, deliberately. Then they began to tear that page in half and then in half again and again. The paper hissed in protest, but it made no difference; soon all that remained were little flakes of white, speckled with black. They rained down all over the writing table and onto my lap and shoes. Once the hands had finished with the first page they began on the next, and the sound of all that paper tearing was more exquisite to my ears than the singing of angels.

IO.

AFTER DESTROYING THE MANUSCRIPT I FELT WONDERFUL, BETTER than I had felt for months, but this feeling did not last. I knew that my act of destruction was meaningless and by the next morning my depression had descended once more. A heavy fog had settled over my mind and, rather than being able to concentrate on the problem of Franz to try to solve it, I was totally incapable of any kind of productive thought. I was sluggish, stupid and wanted nothing but to sleep the day through in a room with heavy curtains drawn. But I had been at home now for some days and was due to return to the post office. I was reluctant to return, but once I had I was grateful for the rhythm of the familiar routine. I performed the necessary tasks of my day mechanically—I got up at the usual time, dressed, ate my usual meals and completed my work with ease—but all the while I felt nothing inside.

Days passed. It was as though I, the part of me that I called 'I', had become independent of my body, which carried on with my usual routine as if from some intelligence built into the bones and the muscles. My real self floated somewhere in the air around my body or had retreated to somewhere in its depths. I appeared to be normal; that is, no one seemed to notice any difference. People's faces looked the same as they usually did when they greeted me, and no one started in surprise at the spectacle that I presented: of a man of animated flesh, of walking and talking muscles with no one at the helm. In my office at work I would sit very still and listen to my own breathing, breath after breath, in and out, as inexhaustible as the waves of the sea. Occasionally I took out the notes for my book and looked over them, but all I found there were some dead black marks on the dust-covered page, like hieroglyphics.

Thoughts of Anja pained me, though only in a theoretical way, and I avoided the streets close to her house and the grounds of the university, more from their association with my former bliss than the desire to avoid running into her. She came to call on me in any case a few weeks after I had returned to work. She arrived at the house shortly after I had come home from the post office, bringing with her a tray of biscuits from the Café Louvre. Her voice was kind and gentle, and I thought I could read regret in her eyes, but perhaps it was only sympathy.

Elsa made coffee and Anja and I sat in the living room and ate the biscuits. The anaesthetised feeling that I had maintained for days began to falter and images from Franz's Gregor flashed into my mind at random, each bringing a stab of pain. I pictured Gregor as a monster with my face, wearing my clothes, and the whole story playing out in the rooms of this house, in my own bed, under this sofa.

I was besieged, too, with jealous thoughts about Franz. His straight body, his elegant features haunted me. How could she ever prefer me to him? The spectre of my ruined body returned to me and I viewed myself as if from the outside, a lumpish, repulsive figure slumped beside Anja's delicate form, like a rude lump of clay beside a Meissen figurine. I strained to keep my body as upright as possible so that my hand shook as I lifted the little coffee cup to my lips.

Anja seemed to have noticed nothing amiss and carried on as if everything was as usual between us, as if the episode with the comb had not occurred. I felt grateful to her for this, and also for the sense of calm that she exuded. She leaned forward to take a wafer from the tray. The disturbance of the air wafted her perfume towards me and all the smells of summer came to me: plums and dusty grass heated by the sun. The smell unknotted something in me and my head was suddenly tight with tears. A great sadness unfolded itself over me: the sadness of regret, as though Anja had died, or I had, and there was no going back.

I wanted to tell her about Gregor, confide my fears. I wanted to ask her about Franz and have her laugh away the suggestion. I wanted to sink into the sofa cushions and cry and have her smooth away my pain with her white hands. But I did not know where to start the story. She knew me only as Max Brod, the successful writer. I had never spoken to her of any of my difficulties, either with writing or with my life in general. She knew nothing of my childhood, of my being a cripple. I had pretended to myself that she had not even noticed my deformity; a fantasy, of course, but it was also true that I had never seen her eyes fasten onto my body and slide down it the way the eyes of others did. While she had told me every tale of her own childhood and a thousand details of her experience, I had largely remained silent or else presented her with carefully curated scenes. To break down now and flood her with my misery would be to edge close to madness. I wondered if I could simply show her Franz's manuscript, and whether she would then understand about Gregor. Would she? And would she then laugh the thing away? Or would she turn towards me with her eyes crumpled in concern? She had the power to allay my fears but also to give them life.

Instead of crying, I sipped the bitter coffee and crumbled a biscuit to sugary dust between my fingers. Anja began telling me about Herr Liška, who had been making repeated visits, apparently having renewed his offensive. All I felt was relief; Liška was better than Franz, after all. My apprehension of Liška had changed, and I no longer believed that Anja was using him to rouse my jealousy. I noticed that she asked me for clarification of Liška's actions and words as though I were that man himself, or a close friend of his who would know his mind. Perhaps she thought that the minds of all men were the same.

'Max, I've missed you these last days,' she said then and reached to take my hand. Where once I would have felt excitement now there was only wariness, tiredness. Both of her small hands enclosed mine lightly like warm water. If only I could forget her. And yet, at her touch I felt an involuntary rush of warmth flood the region of my heart. It was painful. That summer smell hung all about her and I was drawn now within its warm cloud. I breathed in a lungful of delicate air and held it, as if it might contain some remedy for my pain.

'I don't know what I would do without you,' she went on. 'Who would I talk to?'

She shuffled her body so that I could feel the warmth of her along my crooked side and she leaned her head on my shoulder. I mumbled something indistinct, not knowing what to say, knowing what I wanted to say: *Anja! Anja, you are my love! You alone can cure me.*

But then she sat up and looked at the clock on the wall. She gave a little start and jumped up. I felt a rush of coldness as her body was withdrawn from mine. I remained sitting there.

'Oh no!' she said. 'Look at the time! And I promised Aunt Ilse . . .' Her voice trailed off as she dashed a few steps towards the door and then swooped back to touch my shoulder gently with her fingers.

'Goodbye, Max,' she said. I felt the warm breath of her as she leaned down and lightly grazed the top of my head with her lips.

She slipped from the room and I sat with my eyes closed and listened to her steps echo away. I heard the front door opening and closing and then silence. Then I heard the steps approach again; she must have forgotten something. I got up from the sofa as the door swung open.

It was Franz. I fell back into the sofa. He did not greet me. His face was stony, almost unrecognisable. He was holding a small paper bag in one hand and he reached inside and took out a handful of something. I stood up, ready to confront him.

'How dare you?' he said, and threw the thing he held in my direction. I flinched and covered my face with my hands, but I felt only something soft brushing against me. I opened my eyes to see a swirl of white flakes fluttering down around me.

'You think your actions are the actions of a god,' he said. He threw another handful. 'But they are useless.' He laughed then, once, toneless and hollow, like a lunatic.

The white flakes had landed on my shoulders and the front of my jacket. I picked some off and inspected them. I saw that they were tiny pieces of paper written on one side in black ink. I was able to decipher the odd word, and recognised the writing as Franz's. It was his manuscript, I realised in a flash: the one I had destroyed.

Franz began to advance on me and I backed away.

'You will read this work again; you will see it soon, everywhere. You can't stop me.'

I felt ill. He was still coming towards me and I thought that he would strike me, but in the end he only threw the empty bag in my face and then walked out.

I immediately crouched down and began scrabbling around to pick up the fragments of paper. I hurried to scoop them up and put them back into the crumpled bag before anyone came into the room. When all the little flakes were back in the bag I threw it on the fire.

All of my old worries returned to me. Had Franz met with Theodor? Had he convinced Theodor that Alexandr was an impostor? If so, I was ruined. But I had a dim recollection of Theodor saying that he would be out of Prague for the next weeks. There was a conference in Vienna that he attended every year, and he generally stayed away a while. And Franz's threat did not necessarily mean that the two had met. Perhaps Franz had only sent Theodor the manuscript at the same time that he had given it to me. And why, indeed, had he given it to me? Was he taunting me?

Over the next days and weeks I agonised over the situation. I waited for the angry visit from Theodor, for the telegram or letter denouncing me. But nothing came. Franz must only have corresponded with Theodor, or perhaps it was all just bluster. Weeks turned to months and gradually I began to relax again.

II.

ONE DAY MONTHS LATER, JUST WHEN THE WHOLE THING HAD faded from my mind, the dreaded letter from Theodor arrived in the morning post. It was nestled among the routine bills and newspapers like a cuckoo's egg. I grabbed at the envelope and tore it open with a trembling hand. Inside was only a small card. My first thought, nonsensical though it was, was that it was Theodor's lawyer's card. I felt everything begin to collapse around me, and the walls of the house were suddenly made thin, insubstantial as pieces of cloth. I pulled the card out. It was not a lawyer's card. It was much worse: an invitation to a party that was to be held in honour of Franz, to celebrate his new work, *Die Verwandlung*. On the back of the invitation Theodor had scrawled an affectionate note for me, thanking me for introducing him to Franz.

I stood, holding the card dumbly. It seemed that there was no escape from Franz. The only thing in my favour was that it was clear that Theodor had not met Franz. Luck must have been on my side for once and Franz's contact with the publishing house must have only been through one of the other staff. However, the invitation presented more of an obstacle than a reassurance. The prospect of attending the party was a horrifying one. I could picture the gaze of a hundred eyes, swinging between me and the book's cover. 'There he is!' people would whisper to each other. 'Look!' they would say. 'It's the real Gregor!'

But, even worse, the party presented anew the problem of my deception being uncovered. I had thought that the whole matter was behind me and I felt extremely weary at the realisation that I had been wrong. It seemed that my act of deception could not be outrun. I would have to face the consequence of Theodor discovering what I had done. I could not even imagine what he would say. My career, of course, would be finished. The party was still a few weeks away. Perhaps I could leave Prague, I thought wildly. I had family in Brünn; perhaps I could request a transfer to the post office there. But in the following days I settled into a kind of lassitude. Instead of considering the situation, I pushed it from my mind and slept, dreaming empty dreams of blackness.

I read the news of the imminent publication in the *Bohemia* newspaper. Early reviews also began to appear and I could not help seeking them out in the morbid way one seeks out the obituary notices. In *Hyperion*, *Der Neue Weg* and *Herderblätter* the reviews were enthusiastic, and the more conservative journals attributed the work to a diseased mind and lamented the decline of literature: a reaction that only increased Franz's fame and notoriety.

The following week, copies of the book began to appear in the bookshops. They were often arranged in the window and would catch my eye when I walked past. I would stop involuntarily and gaze at them as I would have done had the book been mine. I would stand there for a long time, mesmerised by the rows of coloured oblongs arranged in neat stacks, until my gaze unfocused and the colours of the covers had run together into a bright, soft mass. Gradually, I would become aware of my own reflection in the windowpane, a stunted shadow cast over the scene, and then I would hurry on, crumpled with self-consciousness. I had told no one about my suspicions regarding the origin of Gregor. Some things are just too shaming to allow to pass through one's lips.

I knew that by this stage most of my friends would have read the book, and the conversations and conjectures I had imagined had probably already taken place in various hotels, cafés and parlours all over the city. Since reading the manuscript I had retreated into myself; the circle of my days had narrowed to encompass only work and home. I had met none of my friends, gone to no lectures or readings or theatre productions or concerts. All the letters and postcards that came enquiring about me were left unanswered. If I chanced to pass someone I knew in the street I would duck my head and cross to the other side before they could greet me, convinced that the sight of me would conjure the image of Gregor in their minds.

Anja faded from my life along with everything else at this time. She did not call on me again and no longer sent the little cards she used to send when we had not seen each other for a while. I did not seek her out—I was too ashamed and dejected—but I alternately longed for her and wished I had never met her. I thought of her constantly and wondered whether Liška was the cause of her silence, or Franz.

The night of the party drew closer, like a storm coming in over the sea, and suddenly it was only a few days away. I tried to ignore it. I locked myself in my study, keeping up the pretence that I was working, though in reality I was only reading. As usual I had asked Elsa not to disturb me. My thoughts turned occasionally to Franz and the party, but each time they did I forced them away and back to the book I was reading. The lamplight smoothed and rounded out the corners of the room and made the walls curve around me in a dome, like a protective embrace. The fire murmured contentedly to itself and beyond the room I could hear the muted evening activity of the house. I heard a knock at the front door but I hardly gave it a thought. But then someone knocked at the study door, and I saw the door handle twitch as it was tried. I froze and held my breath. The knock came again. I considered sitting silently there and leaving the door unanswered. My recent isolation from society had made me shrink from contact with people somewhat. The knock came again and drove me up from the sofa. I straightened my clothes and hair before I opened the door. It was Anja.

She came in and we sat side by side on the little sofa in front of the fire. The light of the flames made her skin luminous and as smooth as wax. She was so perfect that it seemed entirely possible that she was not even real. I had the urge to reach out and touch her to make sure. But that evening I noticed that there was something different about her, some hesitation that made me nervous. Her eyes moved over my face probingly, as if she were trying to gauge my reaction to something. I guessed that she had come to tell me some ostensibly happy piece of news, such as her forthcoming engagement to Liška.

'What?' I could not help myself asking after a few moments of superficial conversation. 'What is it? You have something you want to tell me?'

Her face had a strange, rigid look. 'No,' she said. 'I only … Well, you know that party, the one for *Die Verwandlung—*'

I knew at once what she was going to say. My usual reserve slipped and I barked at her, 'I suppose Franz has asked you to go with him.' I saw her eyes widen in surprise and I was instantly ashamed of myself.

'Oh no,' she answered in a small voice. 'I haven't been invited to the party. I heard about it from a friend at the university. Actually, I was rather hoping that you might ask me to go with you.'

For a moment I was amazed that she would want to go. To me, the evening was nothing more than an ordeal to be survived. The idea that someone, and indeed probably everyone other than myself, considered it to be a celebration surprised me. Of course I longed to take Anja to a party and introduce her to everyone, to see her lovely face smiling and see the admiration in everyone's eyes, to claim her as mine. There was nothing I wanted more. But it was impossible. I could not face the humiliation. That gallery of sneers and sideways glances. And, even if I managed somehow to steel myself against my shame, there still remained the problem of Franz. I did not wish Anja to be a witness to my shameful unmasking. But she was sitting there looking up at me timidly with her dark eyes and I did not know how to refuse her. I never wanted to refuse her anything.

I protested feebly that I couldn't go, that I had too much work to do, that I was behind in my writing and would not meet my deadline. She looked pointedly at my empty writing table and the copy of *Scheherazade* that lay face down next to her on the sofa.

'Max, you need some rest. You need some rest and you need some fun. You need society. You can't just stay locked up here in your study your whole life, ignoring everyone.'

I knew that what she said was true. She took my hand and slowly raised it to her lips. I concentrated very hard on breathing. How many times I had dreamed of this. I felt the pillowy pressure of her mouth for only a moment, before she took my hand and pressed my palm to the skin of her face. I hoped that she could not feel how my hand trembled. I held her face, and it was so small. The heel of my palm rested under her chin and my fingertips brushed her temple.

'Please, Max?' she was whispering now, and I could feel the warm puffs of her breath against the inside of my wrist. 'Can I come with you?'

I could not find my voice so all I could do was nod.

She left soon after this, and when I had recovered slightly I felt a great surge of strength. I took the hand that she had kissed and held it to my lips, breathing in the traces of her. Now everything looked completely altered. With that one gesture Anja had remade the world for me. I saw myself as Anja might see me: intelligent, misunderstood perhaps, but powerful and mysterious.

I imagined walking into the party with Anja on my arm and my breast swelled. Perhaps I could go. With Anja by my side, surely I could. If people thought that I was the model for Gregor, so what?

To hell with them. Even if someone asked me about Gregor, what of it? And at least if I did go the horror of seeing everyone would be conquered in a few short hours. I would not die of shame. And Theodor, well, I could not run from him forever. He would have to be faced sometime. At least on that night he was sure to be in good spirits.

I sat and considered the situation. I could not control people's reaction to me, that was true, but perhaps I could take some measures to avoid my act of deception being uncovered. I could always use Alexandr again. The thought edged its way slyly forward. It would be easy to arrange for him to arrive early at the party, before Franz could get there. If he ever did get there: there was always the chance that he would not even come. But I could not hope for that a second time. In any case, I had the upper hand: Theodor had already met Alexandr once; why would he believe some late-coming stranger who claimed to be Kafka, when the man he knew to be Kafka was already standing there in front of him? And, even better, the real Kafka was unlikely to react in a calm manner if faced with this scenario: in all likelihood he would rage and appear as an unhinged lunatic. I remembered his mad laughter when he had last visited me.

I wasted no time, and the next evening I went to the Karlshofergasse again in search of Alexandr. I found the little, dingy pub where we had first met, and I now saw that it was called the Three Boots. This time the place was crowded with after-work drinkers, but Alexandr was not among them. I asked the bargirl, the same pale-faced slattern I remembered from last time, if she knew when he would be in. She shrugged and told me that he had been there earlier and would probably be back soon. I decided to wait. I stood at the bar and drank a glass of schnapps. I felt even more conspicuous than usual among this crowd of working men in their dirty cloth caps and ragged trousers.

After only a short time Alexandr came in. He saw me and came to stand beside me at the bar. I bought him a schnapps.

'Is your friend having another dinner?' he asked.

I told him about the party.

'This one will be easier because you will be in a crowd,' I said. Although, when I considered it, this was not necessarily true. The evening would no doubt be full of people wanting to discuss the book with him. Could I ask him to read it? But perhaps this was not necessary: in my experience, people love nothing more than giving their own opinion and rarely take in what anyone else is saying.

'My rate is a hundred and twenty crowns for the evening,' he said. It was more than I had expected, but we both knew that I had no choice but to pay it. I had come prepared, and handed him half of the required sum with the other half to come afterwards. I arranged to meet him at the St Wenceslas monument in the Wenzelsplatz.

By the day of the party my confidence had flagged somewhat. I became sick with dread. I tried to buoy myself up by thinking of Anja and remembering the touch of her lips, the warmth of her breath, but even that could not entirely dispel the heavy foreboding that lay over me. I sat in my office at work and tried to distract myself with mundane tasks. The hours crawled past. After my lunch break a postcard came for me from Anja. She was writing to say that she could no longer come to the party with me because she was ill.

What was left of my newly acquired energy seeped out of me. I screwed up the card and threw it across the room. Without Anja, there was no longer any reason for me to go to the party either. Except that I had already given Alexandr sixty crowns and there was little hope of recovering the cash. My old apathy returned. Perhaps it did not much matter what I did. People were always going to regard me as a freak, and at well past twenty years of age, this was something that I would have to accept. There was nothing I could do about it. As for Franz, well, either I would be found out or not. I had no control over the situation. I decided to go ahead as planned. I might as well get my money's worth.

At seven o'clock I made my way to the Wenzelsplatz. Alexandr was to be there at half past, in plenty of time for the party at eight. I arrived early and waited.

Now I was terrified of the party, envisioning the array of horrors the evening might contain. I began to walk up the length of the square to distract myself. 'If I walk once up and down,' I told myself, 'Alexandr will be there when I get back.' I forced myself to walk slowly and concentrate on each step, but my thoughts would not be quieted. When I got back to the monument Alexandr was still not there. I walked all around the monument in case he was standing on the other side. It was twenty to eight. Everything was very quiet. Above me the figure of St Ludmila was only a black shape that rose up and blotted out the stars. I glanced at my watch, which was now showing a quarter to eight. I was in agonies at the thought of Franz arriving at the party before us.

There came the sound of hurrying feet and ragged breath.

'Herr Brod?' came a voice, and a man was beside me. I could not see him clearly in the gloom cast by the monument.

'Alexandr?'

'No,' said the man, 'my name is Gustav. Alexandr could not come tonight. I will take his place.'

I felt the muscles on my face slacken with shock and the buildings around the square reeled before my eyes. It could not be true. I cursed Alexandr, and myself for trusting him.

Even in the dark Gustav must have seen the look on my face, for he quickly began to assure me of the similarity between him and Alexandr. He stepped away from the statue and removed his hat to let the light shine better on his face. I noticed that he was wearing what looked like the same grey suit that Alexandr had worn to the dinner. It was true that he did resemble Alexandr. He was dark and had the same upright, martial way of holding himself. But, even if I tried to imagine that it was Alexandr, it was clear to me that it was a different man. However, I had spent more time with him than Theodor, who had only seen him for an hour at the most. There was a chance, I thought, that he would not notice. If I was very lucky. By now it was almost eight o'clock.

'Let's go,' I said.

The weather had turned and a light rain had begun. The lights from the lamps were reflected on the stones of the street, making starry patches under our feet that flashed up at us as we walked. The party was being held at the Hotel Europa, which was only a short walk from the monument—too short, I now felt.

With every step I cursed Franz, who was the cause of all of this mess. I felt like a man walking to his own certain death, but I could not turn away. I was propelled forward, as though swept up in an avalanche, and the weight of all my shame and anger roared at my heels. I heard my footsteps clatter along, and saw my dim shadow swinging back and forth like a pendulum beside Gustav's gliding one. I imagined all the faces at the party turned towards me, looking with disgust at my hulking body, which revealed the true ugliness of my innermost self.

Gustav did not try to speak with me. He just walked along, quietly humming a tune, and though the rain increased he let the light raindrop beads encrust his hat and shoulders instead of putting up his umbrella. The rain had made the cobblestones slippery and my left foot kept sliding sideways on them. I was using my umbrella as a walking stick to steady myself. I was becoming soaked but I knew that if I put up my umbrella it would be difficult for me to keep my balance.

I wanted to ask Gustav to hold my umbrella over me. I formulated the question in my head: *Would you mind covering me with an umbrella? Or could I take your arm? It's difficult for me to walk in the rain.* My lips mouthed the questions. Were they reasonable requests? Or were they irksome? Making another person responsible for my own inability to walk. The more I considered it, the less I was able to determine which it was.[*]

I slowed down to put up my umbrella, which had a mechanism that often jammed. Gustav walked on ahead of me. I succeeded in

---

[*] This paragraph has been crossed out.

getting the umbrella up and immediately felt better. Gustav had proceeded quite far up the road. I could see the raindrops sparkling on his head and shoulders as he passed beneath the streetlamps.

I quickened my pace to catch up with him, holding out my left arm as a counterweight to the umbrella, but of course I had only proceeded a short way before I missed my step. My foot slid away from me and I came down heavily on the stones. My umbrella tumbled away down the street. There was nothing to hold on to and I scrabbled around trying to stand up. An image came to me of myself as Gregor, grovelling on the floor of his house.

Gustav had run away down the street to retrieve my umbrella. By the time I was standing again he was back at my side, holding out my umbrella for me to take. I wanted to cry with self-pity. My right wrist ached from where I had fallen on it and the skin had scraped away. I was too ashamed to tell Gustav that I could not walk while holding the umbrella, and the rain was now too heavy for me to do without it, so I took it from him and we walked on. He put his umbrella up also, and kept pace with me.

I desperately wanted to take his arm to steady myself. I could see it in the corner of my eye, temptingly solid and reassuring, bent in a crook like a purpose-built handle. I even reached out my fingers and brushed them against the fabric of his sleeve, but could not bring myself to grasp it and lean on him.

Instead I concentrated on my feet. Since my illness I had not been much among company and as a consequence I had lost the ability to easily control my gait and posture in the way that I could when I practised it daily. I concentrated on balancing my weight and strained to make an even rhythm of my footfalls.

I tapped my forefinger against my thigh as I walked to help me keep my steps to an even time and counted the number of steps that I could match to this rhythm. I only managed six on the first try before I started to lurch from one side to the other and throw my weight forward from my hip. I concentrated and the wet cobblestones flashed past under my shoes, and this time I made it to eleven.

Gustav gave a tug on my arm and I saw that we had arrived. I stood there dumbly, still counting in my head. Theodor must have been keeping watch for us as he rushed out with his hand extended to shake the hand of 'Franz'. I watched Theodor's face closely for any sign that he had noticed the difference between the two men, but his expression did not seem to flicker when he saw Gustav. In fact, he was beaming, his face pink and satisfied. He greeted me with only a brief nod and then ignored me. He drew Gustav inside and I followed.

The little private room of the Hotel Europa was much brighter than it had looked from outside, and it was hot and full of people. I looked around for Franz, in case he was somewhere there in the crowd, but I did not see him. Theodor had clasped Gustav's arm and was propelling him inside. They were set upon by a loudly talking crowd, some of whom were holding copies of the book. They gathered around Gustav in a little knot and swept him and Theodor away to the other side of the room.

I was left alone, standing exposed in an empty space by the door. I tried not to notice the looks that strangers in the crowd were giving me, or the fact that Felix and Kurt, who were standing by the window, seemed to be ignoring me. In the light of the room I saw that my trouser leg and the sleeve of my jacket were streaked with mud from my fall, and I retreated back to the entrance hall to try to remove it with my handkerchief.

The mud was still damp and all I succeeded in doing was rubbing the stain up and down the lengths of my arms and legs. My heart began to hammer with panic at the thought that someone entering the hall—Franz worst of all—would see me crouched there, cleaning my clothes. I could see how I would appear to others as I stood there: a hunchbacked animal in a dirty jacket, furtively trying to clean itself. For a moment, with my arms and upper back restricted in their movements by my jacket, my limp legs, my weak arms, I felt myself to be the insect Gregor: I was him. Despite myself, I had to commend Franz for the keenness of his perception of me.

No matter how hard I brushed I could not remove the traces of mud from my clothes. I no longer wanted to be at that party, covered in the dirt that was like a badge of my own ineptitude. I stood hovering at the door, uncertain. All the eyes in that room terrified me and I could hear the name 'Gregor' again and again, bobbing like a cork on the sea of talk.

'What are you doing, hiding away in here?'

Kurt and Felix stood in the doorway. Kurt held a tray of schnapps. I let them hustle me into the room and they drank and toasted each other and me. Gustav was lost from view, the invisible centre of a small crowd.

I heard the door open and close, and my muscles tensed like a boxer's. I was standing facing the door, but the view was blocked by Kurt's head. I shifted around, trying to see who had come in, not listening at all to the conversation of my friends. But it was only a man, not Franz, and I could relax again. Felix and Kurt were looking at me expectantly and I realised that someone had asked me a question.

'So, was it you?' Felix said, repeating his question. I was stunned by the barefaced way he asked me, not lowering his voice at all.

'What?' I asked, and then began to stammer that I didn't know what he was talking about, that I hadn't read it yet.

He interrupted me. 'I mean, I'd heard that Franz sent you the manuscript. Was it you who edited it?'

When I realised that I had misunderstood him I felt even more ashamed.

Felix's expression shifted and he exchanged a look with Kurt, only for a fraction of a second, but I knew that I had only succeeded in bringing the comparison of Gregor and myself to his attention. Or had I imagined that too? I took another schnapps from the tray and drank it in a gulp. I didn't know. I had forgotten for a moment about Franz, but suddenly no longer cared whether he arrived or not. I began to drink steadily and dreaded the moment that I would be left alone in the crowd, at the mercy of all those eyes.

Some time later Theodor came over to join us. By this stage I had drunk a great deal and the world had retreated behind a pleasant, rosy mist. Theodor had left Gustav in the grip of a crowd of people whom I could see huddled around him, each talking at him louder than the other. I had a nagging sense that I should somehow be worried about this, but could not recall the reason why. Theodor clapped me on the back, hard, and put an arm around my shoulders.

'Congratulations, Max,' he said. His face was very close to mine and I could see all the details and imperfections of his skin. I gazed at him in wonder. 'You have done a great thing for literature. You have brought us Gregor. He would not exist without you.'

Gregor. It all came back to me. Had Franz told Theodor as much? Or was it so obvious to everyone? Kurt and Felix were standing there, smiling at me. Their lips seemed uncannily rubbery and large, stretched wide like the pink insides of shellfish. Theodor too seemed to have grown and the three men loomed over me, huge and distorted, their heads rising up like the tops of tall trees, bent slightly towards one another to form a canopy over my head, enclosing me. I fought my way free of them. *Gregor, Gregor.* I could hear the name issuing from a hundred lips like a murmured chorus.

I struggled hard to get to the other side of the crowded room, but there was no escape. Bodies pressed in on me from all sides and seemed deliberately to hinder my way. Shards of other people's conversations broke into my awareness, and everywhere I heard my name together with Gregor's. Every laugh, every whisper, was directed at me. I shrunk within my mud-encrusted clothing. I seemed to have become very small, or perhaps it was the room that had grown. It suddenly seemed to be of an immense size, large enough to contain all the inhabitants of Prague. The ceiling was lost from my view, unimaginably high up, wreathed in clouds. I struggled to breathe. Raised voices and laughter rained down on me like physical blows. The lights were suddenly too bright and dazzled me. They were reflected from a million points in the room: from the glasses held in warm hands, from jewels on the necks of the women, from shining eyes. The bright points burned into my eyes and left a cloud of black spots in their wake.

I was still holding a glass of schnapps, of which only the dregs remained, and I stared at it to steady myself. The glass was cut with a bevelled edge that reflected colours from the room in its sharp lines. I gripped it in my fist and watched the skin of my palms and fingers turn white where the wall of the glass pressed into it. I tried to breathe regularly. The walls of the glass were cooler than the air in the room and I pressed the glass to my face and rolled it over my cheeks and forehead. I began to feel calmer. The scale of the room returned to normal.

I felt something touch my arm, and I shrugged it off without turning my head. It took so much effort to control my body.

'Max,' someone said, and I turned slowly, my eyes leading the way. Uta stood in front of me. I instinctively looked around for a means of escape, but I was held fast in the press of bodies. I closed my eyes, as though this would make me disappear. The touch on my arm came again, together with a nervous laugh.

'Maxelein.'

I shuddered at her use of the endearment but I peeled my eyes slowly open. She stood there smiling at me. Her hair was arranged in a complicated fashion and glistened as though it had been doused in some kind of oil.

'Aren't you a regular Sleeping Beauty?' She laughed. I wondered for a moment what she was talking about, then I remembered her many visits to me when I was ill. I shuddered at the thought of her entering my room and seeing me there in my bed, with crumpled sheets and dented pillows in the intimate pose of sleep, feigned or not.

'Or maybe we two are Beauty and the Beast?' Again she gave that laugh, like two sharp hoots of a bird.

Had she actually said that? I wasn't sure. Conversations hummed in the air all around me, punctuated by loud laughter, making it difficult to hear her. She was speaking in a deliberately low tone—contrived, I knew, to entice me to lean closer to her. She continued to speak but the thread of her voice was suddenly like a foreign language and I could only catch a few fragments of what she said. Her fat mouth moved in a way that was both repellent and hypnotic. There was a small patch of transparent hair below her lower lip that bristled as her lips undulated to form words, and I could not keep my eyes from constantly straying to that place.

She edged closer to me and I shuffled slowly backwards to maintain the distance between us, but I had not gone far before I felt the warm resistance of another back pressing against my own. I put my good foot out in front of my body as a barrier and stood behind it, poised like a grotesque dancer.

The perfume she wore had begun to seep out into the stagnant air around her, and I breathed through my mouth to minimise its effect on me, but even so I could still taste it at the back of my throat.

I thought longingly of my soft bed, waiting for me. I thought of Anja, lying in her own bed, her cheeks flushed perhaps with fever, her hair damp, sticking in strands to her smooth skin. The party suddenly appeared to me to be the most inhospitable corner of the earth. Uta was still edging closer and now I had my head tilted up to try to snatch at the unperfumed air above my head.

The knot of people around us suddenly loosened and I could not wait a moment longer. I held up my hand almost in her face to halt her flow of words. Her voice stopped and her face was stunned. She stared at the open palm of my hand as intently as though there were something written on it.

'Excuse me, I must . . .' I gestured vaguely to the other side of the room.

Her face was confused and she controlled it with effort. She managed a creaky smile. 'Oh! I wouldn't dream of holding you up! You must have important business here; all of these literature types.' She dismissed them with a flick of her wrist.

Her voice trailed away as I left her behind, and the space between us became filled with the bodies of others. It was only then that I remembered Gustav. I saw that he was standing close by, talking with Theodor. Gustav was saying something to Theodor, his hands animated as he explained something. I could not see Theodor's face, but I could see him nodding his head, listening.

When I got closer I realised that they were discussing a recent production of Janáček's *Ihre Stieftochter* and were deep in conversation. Gustav's knowledge on the subject took me aback, and then immediately I felt snobbish for assuming that a soldier would be ignorant of opera. Besides, I did not even know whether the man was a soldier. They hardly paused in their conversation to acknowledge me. Far from being bothered by this, I felt relieved that the two were getting on so well. I looked around the room for Franz, but I could not see him. It appeared that my luck had held. The thought that I might have pulled off my plan that evening was intoxicating. I felt a greater sense of achievement than any I had felt with the completion of my creative works. I must have been standing there with a foolish expression on my face, for first Gustav and then Theodor gave me an odd look.

'So, Max,' said Theodor, 'I have been wanting to ask you: how was it that you two first met?'

'At a Schopenhauer lecture,' I said, without thinking. Then it occurred to me, too late, that the question might have been a test. Theodor was nodding slowly, his face inscrutable, but for a brief moment I thought I saw something flash across his lips and eyes; the ghost of a smirk, a certain fixity of gaze, which chilled me. I rapidly changed the subject, trying to distract Theodor by bringing up the Schopenhauer book, which was by now far behind schedule.

'You must be mightily sick of Schopenhauer,' he said, and I laughed nervously.

'Franz' and I left the party soon after that, and after we were a few streets away I stopped to pay Gustav the rest of his fee. He thanked me politely.

'By the way, Theodor asked me to come to his office tomorrow morning,' he said.

So still I had not escaped. It seemed that this charade would stretch on indefinitely.

'Can you make it?' I asked.

'Perhaps. It will cost you a hundred and eighty crowns.'

12.

GUSTAV LEFT AND I WALKED HOME. IT WAS STILL RAINING AND I made my way very slowly, supporting myself with one hand against the buildings and railings. I felt very tired. My thoughts kept returning to Anja. I imagined her lying weak and fevered in her bed, and I wished I could be with her.

Without allowing myself to notice, I favoured the route that took me close to Anja's house and soon I found that I was standing outside it. I looked up at the shrouded windows. I could hear, or imagined I could hear, the faint sound of piano music and singing and laughter. I stood for a long time with my hand on the wall of the house opposite. The music became overlaid with the percussive ringing of the raindrops falling onto the taut fabric of my umbrella and the hard surfaces of the street. Another faint sound became audible, of sharp footsteps echoing on stone.

At the sound of these I instinctively hurried to the street door and knocked, not wishing to be discovered loitering there, staring up at the house. In the interval before the door was opened I stood there wondering whether I should run away; it was far too late to call on Anja, particularly if she was ill. But the concierge opened the door and I went through to Anja's apartment. As I toiled up the stairs, leaning heavily on the bannister, I imagined Anja's face smiling at me and I recalled the light touch of her fingers in mine, and the staircase seemed so immensely long that I thought I would never reach the top. The maid opened the door of the Železný apartment and I asked breathlessly for Anja, but the maid shook her head and told me that I could not see her, that she was asleep. As she was telling me this, her eyes left my face and she gave a start of surprise. I heard a sound behind me. I turned and there was Anja, out of breath herself and soaked with rain, coming up the stairs.

She stopped at the top of the stairs and looked at us, wide-eyed, the fingertips of one hand lightly touching the bannister, frozen like an animal surprised by a predator. She very quickly smoothed over her look with a smile and stepped towards me, thrusting forward her damp and cold hand for me to take. I could see the beat of her heart pulsing the arteries in her throat, and I felt the undulating motion of her audible breath running through her body. Raindrops slid down the strands of her hair like glass beads down a string and dropped onto the floor around her.

'I thought you were ill,' I said, watching her face closely from under lowered lids.

'Oh, yes. Well, I was. But then I felt better and then I thought . . .' Her voice trailed off. She seemed ill at ease and kept wiping her hands one against the other. 'How was the party?' she asked.

'It was fine,' I said. Both of us were stiff with lies, like bad actors. 'But where were you just now?'

'Yes! Well, I was with Aunt Ilse.' This was clearly a lie. 'I was going to stay there for the night, but then I thought, well, it's better to come home. But now, look! I am soaked through.' She gave a little uncertain laugh.

Something had shifted between us. She seemed to speak to me from a great distance, as though I were standing on a pier and she on board a ship about to sail, leaning over the ship's side. I didn't know what to say to bring her closer.

We remained on the landing and she didn't invite me in. She politely asked me about the party, who had been there, what people had said about the book, and I told her some invented generalities. The words that came out of my mouth were like heavy bricks that fell between us and formed a barricade.

She began to talk about Franz's book and only then did she forget herself and break through the reserve that she had been wearing like armour. How I hated Franz at that moment for having the ability to light her eyes, to animate her fingers when I could not.

Franz. In a perverse flash of jealousy it came to me that the reason for her breathless disarray was that she had just returned from an assignation with Franz. After all, where had he been? I knew that the thought was pure paranoia, but at the same time it seemed perfectly reasonable to me.

'And how is your Aunt Ilse?'

She looked blank for a moment and then told me that her aunt was very well. The life left her again. I felt suddenly very tired. So it was true.

'She has recovered from the flu?' I could not escape from my trap of deadened words.

135

'Oh yes. Fighting fit.'

'The maid thought you were asleep.'

'Did she? Oh, Marie doesn't know if it's day or night.'

It occurred to me that I also had no idea how late it was. The house was very quiet.

'Well, I'm sorry to keep you waiting out here in your wet things,' I said. I wished I had never come here.

'Yes, I suppose I should change. Well, goodnight then. I'm glad you enjoyed the party.'

'Goodnight,' I said. We shook hands again, and she closed the door before I had even reached the stairs.

13.

HOW QUICKLY ONE'S LUCK CAN CHANGE. BUT THEN I HAVE NEVER been a very lucky man. Of what Schopenhauer calls the three great powers of the world, luck is that in which I am most deficient. Sagacity, though, I have in abundance: that is particularly clear now, looking back on these events of which I tell. Strength I never lacked, despite my weakened appearance; in fact it is precisely my weak exterior that is the source of my power. But at that time I suffered from want of luck. I was like the captain of the ship that is constantly blown off course. I could see the landmass towards which I was bound, but how the winds of ill fortune pushed at me. I worked hard at the rudder, adjusting my course again and again, but even as I did this, fresh squalls fell upon my vessel and threatened to engulf me.

Barely did I have time to register the blow dealt by Anja's strange behaviour before I had Theodor's meeting with Gustav to navigate. And that next meeting was to be the beginning of the one of the more violent storms of that period.

The morning after the party I waited for Gustav until our agreed time, but he failed to show, so after waiting too long and making myself late I made my way to the Goldblatt office in the hope that Gustav had gone directly there. The one mercy I could think of was that at least on this occasion I had no anxiety of the real Franz making an appearance.

From the moment the door of Theodor's office building was opened I felt that I was being punished. There was a hostility in the room that had been absorbed into the stale air and the angular furniture that crowded the small space. I was aware of a series of darting glances shared between the office staff. No one looked me in the eye or answered me directly when I asked whether Franz was in a meeting with Theodor. I was made to wait a long time, ignored, in a dusty chair in the corner.

When I published my first novel and had come to this office for the first time my experience had been very different. I had been greeted with enthusiasm by the staff. They had left their desks and crowded around me, heaping such praise upon me that I felt quite ashamed. I was attended to and given the best chair, and tea, and was endlessly fussed over. Every time after this that I had come here had been like visiting the house of a friendly relative. I had always felt, naïvely, that this treatment of me represented a genuine affection, particularly on Theodor's part. To me, he had become almost like an older brother or a trusted friend, but now I saw that this was false, and that for him the relationship had only ever been a transactional one. It occurred to me as I sat there in the uncomfortable chair to which I had been demoted that now Franz was the one who would be getting the special treatment.

I had not really thought through what I would say, or what reason I would give for being there at the office at that time. I remembered the look I had seen steal over Theodor's face the night before when he had asked me how I had met Franz. I would have to be careful not to arouse his suspicions. The only excuse I could hit upon for my unexpected appearance was to beg for more time on Schopenhauer, which would be a useful thing in any case, if it were granted.

Theodor called me into his office. Gustav was not there.

'It seems your friend has great difficulty keeping appointments without you. Perhaps he should employ you as his personal assistant.'

We sat staring at one another for a while. I tried to sit up very straight but could not look him in the eye for long. My gaze dropped to the surface of his desk, which was littered with papers; clipped-together manuscripts, notebooks and loose pages lay in piles, presumably in a kind of order known only to Theodor. My eye was caught by a bundle of loose sheets of paper covered in handwriting, of which only a small corner was visible. The sight of the blue ink of the handwriting caused my heart to jolt when I recognised it as my own. I realised it was the story that had been the product of my fainting fit some months before.

'What can I do for you?' asked Theodor.

I tried not to stare too much at the pages as I explained the difficulties that I was having with Schopenhauer, but only half of my attention was on my words.

The blue handwriting loomed in my mind and I cringed at the thought of Theodor, or anyone for that matter, reading those private lines that had come directly from my locked-away secret self. I could not understand how the pages could have come into

Theodor's possession and I tried to remember the last time I had seen them. My gaze darted again and again to the blue lines, but now I was no longer certain if it was, in fact, my own writing. I wondered whether I should ask Theodor if I could read it, but I did not dare. What excuse could I possibly give for such a request? And what would I say if it was indeed my own story that lay there? I could surely make no claim upon it.

I had this whole time been continuing my rambling explanation of my difficulties and I came out with my request for more time; another month.

There was a silence. I sat hunched over, now staring openly at the handwritten corner of the pages.

'I see your attention has been riveted by Franz's newest story,' Theodor said, and his voice was hollow with irony. His hand burrowed among the papers and he pulled out the handwritten bundle.

'I too was struck by it. It is vital. Compelling. Brutally honest. Honesty: this is the substance of real art.'

I nodded stupidly. My hand reached out timidly for the papers he held. Narrowing my eyes I tried to discern the writing. It looked from this closer distance identical to my own, I was sure of it.

'May I . . .?' My voice came out in a squeak that was ignored.

'You see, Max,' Theodor said, sounding tired, 'you may be well known now, but the reading public is fickle. They will so very quickly forget you. The mileage of a book is only so long, and you must never forget that there are young writers, new writers, writers like Franz, coming up at every moment. It is imperative, if you want to survive, that you keep on producing work. If you want to survive.'

My eyes were still fixed on the papers. I thought that I could pick out a few phrases there on the page that seemed familiar. I wrestled with a fresh wave of shame at the recollection of the story's content. Perhaps it was better that it had been attributed to Franz. But how could Theodor have got hold of the thing?

'But of course,' Theodor went on, and his voice had now softened, 'I am eternally indebted to you for introducing me to Franz.' He put the pages back underneath the pile of papers on his desk, appearing to be lost in thought for a moment. I had shrunk into the chair. If it really was my story that he held, there was absolutely nothing that could be done about it. I glanced up at Theodor's face and saw that he was giving me a long, appraising look.

'Well, I am prepared to give you the time you ask for, but only if you will do something for me,' Theodor said.

Now he looked sly. I waited for him to go on.

'There appears to be an emerging interest in travelogues.'

I had no plans to travel anywhere. I am not a man who romanticises travelling; not through any closed-mindedness or lack of imagination, but because it causes me such considerable bodily suffering. Being confined in too-small chairs, uncomfortable beds and jolting carriages are the chief memories that remain to me of most of the journeys on which I have embarked.

The thought also crept into my mind that writing a travelogue was beneath me. I was not some Baedeker hack,* touring the cities of Europe and rating it in stars. But I could see that I was in

---

* A copy of the 1905 Austria–Hungary Baedeker guidebook was also found among the manuscripts.

no position to refuse him. I feigned some enthusiastic sounds and repeated, 'Travelogues,' in a satisfied tone that I hoped was believable.

'They are becoming very popular,' he said. 'A travelogue written by a well-known author would be even more of a success. However, I think we could do one better than even that.'

I hoped he was not going to ask me to travel to some inhospitable, far-flung place. Images came to me of my crooked form toiling across narrow jungle paths crowded with wild animals, over jagged snow-covered mountain peaks, through windy deserts.

'Africa?' I asked.

He ignored me. 'What is better than a travelogue written by one well-known author?' He paused and bared his teeth in a smile. Then he answered his own question. 'A travelogue written by two well-known authors.' His teeth flashed.

He was going to ask me to write a travelogue together with Franz. The problems with this scenario came rushing into my head one after the other. I was by this time so weary of the double dealings and trickery in which I had been engaged. And the cost! It would be ruinous. There was no way that I could afford to pay for Gustav or Alexandr to accompany me on a tour that might last weeks. There was, I thought, always the possibility of going with the real Franz, but the thought of seeing Franz for a few hours, let alone spending weeks with him confined in train compartments, restaurants and museum exhibits, was too terrible to contemplate. And then there was Anja. I could not bear to be separated from her. I pictured her again as she stood there laughing on the landing, her face pale with cold. To go away from Prague now would be a mistake, of that I was sure. I desperately cast about for possible excuses.

Theodor took my silence for assent. 'Well then, that's settled. I thought a tour of the spa towns of Bohemia would be popular. You'll begin with Karlsbad and then go from there. I will arrange the tickets and bookings.'

He began to shuffle his papers around on his desk in an attitude of dismissal.

'Oh, one more thing—I will, of course, need to ask you to sign an agreement committing to the completion of Schopenhauer by the revised deadline. And also for the travelogue.'

He pushed a sheet of paper across at me. He had never before insisted on such formalities and the request was like an official withdrawal of his affection. I was much too agitated to read the agreement and only scanned the page mechanically, taking nothing in. My hand was numb as I signed.

'Good,' he said as he took the paper back from me. He gave me a carbon copy and also a sealed envelope, very thick. 'This is also for you: some information about Karlsbad and Marienbad.'

He then opened one of his desk drawers and took out another envelope. He sat weighing it in his hands for a moment while he looked out of the window, before turning and fixing me with a narrowed gaze.

'And I wonder if you might also pass this on to Franz for me?' he said. He handed me the envelope. 'It's a cheque.' He seemed to be watching me closely, no doubt looking for any signs of murderous envy. I wondered if he had given me the envelope with the purpose of provoking me. But I gave him no satisfaction on that quarter. I accepted it with a smile and politely took my leave of him, keeping my smiling mask intact until I was well away from the building.

14.

A FEW WEEKS LATER, FRANZ—THE REAL FRANZ—AND I WERE sitting side by side in a train compartment bound for Karlsbad. I had visited Karlsbad before, long ago in my childhood. My mother had taken me there, and on to Marienbad, and any other spring or well that promised miracle cures for those who took its waters, in the vain hope that my crooked spine might be cured. She had approached each new place with shining optimism, completely convinced that it held the power to cure me. She patiently held me in the various pools and under the springs, she consulted a variety of doctors, and fed me foul-tasting water from cups and bottles of numerous designs, but each time the treatments failed to have any effect.

Somehow this failure never seemed to deter her or diminish her certainty, so when she met an old woman in a restaurant in the town who told her of an even more beneficial and healthful spring just over the hills she simply transferred her conviction and we set off to this new location. As a child I found this very confusing. I had always interpreted her certainty as absolute—if she were certain about something then it was sure to be a fact, beyond question—so I was perplexed when my body remained exactly the same as we went from town to town, spring to spring. It seemed to me to be an inexplicable failure in the mechanism of the universe, as though the constellations had suddenly begun to turn on a new axis or the seasons had reversed. I could not understand her continuing composure in the face of such chaos. At the same time it had also seemed like my personal failure: a failure to control my own body. Other people had no trouble mastering their own bodies, but I was mysteriously powerless to do this and was held instead within my body's rigid walls like a prisoner.

Only vague memories remained to me of Karlsbad: mostly of the damp and grey atmosphere and that feeling of guilt, a vague panic of things going wrong and it perhaps being my fault, all of which was connected to that penetrating, sulphurous smell that lingers like mildew in the streets and houses of all bath towns. I could recall that oppressive odour with remarkable clarity, as though clouds of it were blowing into the train compartment through the slit of the opened window.

Sitting there next to Franz was a strange experience. I had to keep reminding myself that he was not Alexandr or Gustav, and I took care not to say anything which might give me away. Fortunately, he was not much disposed to talking, and after greeting me he had settled into silence behind a newspaper. He was acting towards me with neutral politeness, as though our last angry encounter had not occurred, which puzzled me. Perhaps he felt that he had triumphed over me with his publication of *Die Verwandlung*.

The thought of that book still smarted, but I sat and soothed the pain by gloating over my successful deception of Theodor. I imagined how much worse it would be for me now had Franz known about the scope of his success. Of course he knew that his book had been successfully published, and this was bad enough, but, if I continued to carefully manage the situation, hopefully this would be all that he would ever achieve. Franz was on his way out. I still had his cheque in my pocket.

I sat and looked out of the window, not making any conversation. I had put a notebook in my jacket pocket with the idea that I would take notes about the landscapes that we encountered on the journey. I took it out and sat with pen poised, ready to note down my impressions. I assumed that Theodor was expecting us to produce a travelogue illuminated with golden scraps of poetry, but I could find nothing to say about the unremarkable springtime hills and trees as they sped past, beautiful though they were, so my page remained blank.

I saw Franz take out his own notebook and begin to write. He sat over it for a long time, his head lowered with the effort of concentration, jotting down small amounts at a time, but very consistently. Soon he had filled several pages. My page was still an empty space. When he saw me watching him he slid his notebook back into his pocket and looked studiously out of the window. I wanted to ask him what he was writing, but I didn't know how to without sounding jealous and peevish. I shuffled around in my seat and leafed through the empty pages of my own notebook. Franz gave a sudden laugh, turning to me and holding out his notebook.

'Never mind, Max, it's not my magnum opus.'

He snapped the book shut and stowed it in his pocket. I sat staring straight ahead. We both remained silent for the rest of the journey.

15.

IT WAS EVENING WHEN WE ARRIVED AT KARLSBAD. WE WERE TO stay at the Hotel Kroh, which was close to the Kurhaus baths. The journey, and Franz's presence, had exhausted me and I was looking forward to a few moments alone in my room. As we pulled into the long drive of the hotel I had tantalising glimpses of cool gardens and arched windows looking into dim rooms in which yellow lamps glowed. My body, tired and sore, vibrated with anticipation.

Franz had hurried to the hotel desk ahead of me, leaving me to struggle up the staircase in his wake. My body was frozen and rigid and my blood seemed to have stopped flowing. I had to stand there in the yard and make a spectacle of myself chafing each of my legs with my hands before I could even attempt the stairs. A porter in a dirty jacket appeared at my elbow and tried to help me, but I rudely ordered him away, ashamed.

Labouring up the stairs, I realised that my glimpse of the hotel's opulence must have been a glimpse into the hotel's past. At close range I could see it was a shabby place, past its prime and gently decomposing. The wide carpets were spotted and crusted with dirt, the brass fittings tarnished and every surface overlaid with a furred layer of dust. A strange smell pervaded the hall, of vinegar and the insides of old books.

By the time I reached the desk Franz had already received his key and was signing himself into the register. I stood to one side until he had finished and had turned to go, saying over his shoulder that he would meet me in the bar later.

The hotel clerk was an elderly man with a face as naked and pink as a baby's. He searched and searched through his papers and ledgers, but my name did not appear anywhere. There was much fussing. Several other clerks were called for assistance and together they hunted through drawers and the wall of little pigeonholes as though they were conducting a burglary. Then they came back to me, shaking their heads. There was nothing under my name and the rooms of the hotel were completely full. The pink-faced clerk showed me the ledger; Franz's name was the last one written on the list.

I had propped myself up on the desk with my forearms to take the weight off my cramping legs while they searched, and now I hung there like a shipwrecked man clinging to a piece of flotsam. My head ached and the fumes from the spring, strong even here inside the hotel, were making me nauseous. I could not face another carriage ride to a different hotel. I decided to ask Franz—to beg him if necessary, or pay him—to give me his room while he found accommodation elsewhere. Franz was sent for and I sank into a dusty sofa.

I remained sitting there while Franz came down and had an argument with the clerk. The clerk kept gesturing to me, his pink fingers delicately curled, but Franz never turned his head, although moment by moment the violence of his gestures increased. I closed my eyes.

Theodor, it transpired, had booked us into a shared room, which was the cause of Franz's ire. Not only was it shared, but it was tiny: barely larger than the train compartment we had arrived in.

'This is certainly going in my review,' Franz hissed at me as we climbed the stairs together, as though it were my fault, or the hotel's. I ignored him and lay down on my tiny bed, fully clothed.

When I woke up it was to the relief of an empty room. I went downstairs and found Franz in the dining room with notes and brochures spread out on the table all around him. It was still early and the dining room was almost empty. I sat down and he handed me a piece of paper covered with complicated ruled columns. He explained that it was a schedule that he had arranged for us, which would specify times for touring the town, writing the travelogue and doing our own writing.

Franz went to see about some food and left me to decipher his schedule. My head was still thick with sleep and I squinted at the rows of sharp numbers in Franz's handwriting, unable to make sense of them. As I gradually woke up it occurred to me that the schedule, even the very idea that Franz would take it upon himself to write one for me, was totally outrageous. I whipped out my pen to make amendments.

'Herr Kafka?'

I was still scowling when I looked up into the face of a youngish woman. She was standing bowed slightly towards me, inclining her body forward from her hips, waiting for a response. She reminded me of Uta, although this woman was younger, with her hair too tightly curled, too elaborately arranged, her dress too flounced and her lips too artificially pouted.

'Yes,' I said without thinking, while I continued to assess her attractiveness.

She cooed and with fluttering hands started to tell me how much she admired my work, while looking greedily down at the paper-covered table. Her eyes flashed her desire at me, which restored my temper. She was clearly angling for an invitation to sit with me. Despite her affectations, I discerned that her figure was most shapely and her fine-grained skin reflected the light with a pleasing sheen.

'I mean no,' I interrupted her monologue, remembering her question and my name. 'Kafka has just gone out. I am Brod; Max Brod. Please, join me.' I offered her the chair that Franz had just vacated.

'Oh,' she said. Her body sagged in disappointment. 'Oh, no, I really can't.'

Her eyes darted around the room as if she were hoping to catch a glimpse of Franz coming back. I too looked towards the frosted glass of the door and thought I could see the outline of Franz's dark head appear at the other side. I was humiliated at having exposed my interest to her, and the possibility of Franz appearing and finding me with her there waiting to see him was too much. Rudely, I got up and pushed past her out of the room.

16.

ALTHOUGH I DIDN'T KNOW IT THEN, THAT FIRST EVENING AT Karlsbad was to be the model for the rest of our time there. The news that a famous writer from Prague was in residence had apparently spread instantly through the hotel the moment we had arrived. This gossip was a welcome distraction for the bored well-to-do women who populated its rooms, and hunting for Franz must have filled in time between massages, doctors' visits and comparing ailments, and indeed perhaps formed an invigorating part of their cure.

Any movements that Franz made around the hotel were observed and shadowed by dozens of people who tailed him in the hope of claiming a moment of conversation with the celebrated artist. The resulting encounter was then loudly flaunted by the victor at dining tables and along the spa colonnades for days afterwards.

Maddeningly for me, although news of Franz had rapidly spread, I remained anonymous. People began to take me for Franz's assistant, and I became drawn into the hotel guests' hunt for him, as they followed me to discover Franz's whereabouts or tried to befriend me in the hope of wangling an introduction to Franz or, better still, an invitation to dinner with him.

Although Franz must have been greatly surprised by this behaviour he never said a word about it. I tried as best I could to shield him from the interest that he aroused, and when this was not possible I would trivialise it, putting the fascination down to boredom or the small-minded fads that thrived in spa resorts.

I am sure, of course, that at first Franz enjoyed this unfamiliar attention. Women were constantly employing flimsy ruses to entrap him, their fluting voices teasing and flirting with him; men at the bar offered to buy him schnapps or the town specialty, Karlsbader Becherbitter, and wanted to talk politics. Ignored, I looked on with gritted teeth. Franz began to be engaged in a fury of letter-writing in answer to the endless little notes that were left for him at all hours at the hotel desk or in our room or at our usual table in the dining room. I was used to being on the receiving end of such adulation, and felt bewildered and offended by how quickly Franz had taken my place as the centre of attention. Indeed, if I was honest with myself, I would have to admit that the attentions that I had received even at the height of my popularity could not equal those that Franz enjoyed at Karlsbad. He was treated like a film star, a king.

However, to my surprise, after a few days of this I found that, following the initial sting, Franz's eclipse of my own popularity became easier to bear. I found that I was even quite grateful to slip into the restful role of anonymous spectator. A great and unexpected sense of freedom and lightness came over me, as though I were only arbitrarily connected with the world and floated through it like a ghost, completely free and invisible.

Franz also treated me as if I did not really exist. Aside from discussing places to visit for the travelogue, he completely disregarded me and went about the routines of his day as if he were alone. I had never lived in such close proximity to another person for such a length of time and I observed Franz's habits with all the interest of an anthropologist. Franz to me had always been a model of the urbane gentleman: supremely elegant of figure and dress, fluid of movement, immaculate at all times. From our first meeting and every time I had seen him after that I had always been struck by his physical presence. I had often imagined the lives of others, of those not plagued by defects such as mine, and had dreamed that they lived lives of easy simplicity and naturalness, but I was surprised to find that there was a great deal of stage-managing that went on behind the scenes, even for Franz.

Every morning on waking he would embark upon a series of physical exercises performed on the bare boards of our room. My wake-up call of those mornings at the Kroh were invariably the thumpings and groanings that Franz made as he jumped and stretched and pushed and pulled his own body about. I would lie under my bedclothes and watch the proceedings with interest. He would perform the sequences in his underwear and they would conclude with a series of noisy breathing exercises performed at the open window. After this, Franz would pull out a small tape measure and take note of his statistics—the circumference of his thighs, his waist and his chest—and jot them down in his notebook.

He was completely heedless of my presence in the room: a lack of delicacy of which I was quite envious. He followed his exercise schedule regardless of circumstance; the cold did not deter him, and if the rain blew in the open window and soaked him as he breathed aggressively at the air, he seemed oblivious. The exercises took precedence over all other things; breakfast and any morning appointments were all postponed until Franz had completed his circuit. I now saw his perfect physical form in a different light and being made aware of the work that went into it was strangely comforting to me, bound as I was in my own imperfection.

Franz had another habit in which he engaged less regularly, one that I was not privy to until we had cohabited for more than a few weeks. One afternoon I came back into our room to find it empty. I noticed that the wardrobe door was ajar, and a second later realised that Franz was there in the room after all, crouched next to the wardrobe and obscured by the open door. He was so engrossed in something that he had not noticed me come in. He was standing in the beam of sunlight that came through the window in front of the long mirror that was fixed to the wardrobe door. He was fully dressed and looked ready to go out. He was peering anxiously into the mirror, his face inches from the glass, his breath making white clouds upon it. Then he held something up to his face and began angling his head and his body awkwardly around, turning in a slow circle. He kept pitching his head at odd angles, his eyes on the object in his hand. I saw that it was a tiny hand mirror, which he was using to view himself from all angles. He turned to look at himself in profile and tested out various expressions, smiling and looking serious, tilting his head up and down. He turned and viewed himself from the back.

I felt ashamed for him, to have caught him in such a private moment, but also surprised, because his actions spoke of a vulnerability of which I had not thought him capable. I also felt the shock of recognition. In my younger years, and still now at times of nervous unease, I have engaged in a similar obsessive looking; to what end, I do not know. Perhaps I looked to try to gain control of my image, as if the offence it could cause were a finite physical thing that could be used up by my eyes alone. Or perhaps I looked to assess the exact sum of my hideousness, to quantify it. But in this I was never successful, because all proportion disappeared in front of the glass, and with my exposed self before my eyes my sense of judgment became confused and useless. Was I a complete monster or only mildly unpleasant? The answer always eluded me; the more I looked, the less I knew. What could Franz possibly be looking for? I wondered. He surely had no need of it in the way that I had.

I quietly took hold of the door handle and silently opened the door a small way and then noisily pulled it shut behind me, pretending that I had only just come into the room. I had expected him to jump hastily from the mirror and I gave him time to do so by lingering with my back to him while I hung up my hat and coat. But when I turned to face him I found that he had not moved; the only concession to my presence was his gaze sliding briefly over to me and then immediately back to the mirror's surface.

During the time at Karlsbad, my thoughts often drifted to Anja. My feelings for her had the effect of inoculating me against the charms of the women in the town. The days of pleasant reverie about my relationship with Anja were long over and now my thoughts circled menacingly. Now I relived each one of our encounters obsessively, trying to discern the point of collapse, the moment when that first germ of destruction had entered into our relationship. There were so many things I would have liked to ask her.

As soon as we had arrived at Karlsbad I began to write letters to her, filling pages with questions and recriminations, with my own interpretations of looks she had given me, of phrases spoken. It became difficult to gather up the facts of the situation and I could no longer remember the exact nature of our relationship, how much of it was real and how much was lived only in my mind. I relived scene after scene of our days together, each time arriving at a different conclusion as to what was between us. Now I thought that she loved me; now that she barely saw me as a man. In the letters I was by turns abject in my sadness or crowing with accusations. Herr Liška came back to haunt me and I imagined him as a young Jan Žižka, still with both of his own eyes, austere and determined. I pictured encounters with him and plotted out what I would say to him if we chanced to meet. Of Franz too I was jealous. I remembered how she had looked that night on the stairs and how my mind had leaped immediately to Franz as an explanation. But I could not allow myself to dwell on that—I would have been driven mad—and I tried to I push all thoughts of him and Anja from my mind.

Although I wrote Anja letter after letter, I could never grasp the heart of what I wanted to say. Words are such imprecise tools, particularly words fixed in time and written black on white. Far better to expose one's bare breast, to tear it open and display one's heart, quivering; to show a naked eye, bathed in salt tears, or open late at night, dry and staring wakefully at the ceiling.

Of course I never sent Anja any of these letters. I screwed the pages into tight little balls and threw them away. Instead I sent her a few postcards and letters of the most conventional sort, recounting some amusing goings-on, or describing a local attraction as if in rehearsal for the travelogue. I never received any reply.

17.

FRANZ, AFTER SOME WEEKS AT THE HOTEL, HAD BEGUN TO TIRE of the attention that came at him from all sides. The turning point came as a result of some encounters with a certain doctor who was also a visitor to Karlsbad. I first came across Dr Klopstock in the gardens of the Kurhaus bathhouse one afternoon, where we were sitting in adjacent chairs, he sunning himself and I making notes for the travelogue.

We fell into conversation, uneasily on my part. By this stage of our trip I had become somewhat wary of people attempting to use me as a means of getting close to Franz. But Klopstock seemed to be a perfectly ordinary man and did not strike me as one likely to be given to such obsessions. He was of early middle age and his neatly combed, uniformly grey hair was the only tidy thing about him. He slouched casually in his chair and both the suit he wore and the newspaper he held were comfortably rumpled and a little the worse for wear.

When I introduced myself he told me that he had read my first novel, but that he could not venture any opinion on it because he could not remember it. This comment cheered me immensely, suggesting a lack of interest in either literature or any flattery of me that might have made him a potentially troublesome acquaintance. At some point in the afternoon he mentioned quite calmly that he had heard that Franz was staying at the town, and that he thought he had glimpsed him at the baths but had not realised that I accompanied him. I explained about the travelogue and we then had a pleasant conversation about the baths and he recommended various sights in the region of Karlsbad that might interest us.

We spent an enjoyable few hours together, and as we were about to part the doctor invited me for dinner the following evening, together with Franz. The mention of Franz put me on my guard, but I accepted, after warning him that he may be dining alone with me if Franz was not able to attend.

The evening of the dinner came and, sure enough, Franz was nowhere to be found. I did not wait, but went to meet Dr Klopstock on my own. Relations between Franz and me were still rather strained and our conversation was still restricted to the practicalities of the travelogue. I was looking forward to the dinner; to have some conversation on subjects other than schedules, museum opening times and train timetables would be a welcome relief.

The meal was quite unremarkable and Dr Klopstock was an attentive host. He was not excessively disappointed that I appeared alone. I had a pleasant evening and then I promptly forgot the occasion. Over the next few days I did not see the doctor again at the bathhouse or around the town, and as I was busily touring the area and reviewing the sights he disappeared from my mind.

The following week I was hurriedly dressing in our little room one morning, taking advantage of Franz's visit to the bathroom, when I was startled by a noise at the window. It sounded as though a bird were on the other side, tapping its beak against the glass. When I had put my shirt on, I drew back the curtains to look, but the window revealed nothing more than an early-morning spring sky with a few reluctant clouds. I opened the window and heard a shout from the lawn below. A man was standing there on the grass and waving his arms energetically over his head, apparently trying to get my attention.

He was shouting something over and over, and I thought at first that there had been some kind of accident and he was calling for assistance, but then I realised that it was my name he was calling. I had no idea who the man was.

Windows on the floors below ours were beginning to swing open and curious heads to emerge. Other windows were being angrily slammed shut against the noise of the man's shouts. I noticed a group of porters in uniform running towards him across the lawn, accompanied by a small bald man. I gestured to the shouting man that I would come down.

When I reached him he was surrounded by a ring of the porters, and was silently fighting his way out of the grip of the bald man, who I now saw was wearing pyjamas. His face and scalp were still scored with vivid purple runnels from the imprint of the creases on his pillowcase. The shouting man was the tallest of the group, but was nevertheless impeded by the bald man, who had his arms wrapped entirely around him, pinioning his arms to his trunk and trying to throw him off balance like a professional wrestler.

I realised then that the shouting man was Dr Klopstock. He totally ignored the bald man clinging to his waist and casually hailed me as though we were simply meeting by chance in a café or on the street. He looked so dishevelled as to be unrecognisable. His hair was now like a cap of furze over his hollowed face and his clothing was covered in dirt.

'Brod, I have been meaning to tell you that I have moved into your hotel. A room came up and I thought it would be good to be closer,' he said, quite calmly.

The wrestle was still in progress, but Klopstock was managing to keep his voice on a remarkably even keel.

'Do you and Franz fancy a morning walk? That's what I wanted to ask you.'

My face must have communicated the disorientation I was feeling, because he indicated the bald man with a tilt of his chin, and said, 'Oh, Jensen. You mustn't bother about him.'

The bald man, Jensen, succeeded in pulling Klopstock to the ground. He lay there quite sedately, ignoring everyone and staring up at the sky. Another group of men had arrived, some fully dressed and some still in dressing-gowns. They huddled around the fallen Klopstock, blocking him from my view, and began discussing something in urgent tones. Occasionally one of them would turn and glare angrily at me and at the small knot of porters. I made my way back to our room.

Over the next days, Dr Klopstock came to be a regular feature in our lives. He tailed Franz with a ferocious tenacity that exceeded that of any other hotel guest. The apparent lack of interest he had shown in Franz in the beginning had given way to an all-consuming obsession. He seemed to spend all his time trying to get near to Franz and he seemed convinced that there existed between them some close relationship.

In the mornings I would open the door and discover him waiting outside on the landing, as if he had been standing there all night, which perhaps he had been. He would write letters to Franz, leave him small gifts, and send endless invitations for dinner or to the theatre. In the afternoons he would take a chair out onto the middle of the lawn, place it under our window, and simply sit and look up at it for hours. I had no idea how he had even found out which window was ours. He somehow managed also to discover which places we were to visit, and we would chance upon him in the corridors of museums, standing silently among some Roman sculptures or sitting on a park bench in Karlsbad, or we would catch sight of the top of his hat bobbing up and down at the other end of the train compartment.

He was always perfectly polite and reserved when we met him, and would calmly discuss some point of interest in the museum or the park as though his obsessive attentions did not exist. This was completely unlike the way he expressed himself in his letters, which were more like ardent declarations of love. I found this dissonance extremely unnerving.

To Franz, the whole thing was highly amusing at first; guessing where Klopstock would next appear became like a little game between us, the reading of his letters became a daily ritual, and these diversions greatly improved the cooled relations between

Franz and me. Before long, the frequency of Klopstock's letters increased and he began to outline his plans for moving to Prague to be close to Franz, and then at last Franz began to feel uneasy.

I was able to track down Dr Jensen and discovered that Klopstock was a psychiatric patient in his care. Jensen was a keen proponent of therapies that involved building a healthy body to build a healthy mind, and he was much given to experimental treatments for obsessive psychiatric disorders. He was insistent that Klopstock remain in the town for the planned duration of his cure, saying that to move him away now would have fatal consequences for his recovery.

The situation began to wear on Franz's nerves. As well as Klopstock, amusing though he may have been, Franz also continued to be courted by the other guests. He still spent his time endlessly writing letters and fending off advances from all sides. It became unmanageable and he began to barricade himself in our tiny room to avoid encountering anyone, and had his meals sent up to him.

One result of this was that Franz felt unable to make the necessary tours of the area, so I spent long afternoons trailing through empty museums and dark churches alone, noting down every detail. I spent one whole day sampling each variety of spa wafer, both hot and cold, and weighing their relative merits. It took days to taste the water at each of the town's thirteen main springs, mostly because the taste was so vile that I could only manage to force the stuff down a few times a day. Even today I can still recall the taste of those springs: a warm mixture of citrus and rust that lingered on the palate for hours. I was pressed by competing local shopkeepers to try out any number of patented cups and drinking vessels designed especially for the Karlsbader water, each claiming to provide the best way for the body to absorb the water's healthful magic.

I took various bath cures at the Kurhaus, of varying levels of ignominy. I had my gums irrigated. I tried hydrotherapies of various means: being sprayed with a hose attached to a pneumatic pump in what I found to be a most undignified procedure, and being immersed in pools and springs. I was locked in a kind of sauna, which was referred to as 'a cupboard for sweating'. This was a wooden box that fitted around the body and had a small opening that clamped around the neck. Steam from the springs was pumped into this box, but I failed to reap the miraculous benefits of rejuvenation that it promised.

I was initially self-conscious at the thought of exposing my body to the nurses and physicians at the Kurhaus, but even a few short hours of walking around the streets of Karlsbad allayed my worries, for it was immediately apparent that the place was a carnival of illness and deformity. I was certainly no longer alone in my difference in that place, for the streets were teeming with the diseased, the misshapen and the infirm, many of whom could not even walk, all hoping for a miraculous cure. We physical freaks seemed to dominate in number over the ordinary able-bodied. And indeed, even those who appeared to be normal from a distance would often on closer inspection be plagued with wheezing breath, rheumy eyes or lurid crops of facial pustules.

I was partly relieved at being spared Franz's company on all these outings I made in aid of the travelogue, but at the same time his absence annoyed me. For all those hours that I was searching my way through unfamiliar towns to discover a recommended place or enduring uncomfortable treatment regimes, Franz was locked up in our room diligently writing. I would come back from an exhausting day of sightseeing or hydrotherapy and interrupt his scribbling. The very sound of his pen scratching across the page filled me with resentment. A few times I asked him what he was writing, but he would never tell me.

The only writing that I was managing to complete was my sightseeing notes and the letters to Anja that I never posted. Franz and I had made the arrangement that if I was to undertake the sightseeing, then he would transcribe the notes that I had made on the trip, in order to balance the workload between us; an arrangement that I still felt to be unfairly weighted in his favour.

Every evening I took out the notes that I had made during the day, together with brochures and maps that I had collected, and placed them on the little writing table in our room.* After more than a week these papers had amassed into a vast pile that grew larger every day, never appearing to make the transformation into the elegant prose that Theodor was expecting.

I asked Franz a few times about his progress with this, whether he had finished any transcriptions that he would like me to proofread, but he never had anything to give me. He complained that my handwriting was too difficult to read, and blamed this for his slow progress. I asked him then if he would like me to proofread any of his other writing. But no matter how often I asked Franz always declined to pass on any of his writing. He had

---

* Blank postcards of Karlsbad and train schedules were found between these pages of the manuscript.

become uncharacteristically evasive about it, and for some reason this nagged at me. Perhaps my nerves had been affected by living in the tense atmosphere of that hotel, constantly on guard against overfamiliar strangers seeking me out, not to mention Klopstock's enduring obsession. I found myself constantly worrying about the question of what Franz was writing as though it would have some catastrophic consequence for me.

Possibly this reaction had come from the Gregor situation, which had put me on edge. Whenever I thought of Gregor I became stilted and silent in Franz's presence and tried to reveal as little of myself as possible, frightened that he might again be observing me for idiosyncrasies with which to pin me to the page. As the days passed I became more and more paranoid about the subject of his writing. When I came back to the hotel in the evening, I could hear him at work from the other side of the door to our room. The pen made a jagged scrabble on the paper, like an animal sliding through dry grass.

I stood silently outside the door of our room and held my breath and listened, as though the pen were a voice that could speak to me through the wood of the closed door. I would stand there for a long time before I proceeded to open the door with care. This was a delicate procedure. I laid my fingers lightly over the lever of the brass handle at first, slowly increasing my grip until my knuckles shone out white. The door was never locked. I would depress the handle with extreme slowness, as the spring mechanism inside ticked. I held my breath and swung the door gently on its hinges, millimetre by millimetre, my eyes on the slowly growing wedge of our room that emerged from between the door and the doorjamb.

I strove for total silence, so that I could surprise Franz. I had no clear idea what I was expecting to happen when he turned and found me there in the room with him. The writing table was opposite the door, under the window, so that even if I had succeeded in surprising him all that would have been visible to me would have been the back of his head and his body hunched over the table.

But, in any case, I never succeeded. Even on the occasions when the metal hinges slid over themselves as silently as the wings of a moth, some movement in the air or a change in temperature alerted him to my presence, and the slit of the door would always widen to reveal him turned in his chair, facing me.

By the time I had stepped into the room he had always slid his papers away and there was no hope of catching even a glimpse of them.

On occasion, usually when I lay awake in my bed at night, the idea would come to me that I could simply take advantage of his absence from the room—when he was washing in the morning, for example—and read through his papers then. But somehow I did not have the heart for this. The image of myself actively hunting through his papers seemed cheap and sad, like one thief stealing from another. I also feared being caught. I had many opportunities to consider it; more and more often it happened that when I returned to the room in the evening I would find him absent. I would stand outside the door and still my breath, straining my ears for the sound of his pen, the creak of his chair as he shifted his weight, but there would be only a rustling silence. The door would be locked and when I had opened it the room empty. Now, I would think, my heart racing. Now.

But I would hesitate. He could come through that door at any moment. On some days he would arrive back at the hotel much later, after I had eaten and undressed for bed; on others he would arrive a moment after me. He never explained where he had been, and I could not ask him.

One day I returned later than usual and found that he was not there. I added my sightseeing notes to the pile on the writing table and casually shuffled through it, as though I were being watched. The hotel was very quiet and I could hear a nightjar call. I stood with one eye on the door, ready to leap away the moment I heard a sound. I looked through the heap of papers, but they were all mine. The ones at the bottom of the pile were already gathering dust.

I rifled through the drawers of the little writing table. I looked around the room for likely places for him to stow his papers; in such a small room there were not many. I stooped to look under his bed. I shifted his pillow and looked underneath. I hunted through the wardrobe. His suitcase was with mine in a storeroom of the hotel, and I wondered how likely it was that he would venture there twice a day to take out his papers and then lock them in again. The wastepaper basket was full of crumpled pages. I took out a compact ball at random and opened it out.

The familiar sweep of Anja's writing covered the page. My skin hardened and my heart was a sharp object in my chest. It was a letter, not the first page, and contained a detailed analysis of some poem or section of prose. Anja was in rhapsodies about it, and the cadences of her voice rang painfully in my head as I read the words she had written. I imaged her small hand holding the pen and guiding it to form the letters that stood there against the paper.

I immediately upended the wastepaper basket and began smoothing out all the pages it contained. Among them were many empty sheets, some containing a few words written by Franz, mostly columns of figures being added or subtracted, or what appeared to be lists of food eaten throughout the day, but there was nothing more of Anja's. I searched through each sheet again to make sure. I read the page of the letter and read it again and then put it in my pocket. I did not know what it meant. I stood in the room, aware of the walls around me, enclosing me. Then I went out into the gardens.

The smell of the springs, to which I had become largely accustomed over the past weeks and rarely noticed now, was extremely strong that night and as noxious as a poisonous gas. I breathed it in with difficulty and could feel the odour penetrate into the fabric of my clothing and the strands of my hair. I walked around in the stench for as long as I could bear it, with one hand in my pocket, the fingers pushed into the folds of the letter, a paper pocket inside the cloth one. Naturally the letter was meant for me; it was the reply I had been waiting weeks for. I thought of Franz coming into the room every day with piles of letters addressed to him, from Klopstock, from the plump lady in the dining room, from any number of strangers.

'Nothing for you,' he would say, and laugh. And I would laugh, right through the stab of pain brought by Anja's silence.

Had he discarded my letter by mistake? Or did he stand there in the hall and sort out her letters to me and put them in his pocket, smiling to himself, leering, or with a mechanical gesture, blank-eyed? Had she been writing all this time? Did he read them? I took the page out again to look for a date, but there was none.

I made up my mind to ask him about it. I had every right to ask him. Unable to wait a moment more, I hurried back to our room. I was shaking and out of breath when I reached the staircase. As I came up the stairs, I knew that the room would be dark and empty, and so it was. I took out the letter and, gripping it like a talisman, settled myself in the chair to wait for him to appear.

I had only been sitting for a short time when I heard the creak of the top stair and the sound of the door handle squeaking as it opened. Franz looked at me without greeting me. I unfolded the letter, smoothed it with my palm onto the surface of the writing table. He watched me, still standing in the doorway with the door open and his hand on the handle. Neither of us spoke. Earlier, out in the garden, I had felt ready to shout and rage at him, but now something made me hesitate. His face was blank, but held a look of slyness, of mastery. Once again, his handsomeness came into focus for me. Seeing him every day for the past weeks had habituated me to it somewhat, and made me forget it, but now I could hardly see him for all his beauty. It struck me then that I had been mistaken. The letter from Anja was not my letter—of course not. It was his.

I pictured myself sitting on trains and park benches writing to Anja, while at the same moment he sat here, in the same chair in which I now sat, and wrote too. I saw our letters being collected in tandem by the postman, and being processed and delivered together also; twins, arriving in her letterbox at the same moment. The thought made me sick. I slid the still-crumpled page of the letter into the pile of notes in front of me.

'Still awake,' he said; an observation. He had come into the room, hung up his hat and was taking off his jacket. I could not speak. My guts roiled, I feared my veins could not contain the sharp surges of blood sent from my heart, the edges of the room turned black. I nodded. Yes. Still awake. Then I undressed and lay in my bed, with the darkness pressing in on my opened eyes.

Morning came and I pretended to sleep while Franz rose early and left the room. After he had gone I slept a little, and as soon as I woke I took the letter out from under the pile of papers and read it again. I no longer knew where I stood in relation to Anja. I thought again and again of the last times I had seen her, but I could not understand it: the kiss, and then her rain-soaked face on the stairs. I had to keep on arranging the facts in a row in my mind, but I could not hold them there long enough to evaluate them, to discover their meaning.

I abandoned my plans for the day, washed and dressed and then went to the hotel desk to ask for the morning's letters for our room. My hands were shaking as I shuffled through them. I did not recognise Anja's writing on any of the envelopes, but one of the letters was addressed to me. I turned it over and saw that it was from Theodor. Of course he would be expecting a draft of our travelogue by now, and all we had was my dusty pile of notes. I cursed under my breath as I remembered the agreement I had signed. Back in our room, I opened each letter one by one, Theodor's also. I crumpled the pages without reading them and threw them into the wastepaper basket. It seemed to take a long time, and when I had finished I felt more alert.

I had to see Anja. I packed my clothes and hesitated before the pile of travelogue notes.* In the end I took them, thinking that it would not take me long to write them up. I took out a sheet of notepaper to write to Franz, but I could think of nothing to say. In the end I left it there, blank, a square of white on the table's surface.

---

* These notes were located among the manuscripts. They are unremarkable, and written in a shorthand style. Their content mostly paraphrases the information that appears in the 1905 Baedeker.

18.

ON THE TRAIN, WITH KARLSBAD RECEDING INTO THE DISTANCE, I felt an immense sense of relief. I opened the window of the compartment wide and stood up to better breathe in the clean air, to rid my lungs of the sulphurous fumes that I knew still lingered there, and in my hair and on the tips of my fingers. I watched the wooded hills speed past. My head was clearer and my whole body felt clean and true, like an arrow being shot from a bow, sure of the target. If I am honest with myself, I was also relieved to be returning home because it would allow me to peel myself out from under the heavy shadow of Franz. Although the anonymity at Karlsbad had the benefit of concealment, I realised as soon as my feet were back on the streets of Prague that I much preferred to be recognised, even though this meant that I lived with the weight of the world's appraising eyes on me.

Prague was bathed in sun and the droplets of a recent shower, and the stones of the familiar streets and buildings were softened and gathered tight around me like an embrace. On the train I had been planning to go directly to Anja's house, but on catching sight of myself in the compartment window I decided to return home first, to wash and change my clothes.

Even so I could not help taking the route that passed Anja's house, and as I turned into the Martinsgasse my heart quickened in my chest. I walked on the opposite side of the street to her house, to be able to see it more easily. The thought that Anja was only a few metres distant from me, separated perhaps by only a pane of glass and the thickness of a curtain, calmed me. I imagined her sitting in her room, brushing her hair, or talking with her mother, drinking tea. My sense of urgency evaporated. It occurred to me that my formulations of the previous night might have been paranoid. The whole thing was probably nothing more than a misunderstanding. In the sparkling light of my beautiful city, all the anxieties of the time at Karlsbad shrank and became nothing more significant than an unpleasant dream.

§

Although I had intended to call on Anja on the day of my arrival, I did not make the visit until a few days later. When I returned home I found that I had many responsibilities requiring my attention: I had work waiting for me at the post office, and Theodor, who had somehow already got wind of my return, was demanding explanations. I began to develop a strange, almost superstitious, reluctance to see Anja. I had not seen her for so long that a part of me preferred to keep her in the sure realm of my imagination, where I could control what happened. I began almost to fear meeting with her, an event which would decisively clarify the situation for good or ill.

On the day of my visit to her I dressed with care and made a detour to buy a bouquet from a flower seller. My hands were trembling as I walked up the Martinsgasse. The street was completely deserted and the houses were silent. Everything had an abandoned air, including Anja's house, when I arrived.

I had to wait a long time for the concierge to open the door and, when he did, it was only to inform me that the Železnýs were not at home, and then slam the door in my face. I stepped back out into the street and looked up at Anja's curtained windows. I stood for a long time, but the curtains never shifted and the folds of fabric fell across the glass like rolls of iron. I returned home and gave the bouquet to my mother instead.

When I'd left Karlsbad, I had thought that I was leaving Franz behind. I had looked forward to existing once more in my own right, rather than as an appendage to him, but it was not long before I realised that he had followed me here; it was impossible to escape him. He was everywhere in Prague. Everyone was talking about him, his stories appeared in the journals to which I subscribed, friends of mine reviewed the stories in other journals, and people were constantly asking me about him and begging to be introduced.

When I went to see Theodor I found the whole office completely altered. The furniture was new and modern and in a different arrangement, and the workers too had been replaced with new ones. No one recognised me, no one knew who I was, and the head clerk, on glancing at my card, called out to Theodor that Franz's agent was waiting to see him.

The other strange workers at the office began to bustle in and out of the hall, glancing curiously at me as I sat waiting. I could hear them whispering in the back room, and presently the youngest-looking one came towards me like an envoy, holding out a copy of Franz's book. He shyly asked me to sign it, which, though slightly puzzled by the request, I did, before realising that he had misunderstood and taken me for Franz.

I felt terribly ashamed when I became aware of my mistake; that I had defaced his book with a nonsensical inscription. After the initial confusion, he also seemed embarrassed, and, eager to cover his embarrassment with pleasantry, told me that he would simply cut out the page and then paste it into my first book when that was published.

Even in the realm of sleep there was no escape from Franz. His face floated in front of my eyes when I drifted off, and in my dreams I would find it superimposed onto other faces: those of small children playing in the street, my mother's face, and even my own in the mirror. I began to dread going out lest I be asked yet again about Franz, and I remained sequestered either in my office or at home.

Although it was unpleasant, this enforced isolation ultimately worked in my favour. The weeks had sped past and the deadline for Schopenhauer was almost upon me. Now I could not avoid the many hours of joyless work that awaited me, and I set myself to the task of marshalling my notes into a vague shape to produce something that might make a book. All my optimism at the outset of writing this book had melted away, leaving only a kind of sick fatigue. How I hated Schopenhauer now. I went about the work passionlessly, all of my lofty ideas gone, aiming only to finish it. I set a strict daily quota of two thousand words and mechanically kept to it with no excuses. I finished exactly on the day of the deadline. I sent the papers off to Theodor, but there was none of the usual euphoria of achievement; only a dull sense of relief. That night I fell into bed at six o'clock and slept a blank, anaesthetised sleep.

19.

BY THIS TIME I HAD BEEN BACK IN PRAGUE FOR MORE THAN A month, and Anja's house still remained empty. I called on her twice a day, on my way to and from the post office, and soon I was such a familiar figure on the Martinsgasse that the concierge stopped even bothering to open the door to me. Instead his grizzled head would appear in the glass panel beside the door and he would peer at out me, frown, and then make an impatient movement with his hand before turning away.

After this silent exchange, I would take up my post on the opposite side of the street and watch the windows of Anja's apartment. I could not tell you why I did this. I would stare at the pattern of the curtains' folds until I was hypnotised by them, and then nothing else—not Prague, myself, Franz or even Anja—seemed to exist anymore. Inevitably, just when I had made up my mind to leave, I would imagine that the curtain had moved, or the shadow of a person had appeared at the window, and I would remain there in the street, looking up.

Anja's continued absence obsessed me. I searched for her everywhere. I walked through the halls of the university, hoping to run into her, but the campus was closed for the summer and the empty corridors echoed with my lonely footfalls. I lingered in the cafés, museums and parks that we had visited together, waiting for her to appear, but she never did. Her ghost began to haunt me, appearing all over the city. I would constantly see girls with hair of exactly the same hue or with the same supple figure walking down the street or waiting at shop counters, and the sight of them would stop my heart. I would hurry along the street, or open the door of the shop, my heart racing, but the girl would disappear or turn her head to reveal that she did not resemble Anja in the slightest.

I asked everyone I knew where she and her family had gone, but no one could tell me, or they gave me contradictory information about the summer-holiday destinations of the family. They were in Vienna or Paris or Berlin, or they had seen Anja yesterday, trying on hats in a shop in the Little Quarter. When I lay in bed at night I began to have paranoid thoughts that she was with Franz, in Karlsbad or in some other place. I pictured the two of them sharing our little Karlsbad hotel room. This would drive me into such a frenzy that I would be ready to leap up and return there by the next train. Consumed by jealousy, I wavered between intense feelings of love and hatred for Anja. I continued to write to her, despite my awareness that the letters would not find her and would instead be collected by the impatient hands of the concierge. It occurred to me that if Franz was also writing to her, at least he was in the same situation as me. As sad as it was, the thought cheered me immensely.

20.

AFTER I HAD SENT MY DRAFT TO THEODOR, SCHOPENHAUER AND the book completely left my mind; and a tranquillity settled over me. A few weeks later, however, my manuscript returned to me once again, its pages disfigured by crossings-out, question marks and notes that were scrawled in every margin. I was given a month to set it to rights, and for the whole of that month I rued the day I had conceived of my exalted notions of an avant-garde philosophical novel.

Usually after a time away from a piece of writing, even one with which I had been fatigued, I had always returned refreshed, with new eyes that could see the flaws but also appreciate the merits of that writing. But this was totally demoralising. There was nothing of much merit that I could see. The pace limped along, no matter how I laboured, scenes followed each other in a confusing order and even I was bored by my own voice. I worked and reorganised and deleted and expanded up until the last day, and then sent it on its way. I was expecting more challenges from Theodor and requests to rewrite it, but I had the sense that he had given up on me, and the book went to print without other changes. I cannot say whether I was relieved or saddened by this.

While I was waiting for the book to come out, I tried to reassure myself that it was not as bad as it seemed, and perhaps some deep part of me believed this and even felt confident of the book's brilliance, because its trajectory came as an extreme disappointment. The week that it was due for release I eagerly watched the usual newspapers and journals for reviews, but nothing appeared. The day of the release came and went, and still the papers were silent. Surely, I felt, there had been some mistake. I furtively made a round of the bookshops and saw the book lying in all its printed glory in the 'new release' sections in the windows, but I never saw any browsing bookshop customer take up a copy.

Another week went past, and at last some reviews appeared. One was a critical piece in *Der Neue Weg* by that turncoat Franz Werfel, who labelled the book 'a compendium of mediocre twaddle, clearly the product of a confused mind'. The same day there was another more neutral piece in the *Bohemia*, which commended the work on its meticulous research but concluded that it was an 'essentially soulless work', far inferior to *Nornepygge*. Apart from these two reviews, as far as I could see the novel was completely ignored. The sales were dismal. The book was moved to the regular shelves, and then away out of sight.

I could almost have laughed to think that I had devised this project as my great masterpiece, a work that would fix my place in the galaxy of literary intellectuals. I could not bring myself to look at it again; it was far too painful.

I tried not to dwell too much upon it. Although at that time I wished never to have to write another word, unfortunately I still had the travelogue to contend with. I had expected Franz to contribute to this, but having heard nothing from him I set about writing it up myself.

While I was sifting through the notes from Karlsbad, I pulled out a crumpled envelope with Franz's name upon it. At first I thought that it might be a letter from Anja, and my heart tightened, but the envelope was too thin to be a letter. I opened it and saw that it was the cheque that Theodor had asked me to pass on to Franz. It was for an odd sum, not a rounded figure, and I thought that it might be some kind of reimbursement. It was also not made out to Franz in name, but to cash. It was quite a large sum: three hundred and fifty-three crowns and twenty-two heller.

There was no note or letter that might give any clue as to the reason for the payment. It certainly was a bit of money. I could have done with such a windfall. I put the cheque away and tried not to think about it. But, in the next days, my thoughts kept returning to it. It was so much money. It was most likely, I thought, that the cheque was for expenses incurred, or expected expenses, in Karlsbad. If that were the case, I reasoned, then I was entitled to at least a part of that sum. Most of it in fact. After all, I had been the one who had done almost all the work while we were there; I had been the one to pay for countless museums and tours of historical sites, and now here I was writing the thing up too. The more I thought about it, the more it seemed fair that I should keep a part of it. After a few more days of piecing together the travelogue, I had convinced myself that actually I deserved the whole sum. Probably,

I told myself, this was what Theodor had intended by making the cheque to cash in any case. And besides, my finances were quite severely drained what with Karlsbad and the money I had spent on Gustav and Alexandr. I cashed the cheque and did not feel the tiniest bit of guilt.

21.

THE HEAT OF THE CITY WAS BECOMING UNCOMFORTABLE AND I fell into the usual state of depression that dogged me each summer. A heightened awareness of my body added to the dark thread of unhappiness that ran through my days. I shrank into myself and kept busy with my work at the post office.

In the mornings on the way to work I would stand on the tram and sweat into my padded jacket, too ashamed to remove it in public. I tried to ignore the looks thrown at me as I stood there with sweat running down my face and the imprint of my hand darkening the leather handles. I would smell the odour of the damp jacket, so often worn, gradually steeping the air around my seat, and I always tried to secure the place closest to the window to spare my fellow passengers.

On the hottest days I would forgo the tram, and instead walk the distance to the office. I would leave my house very early in the morning, just after it was light, at a time when the city was still waking for the day. Remnants of night-time mist clung to the sides of buildings, waiting to be burned up by the sun. The sky was stretched white over the rooftops and I breathed the stagnant air that was like a layer of damp cotton.

I told myself that the reason I took this early journey on foot was because the tram frequently broke down in hot weather and I wanted to be sure to get to my office early, to have some time alone in which to start my day. This was partly true, but it was only the varnish with which I covered my shame at the real truth of my unsightly self. However, walking at this hour was one of the rare times in the day that I was able to escape the harrying thoughts and unanswerable questions that plagued me. Anja and Franz would fall away and my body was significant only as a collection of sensory organs. The air moulded itself around me, as I propelled myself forward, and closed off behind me in my wake, like warm water around a swimmer. This relaxed me, and I was lulled into a trance as I walked.

When I was a child and had first learned to swim it was as though the world had finally opened to me; for the first time I had found a place where I felt at home. I had been a self-conscious child from the moment I noticed my difference from other children and realised it was not something that could be overcome with the passage of time. My lumbering movements were mimicked by the other children in the schoolyard, and adults and older children would look at me with a kind of fear. My offensiveness to them pained me, so I withdrew into myself and tried to erect boundaries with which to contain my difference. I tried to police my own movements and began the long process of learning to control them as much as I was able.

My mother, for the first years* after I was out of the harness, and after the death of my brother, Otto, guarded me as one would an invalid, which was how I thought of myself. I was not allowed to join the other children for games and sports at school, and, instead of allowing me to participate in the gymnastics lesson, the teacher ordered me home for the hour. Although this action on my mother's part was motivated by a desire to protect me, it only served to emphasise my difference and exposed me even more to the cruel taunts and violence of the schoolyard. I hated returning home for that afternoon hour; every day it felt like coming home from a defeat. One spring, instead of going home, I began to spend the hour walking around the streets, or lingering in parks. I crossed and recrossed the Moldau on each of the bridges by turn.

I loved the river, and would find a quiet place on the bank where I would weave small boats from reeds and twigs and sail them in the shallows. Or I would just sit for a long time, silent and still, watching the birds and listening to their song, and that of the whirring insects and the wind hissing in the leaves. Sitting there, silently listening, I seemed to fade away into the undergrowth and lose awareness of myself. My body and my external life floated away from me and I became a part of the riverbank, another animal life among so many others, no more or less important.

As the weather grew warm, I would see the occasional swimmer making his way down the river. I would sit hidden in the long grass, transfixed. The swimmers were like other river animals, like larger

---

* Two pages have been torn out of the notebook and have not been recovered. The first part of this sentence is an approximation.

otters; I didn't relate to them as people. On warm days I would sit with my eyes on the water, looking out for them, and when one appeared I would creep quietly down to the water, as though I might scare them off if I made a sound. I would lean out over the water and watch them glide past, craning my neck to keep them in view for as long as possible. I drank up the sight of their sleek motion with a fierce envy that originated in my flesh and muscles rather than my mind. I would feel the beginnings of tears sting my eyes.

I wanted to rush out and join them, and indeed in my imagination I was already out there, swimming with them; water gurgling past me, cool against my face and with soft strings of bubbles rising from my lips like pearls. As the days passed I became determined to swim. I began to study the motions that the passing swimmers made with their arms and head, and practised them while lying face down on the grass. After a few days of this, I undressed and walked naked and shivering into the water, which was colder than seemed possible. I found a place with a partly submerged tree trunk that extended out into the river, and which I could hold on to as I ventured out into the deeper water.

At first, the touch of the water frightened me, but gradually I became accustomed to it. After a few days I was even quite comfortable with the sensation of the water lapping around my chin and lips, and even of being submerged, but I had great difficulty launching myself from my standing position into a horizontal one. This took many days of practice, and the unfamiliar orientation confused me at first, expelling the breath from my body like a reflex.

My difficulty was that, although I had learned from the passing swimmers to move my arms around and around like the wheels of a mill, I had no idea what to do with my legs. All I could see of the swimmers' legs was a fizzing wake that seemed to propel them forward. My legs were the weakest part of me. At first, when I tried to kick off from the riverbed they would drift behind me like a heavy train, floating for a short while but then slowly sinking down to the sandy bottom again. I experimented with different movements; I tried rotating my legs as though on a bicycle, in time with my arms, or rotating my feet in tiny circles. It was extremely difficult for me to control my right leg, which was only a soft, spongy thing, lacking any muscle. Eventually I hit upon the notion of kicking my legs up and down, and I practised this motion first holding on to the tree trunk, which had become like a friend to me, its knots and footholds familiar and reassuring. Over the weeks of that summer I slowly learned to propel myself along.

Soon I could even swim few strokes underwater, my belly gliding close above the riverbed. I came up laughing; it was like flying, and for the first time in my life I did not feel restricted in space. I floated and rolled around in the river's grip, and my limbs, glowing white through the dark water, no longer seemed to be objects of pity.

Hearing the clock in the Old Town square strike was the signal for me to return to school, and the sound of it was more awful to me than any early-morning alarm bell. The realities of my life came rushing back to me. Reluctantly, slowly, I would swim ashore; school, my mother, every hardship I endured seemed to be waiting for me on that riverbank. I would dress hastily and hurry back to school, late, my hair still wet, my toes inside my socks ringed with river mud.

So many years later, in my early-morning walking to the post office, I was able to regain the same sense of freedom that being in the river that long-ago summer had given me, and for at least a short while I could lose myself in the world. On those walks I was no longer anyone. I breathed the air, I felt it on my face and my hands, my feet moved along the cobblestones, and that was all. Only when the walls of the post office came into view did I come back into myself, and my life opened its wings again and enclosed me. The dull sound of the heavy double doors swinging closed behind me was like the sound of the clock chiming in my childhood, a grim herald of what it meant to be me.

After arriving at the office, I could usually count on having at least an hour to myself before the other workers began to arrive, and even then it was rare that anyone would bother me for another hour after that. If I was writing, I would allow myself fifteen minutes or so to read the newspaper or a review in a journal and drink a morning cup of coffee, before commencing work. At that time I had finished the travelogue, and Schopenhauer was done with, so I was casting feebly about for some new ideas.

On this particular morning I was preoccupied more than usual with Anja's absence. I was certain that she was back in Prague. The last two times that I had stationed myself outside the house, there had been distinct movement within the apartment. I was sure of it. The arrangements of the curtain over the window had also changed. The concierge continued to dismiss me, but I thought I could discern some shift in his expression, another possible signal of the Železnýs' return.

The idea that Anja might be there but that I could not reach her was maddening, and made me feverish and dizzy. Was the concierge barring me from the apartment out of spite? I regretted calling on Anja so persistently; the concierge perhaps felt he was protecting her from a nuisance, or perhaps even violence. For the first time Klopstock seemed a sympathetic figure to me, and it was with shame that I noted our similarities.

I was interrupted in my musings by a knock at the office door. No one had ever disturbed me at this hour before. It was disorienting. There was a long silence, and I began to wonder if I might have imagined the knock, or if the sound had come from somewhere else. But then it came again. I felt irrationally fearful, as if I were about to be visited by some supernatural presence.

'Come in,' I said.

Theodor came into the room. He was the last person I was expecting. I leaned back in the seat, relieved, and waved him to a chair, but he declined with a shake of his head. It was then I saw his angry face.

'Three hundred and fifty-three crowns and twenty-two heller,' he said. He had not taken off his hat. He stood in the centre of the room with his arms folded. He looked furious but also, I thought, confused.

'Oh yes,' I said. 'The cheque.' He must have spoken to Franz about it. I was thinking fast. The possibility of claiming to have lost it flashed through my mind, but I could not remember if I had signed anything at the bank when cashing it, and Theodor might have checked. Perhaps the best thing was just to admit it. 'Yes, that was for expenses, isn't that right?'

'The cheque was for Franz,' said Theodor.

'Yes, but you had it made out to cash, and I thought, well, it must be expenses.' My voice hung in the air. 'Karlsbad, all those museums. And, you know, I was the one who wrote the whole thing up. Every word!'

There was a long silence. I tried to bring my eyes to Theodor's face.

'The cheque,' said Theodor again, slower this time, 'was for Franz.'

I could not meet his eye. 'I see. Yes. It was a misunderstanding. You have my apologies.'

'Just what exactly is your relationship to Franz?' Theodor asked.

I was stunned, and did not know how to answer. To say, *He is my rival and I wish to destroy him*, was not a possible response, although it would have been the honest one. But Theodor was a man of heightened sensitivity and had no doubt already intuited my true feelings about Franz.

'We are not so close,' I managed eventually.

Theodor nodded, as though he was satisfied with this. 'Please return my money,' he said. 'The exact sum.'

I assured him that I would and he left without saying goodbye. I picked up my cup of coffee, now almost cold, and saw that my hands were trembling. I felt ashamed now of having taken the money. Or, to be accurate, I was ashamed not of having taken it but of having been discovered. But, when I considered of all my dishonesties in the past months, taking the cheque seemed to me to be the most harmless. If I had to be discovered in one dishonesty, this was by far the best. Yet I did not feel reassured. Something about Theodor's manner worried me.

It was still quite early, so I took the morning's newspaper from my briefcase, hoping to distract myself. I skimmed through the political pages, my eyes moving superficially over the surface of the paper, taking nothing in. My thoughts circled constantly from Anja to Klopstock to Franz. Franz had become like a phantom to me, a nightmare figure. I saw him as an insatiably greedy monster, sucking up everything around him, all the women, adulation and attention, like someone emptying a glass through a straw. In my imagination he had become swollen, grotesque, with long, skinny limbs like a spider. I pictured him and Anja sitting in our little room at the Hotel Kroh, laughing together over my letters the way that Franz and I had laughed over Klopstock's. They would take it in turns to read sections of the letters out, imitating my voice, and fall about the room with mirthful tears squeezing out of their clenched eyelids.

The thought agitated me to the point where it became difficult to control my breathing. My clothing, damp with sweat, lay cold against my flesh. I could hear the sound of my heart as an external thing, as if it were an object in the room. Panic rose through my chest, and the connections in the world began to float, loose and elastic. To anchor myself, I riveted my eyes to one phrase in the newspaper—'reliable sources brought to our attention'—and read it over and over, mouthing the words. My hands clamped onto the edge of the desk. When I dared to let go, I took a hurried swallow of coffee, which rolled down my throat like a stone. I turned the page, pretending to myself that I was feeling normal again.

Then I saw Franz's face looking up at me. It was certainly Franz, but his face looked different to me now. His eyes, below his neatly combed hair, were like large black pools and they burned into mine. They seemed to regard me and dismiss me for some wrongdoing. His lips curled, about to speak. I stared at his face. It seemed to rise off the page, expand to an enormous size and engulf me.

Wildly, my eyes seized on the words of the headline: HAS THE SON ECLIPSED THE FATHER? My eyes travelled down the columns of print and there, at the bottom of the page, was a photograph of me, small and grainy, barely recognisable. I gripped the desk again, but this time I could not prevent the room from sliding away from me.*

I became aware of nearby motion and a voice inside my head saying my name. Other voices came to me, and I struggled to open my eyes, which seemed loaded with heavy weights. I saw some yellow object floating on a white ground, and it took me a moment to recognise it as the ceiling lamp. I shifted my eyes to the left, and Stephanie came into view, talking to a man I vaguely recognised as being somehow connected with the post office. They were both looking at me intently and they tried to hoist me into a sitting position. My body became rigid at the touch of their hands. I hated to be touched; even to shake hands cost me an effort.

I felt quite normal, and I wanted more than anything for everyone to leave my office, to be left alone. But they insisted on staying and kept me sitting on the floor, propped up against the desk. There was a soft knock at the door, and it opened to admit a strange man carrying a case: the doctor whom they had called.

---

* There is a newspaper clipping included here, measuring approximately five by seven centimetres, which on one side contains part of a photograph of an unknown face, and on the other an advertisement for Gottlieb coffee.

He did not ask for my colleagues to leave the room, but examined me in their presence. He declared my vital signs to be normal, but took the weakness in my legs as a symptom of the fall. My voice quavered when I was forced to identify myself as a cripple. At last he left, along with the man from the post office, and I was allowed to get up from the floor. But Stephanie still lingered and soon Jelen was at the door, his face grave. He sent me home for the day.

When I left the building I collided with a wall of heat that had already built up, though it was still quite early. I began to sweat as soon as I stepped away from the shade of the doorway. After a few blocks, I stopped at a café, more out of the need for a cool place than the need for a drink, and I ordered tea only because it was still too early for beer. I tried to forget the article I had read, but my thoughts circled unendingly over Kafka, Anja, Klopstock, Theodor, but could not fix firmly on any one. The scale of my problems was suddenly too large to contemplate, and my mind shied from the task. It was useless to try to concentrate. What I would have most liked to do was to go for a walk in the country to clear my head, but the day was much too hot for that. I left the café without drinking my tea and walked home.

When I turned into my street, I could see Elsa's head protruding from the window of our house, and she waved when I came into view as though she had been keeping watch for me. By the time I had reached the house she was standing outside the entrance door. Sophie called my name from the window where Elsa had been earlier and waved at me as though I were returning home after a long absence.

It turned out that Jelen had been worried about my condition and intended to have someone accompany me home from the office, but I had left too quickly, so he had sent a messenger to my house to notify my family of my illness. The messenger was still there when I went up, one of the junior clerks. He looked relieved to see me and hurried off as soon as I had sat down.

I had planned to keep the incident of my collapse from my family, knowing they would worry and fuss over something that was really of no significance. Elsa and Sophie commandeered me as soon as the clerk had left. They made me lie down on the sofa and Sophie began bathing my forehead with a washcloth soaked in rosewater. I allowed them to tend to me, mostly because of the worried expression on Sophie's lovely face.

These kinds of collapses had been a commonplace occurrence in my childhood, and had been the subject of endless speculation by doctors. I used to be afraid of the further illustration that they presented of my lack of control over my own body. I was afraid, too, of the reaction they provoked in others. The experience of the collapse itself was not especially worrying or unpleasant. It usually began with a sensation of sliding, a moment of vertigo, which was very much like the experience of being in a stationary train carriage and looking out of the window at the adjacent carriage of another train, also stationary, and then that other train slowly beginning to move, but feeling for a moment that it is one's own train that is moving. After this sliding sensation, I was aware of nothing until I came to myself again. There was nothing in the interval that I could ever recall; only blackness. Yet I had always felt sure that something must happen to me in those parentheses of consciousness; surely I must go somewhere, in the same way that one visits dream worlds when asleep.

Lying on the sofa, breathing in the scent of roses from the cool cloth over my face, listening to Sophie's and Elsa's murmuring and the dulled street noises, I began to drift into sleep. Instead of Sophie's face bending over me I imagined Anja's, her eyes soft with concern, her hair falling a little over one shoulder. She smiled a slow smile, pulling me into sleep.

22.

AFTER MY COLLAPSE, JELEN HAD INSISTED THAT I STAY AT HOME for a few days. The collapse had an oddly calming influence on my nerves, as if a circuit had been broken, and when I woke from a heavy sleep the following day it was to a state of tranquillity that I had not experienced for many months. Wakefulness came to me gradually, and I became aware of the world of my bedroom. Light pooled in through the window and I saw every object in the room anew. My ears detected a complicated arrangement of sounds, through which I constructed the idea first of the house, and then of the city as it gradually spread out around me; Elsa's steps on the stairs, the sound of my own breath, a carriage passing in the street, the trilling of a kestrel, and a jackdaw singing a complicated response.

I smiled to myself and closed my eyes again. I found that now I could easily fix my mind on the idea of Anja and Franz without it continually slipping from my focus, as it had the day before. The previous day had been the first that I had not called on Anja since my return from Karlsbad, but I was surprised to feel no urgency about this. I wanted to drift off again into sleep, but a persistent sound of footsteps going up and down the stairs prevented me. This became joined by the hissing whispers of Elsa and Sophie, together with my mother's voice, which spoke at the normal volume, only to be immediately shushed by the others.

I remembered then that it was my birthday, and a moment later the bedroom door slowly opened and Sophie, Elsa and my mother crept into my room. My mother began singing 'Happy Birthday' straight away in a loud voice, and the other two joined in. Sophie brought me a breakfast tray with flowers and cards and letters that had arrived in the morning post.

Cups of coffee were distributed and I began to look through my birthday letters. There was one from Felix, and Kurt, and of course Uta, whose was written in a pale violet ink. There was another letter from our cousin in Brünn and a very thick one from Berlin, addressed in handwriting I could not immediately identify.

Sophie clamoured for me to read some of the letters aloud, and I opened first the one from Brünn and read out the birthday wishes and news of marriages and births of the extended family and the activities of the summer.

While I was reading, the letter from Berlin was lying on my lap. Something about the writing looked familiar and made me feel uneasy. After a moment I realised that the writing looked like Anja's. I continued mechanically to read aloud. I wanted to seize the Berlin letter and tear it open, but there were many pages still to come of detailed news from Brünn. My cousin Oskar was an amusing letter-writer, and my audience was laughing and exclaiming at the incidents he described. My eyes kept sliding to the Berlin letter. It suddenly seemed to possess an extraordinary weight that pressed down on me through the bedclothes.

At last I reached the final page of Oskar's letter and my fingers were itching to take up Anja's letter immediately, but it occurred to me that perhaps its contents might not contain birthday wishes that could be read aloud to my assembled family. I had not had any communication with Anja since before I was in Karlsbad. The envelope looked thick and heavy, suggestive of the emotional outpourings I had been both longing for and fearing.

At last I finished reading my cousin's letter and reached out for the other letter, but Sophie announced that it was now time for me to open my birthday presents. She jumped up from the bed and ran out of the room. My mother immediately began a long-winded story from the time of my childhood. Her memory of this period was surprisingly unimpaired and she had a ready collection of anecdotes that she recounted in the smallest details. Her words fell about my ears, while all my attention was on the thick envelope in my fingers.

I had heard the story she told many times before; it concerned my brother, Otto. While she spoke I surreptitiously began to slide my finger underneath the envelope's seal. With one hand, this was a difficult feat. The fibres of the papers gradually gave way to the pressure of my fingers and I felt the paper tear a small distance. I edged my finger further along, extending the tear with a timid, dry crackle that I covered by rustling the bedclothes around over my legs and shifting about in the bed. I continued to tear along the envelope in tiny bursts, striving for silence, pausing to give the appropriate responses to my mother's tale.

When I had torn it completely open, I slid my fingers inside the envelope and felt about in the folds of tissue-thin paper that it contained, all the while keeping my eyes on my mother's face, nodding attentively.

She had reached the end of the story, and in a rare expression of emotion, had stretched out with both hands to take my hand, the one entangled in the hidden envelope. I was forced to discard the envelope, and my hand was caught now in her grasp. She told me what a delightful child I had been, such strength, such promise. Every year at my birthday she told the same tales of Otto's childhood, having mistaken me for him. I never had the heart to remind her that Otto was long dead.

My hand lay limp between hers and she patted it absently, as though it were a small pet. Her eyes were far away in the dim past, while mine drifted to the area of bedclothes under which the letter was concealed. It felt vulnerable and exposed lying there, despite being covered up, as if there was a risk of it slipping off my lap and being blown away. I imagined it flying out of the open window, the folded pages of the letter being released and spreading out into the air like a flock of migrating white birds.

Sophie came back with a pile of parcels and I could at last detach my hand and tuck the letter into the safety of my pyjama waistband. After I had opened a few of the parcels I excused myself and went out of the room to read the letter in privacy. As soon as I was outside the bedroom door I examined the writing; it was clearly from Anja, but she had omitted to write her name over the return address.

While I had been unwrapping the parcels, I had tried to think of the worst possible things that the letter might contain, as though identifying the threat and ruminating on it would prevent it from happening. The worst, I mused, would be the news that Anja was together with Franz in that room in Karlsbad, although I knew that it was unlikely that Anja would write to me to impart this news. Or, worse still, she could be writing to tell me that she and Franz were to get married.

I no longer had any kind of objective view on the situation and was unable to judge what was a likely occurrence and what wasn't. I went into the empty living room, and by the time I had closed the door behind me, my calm of earlier in the morning had vanished and I was in a high state of nerves once again. I stood in the middle of the room and reached into my waistband with hands that seemed not to be mine. My fingers felt thick and rubbery and out of proportion, as though I had a fever, and they fumbled the paper from the envelope. One sheet was folded separately from the others, and I opened this first.

The sight of the page covered in Anja's writing flooded my eyes with tears. I immediately saw that her letter was a short one, more of a note than a real letter.

Her signature appeared two-thirds of the way down the page. I was so agitated that the words scurried like ants over the surface of the paper and I had to concentrate to make sense of them. The letter began with some banal greeting and enquiries about my time at Karlsbad and then a few lines of her impressions of Berlin. Then came the blow.

'I enclose here the newest stories of Kafka, which I very much enjoyed. They are works of true genius, with a humour and a darkness that I find wholly irresistible.'

I read the letter again, but the line was still there. *Wholly irresist-ible.* The beat of my heart shook the paper in my hands. It was just what I had dreaded. Her letter, especially when considered together with the letter I had seen in Karlsbad, was as good as proof of her liaison with Franz. The room whirled around me and my stomach clenched so that I thought I would be sick. I felt a desperate need to see her. I had to go to her. I turned over the envelope and read the return address again: Nostitzstrasse 70, Berlin. I automatically reached for my watch, which of course I was not yet wearing, and was ready to run to the Franz-Josefs-Bahnhof and leap aboard the first train to Berlin.

'Max?' Sophie's voice came through the door. I stuffed the letter back into my waistband and returned to my bedroom.

Sophie was standing outside my bedroom door. She gripped my arm when she saw my face. 'You're ill again,' she said. Her eyes were round with concern.

I smiled at her, but I had seen my face in the hall mirror, the lines of my flesh all directed in a downward motion, the panels of my cheeks hanging flat, my eyes staring from bloodless skin.

'It's only tiredness.'

The bedroom was now even more crowded. My father had joined us. He was standing behind his wife with his hands on her shrunken shoulders, and as I limped into the room I felt a wave of sympathy for him; what a family he headed—a family of cripples and madwomen. For the first time I was aware that he must live with a shame and regret almost as deep as my own.

He stepped towards me and formally shook my hand and wished me many happy returns for the day, as though I were a distant relative, but Sophie pushed him and everyone else out of the room, saying that I was not yet well and that they had all overwhelmed me with their birthday wishes. I felt grateful to her as I climbed back into bed. The letter rustled under my pyjamas as I lay down. Sophie hovered around the room as I settled myself and she came and felt my forehead for signs of fever. I closed my eyes against her anxiously peering face until I heard her leave too.

For hours I lay there, not sleeping, not awake, aware of the letter against my skin and its significance. The words of the letter weighed like objects in the room, dark heavy furniture, crowding the space. If the situation was as I feared then I had nothing left to me. I had no more will to write, not after my last failure. And now it appeared that Anja, too, was lost to me. Franz had won. Once again, the only thing I had which was really my own was my broken body.

23.

ELSA AND SOPHIE CAME INTO THE ROOM SEVERAL TIMES DURING
the day to check on me, and each time they did I closed my eyes and
feigned sleep to avoid having to speak to them. When I was alone I
fell into a kind of daze. I lay staring at a patch of sunlight that shifted
along the wall with the passage of the hours. I listened to the noises
of the street as people went about their unremarkable activities.

At some point in the afternoon I heard someone come in and
move across the room to sit in the chair beside my bed. Sophie,
I thought, my eyes still closed. She whispered my name a few times,
testing the depth of my sleep. Her voice was tense. I think that she
knew I was not sleeping, so I opened my eyes.

'Max, how are you feeling?' She put her hand on my forehead
and frowned as she measured my temperature.

I groaned and closed my eyes again.

'I know you're not well,' she said, 'but do you think you could
get up? We thought—Uta and I—well, it was going to be a surprise,
but we're having a birthday afternoon tea for you.'

Uta. The name fell like a stone. I felt sick at the thought of her coming into the house and inserting herself among my family and friends, as if she were one of them. I pictured her letter, with its violet ink, lying on the floor with the others.

'What, now?' I asked Sophie.

'Yes. We're all waiting for you downstairs.'

I groaned again in protest.

'Please?' she said. 'Everyone is there.'

I could imagine Uta sitting there cosily with Sophie, patting my mother's hand, laughing too loudly and ingratiatingly. The prospect was overwhelming, but I was too weak to refuse Sophie's request.

'Let me dress and then I will come down,' I said.

When she had left the room, I threw back the bedclothes. As I sat up, Anja's letter crunched in my dressing-gown pocket. The sound heralded a flood of images of her that settled on me like a flock of heavy black birds. For a crazy moment I wondered if she might be downstairs with the others, waiting for me to come.

I thought of Anja's apartment in the Martinsgasse and those movements I had seen behind the curtains; perhaps the letter was a mistake, or perhaps the letter had been delayed and since sending it Anja had returned to Prague. I wanted to go to the apartment immediately. I pictured myself shoving the concierge out of the way and making for the stairs. I would throw stones up at her windows. break the glass panel, break down the door.

When I stood up, I realised that I did feel ill. My skin felt tender, and to move was to push through air that was mysteriously thick. I decided that I would dress and then simply leave the apartment and go to Anja. If I could not find her at the Martinsgasse, I would take the train to Berlin. I pulled on my clothes and shoes and put the letter in my pocket. My head ached and my ears magnified every sound. As soon as I opened the bedroom door the noise of Uta's shrill laughed flew at me like a swarm of biting insects.

I could see from the head of the stairs that the double doors to the living room were folded back and Uta's voice reigned. Perhaps I could just walk past, I thought, and no one would see me. I held on to the bannister to lighten my step, and proceeded down the stairs slowly, but the top stair still gave a loud creak, alerting Uta.

'Max?' came her voice.

I froze, still clinging to the bannister, and my heart beat light and fast. There came a dense rustling of fabric and Uta appeared in the doorway of the living room.

'My darling!' she shouted up at me, making a stiff operatic gesture with one hand. She advanced.

My eyes darted around, looking for a way out. I wondered if it were possible for me to simply dodge her and run out of the room, out of the house. Her bulk blocked the stairwell. She climbed up a few steps.

'Your face,' she said when she stood a few steps below me, looking up. 'His face!' she called back to the room she had just left. 'His face is white! Like a ghost.'

She darted forward to seize my arm and escorted me into the living room. There was quite a crowd. Along with Sophie and my parents were Felix and Kurt, and Oskar—the cousin from Brünn whose letter I had read that morning—together with his wife. There was no escape.

I let myself be propelled into the middle of the sofa, where I slumped, dazed. Someone handed me a cup of coffee. Its warmth was welcome in my hands, but when I brought it to my face the smell that rose up with the steam was like poisonous fumes. I abruptly put down the cup and spilled coffee over my shoes and trousers. It burned at first, and was quite painful, but then rapidly cooled. People jumped up and called for towels and cloths but I just sat and watched the brown stain widen into the carpet and drip from my shoe leather.

In our family, what we call 'magazines'* are a tradition. For each family occasion we join together and take various kinds of submissions to assemble a little book, filled with poems, spoof newspaper articles and caricatures of the person who is being celebrated. I had always dreaded these magazines when it was my turn to receive them. I imagined the conversations among my family members when it was being assembled, and all the things that were not said as they carefully sifted through safe subjects to tease me about.

I could see my birthday magazine was sitting, ostentatiously wrapped, among the cakes and fruit on the table. When it could be avoided no longer, I took it down and unwrapped it. Everyone was watching me expectantly. The cardboard cover was overlaid with chequered fabric and covered with designs of cut-out felt figures.

Someone—probably Sophie, I thought—had spent a lot of time on it. Uta exclaimed loudly and craned her neck the better to see

---

* The birthday 'magazine' to which Brod refers has been located among the manuscripts, and will be made available online.

it. I opened it to the first page with a feeling of foreboding. The eyes of the room were on me, watching me for my reaction.

The first few pages were quite harmless, with a sketch by my mother and a spoof newspaper article written by Sophie. There was also a little poem, gaudy and overblown, which I thought must be from Felix. On the following page was a drawing in dark ink, which at first I could not identify. The heavy lines suggested a kind of haystack blown by the wind. I glanced around at the faces of the guests and saw that Oskar was nodding encouragingly as though the drawing were his. When my eyes found the paper again, the lines had resolved into the figure of a hunchback, clutching a swooning damsel in one hand; Quasimodo rescuing Esmeralda. Everyone was looking at me.

I cleared my throat, but could think of nothing to say. 'Quite a resemblance,' I managed after a moment. My voice sounded very loud in the room. Everyone's eyes had been fixed on me, but now they bounced away in shame.

'Quasimodo,' Sophie said by way of explanation, 'is a man of gentle heroism and a pure heart. Like you, Max.'

I found the truth of this comment to be negligible, but poor Sophie's face radiated such concern that I tried to smile at her.

'He is quite like you, Max,' Uta broke in, examining the drawing. 'Very like.' There was a silence. 'That muscular back, those strong hands.' Her faltering voice crashed around the room and then dropped away, and no one filled the emerging silence.

I turned the page and everyone exclaimed and laughed too loudly over the next piece, a long ballad that recounted my achievements of the year in the style of a heroic saga.

After the ordeal of the magazine was over I wanted nothing more than to retire to my room. My body felt frayed and ragged and at the back of my mind the problem of Anja's letter called for my attention. I could feel the sharp edges of the paper in my pocket, and it crackled with every movement I made. More cake was passed around and then Oskar came and sat beside me on the sofa. He seemed wholly unaware of having caused any offence with his drawing; on the contrary, he thought it was a great joke, and was, moreover, pleased with himself at having surprised me with his attendance at the party. The long letter I had read that morning had been a carefully designed ruse to make me unsuspecting of his visit.

He asked me familiarly what I was working on, and then without waiting for me to reply told me that he had heard that I was helping Franz write a travelogue and wondered what it was like to work with such a celebrated writer. I was too tired to do anything but nod. I was lucky, he said, to have the support of such a well-known literary figure. I just nodded. Yes. Very lucky.

There was no escape. From the corner of my eye I could see Uta hovering a short distance away, waiting for the moment she could break into the conversation. I looked at her and felt a great weariness. Her face was fat and shiny and framed by her frilly pink collar and yellow hair. She was my fate; perhaps there was no reason to continue to struggle. I thought of Oskar's drawing and I imagined the life of Quasimodo in that church, ringing the bells and, dog-like, feeling only devotion. I had never read the novel, afraid that I would recognise in it a too-accurate portrait of myself, but somehow, despite this, the story had still filtered through to my awareness. That afternoon, in the overheated room filled with the cloying smell of oily pastries and close bodies, loud laughs and voices echoing from the walls, a solitary life in a damp church or upon some mountaintop seemed an idyll beyond imagining.

Oskar was still speaking to me, but I had stopped listening to him long ago. Now I turned and smiled at Uta and she joined us on the sofa. Uta and Oskar's voices issued from their mouths and rose up into the air, like sticky condensation that adhered to the surfaces of the room and the skin on my face. I was much too tired to think now of anything except lying down, and fortunately my illness was a ready excuse for me to soon retire to my room.

24.

THAT NIGHT, DESPITE MY FATIGUE, I COULD NOT SLEEP. I LAY ON
my bed and looked at the patterns that the light from the streetlamp
made on the ceiling and the walls of the room. I had put the letter
on my night table, where it glowed like a little moon. As I lay there,
my head full of night-time terrors, the awful thought came to me
that Franz might be in Berlin with Anja. Perhaps it had been he,
gloating, who had asked her to send me the stories. I thought of the
house in Berlin, its thick walls enclosing the bodies of Franz and
Anja. I found that at first I could consider this horror with a degree
of equanimity, but the more I pictured it, the more uncomfortable
I became. The thought that they could be, at that very moment, in
the unknown house, living, breathing, perhaps sleeping, perhaps
reading, was as strange and awful as considering the unknowable
details of one's own death.

I had put my watch on the night table and took it up from time
to time to squint at its face, but it had become an indecipherable
object, its hands indicating an illogical sequence of hours. The

ticking of the watch became louder and louder and, it seemed to me, slower as the hours passed. The interval between each tick became longer and within this suspended space a host of other mechanical noises made by the watch gradually came to my attention: clicks and whirrings and the musical notes of tiny springs, like the calls of metallic birds.

In the dark, the dimensions of the room altered themselves and became strange to me. In the short time between closing and opening my eyes the distance between the pieces of furniture became unfamiliar, as though I were seeing the room for the first time. The wardrobe was like a dark elongated box rearing precariously over me, and the legs of the dressing table had grown long and spindly.

I thought of Franz and Anja moving through the house in Nostitzstrasse, going from room to room. The house became like a dolls' house, with one wall that swung open so I could easily observe the pair and manipulate them like miniature dolls. I pictured the Franz doll and the Anja doll arranged in different tableaux, in all kinds of vulgar embraces and poses, while their faces smiled silently at me and the ticking of my watch reverberated around the room.[*]

I threw off the bedclothes and looked down along my body spread on the white sheet. It looked just like a normal, straight BODY. I shifted my feet back and forth and they obeyed me. I had

---

[*] The following pages were written on blank writing paper torn from a different notebook and clipped to the pages of the exercise book. The writing is written in a small hand, and is in several places barely legible. The following section contains a number of unclear words, which have been approximated and are indicated in SMALL CAPS.

made up my mind. Without turning on the lamp, I gathered my clothing from where I had discarded it around the room and dressed. I put the letter and the now-booming watch in my pocket and left the house.

Then I was at the train station and the little lighted cabins of my train pulled up and I got on and there was no one in my compartment but me. My watch was making a slow thud from my pocket and my whole BODY vibrated with each shift of the little golden hand. I placed my hand over my pocket to dull the sound. I sat next to the window but could see nothing of the dark landscape that passed, and even if I pressed my face up against the glass all that was visible to me was a series of rushing shapes, like night ghosts, that formed a shifting background to the image* of my own white face looking back at me.

The exception to this was the few stations the train passed, which were like little lighted islands in the night. They were always empty, with not even a porter or a conductor visible, and I could never see the sign with the station's name. I lost count of the number of stations we passed and then the train stopped. It stood still for a long time, hissing steam, and I got off and saw I was at Berlin's Schlesischer Bahnhof.

The station was as bright and as crowded as though it were a busy morning with people hurrying to offices and shops and schools, but when I exited the station I was surrounded again by darkness and silence. I asked a passing MAN the way to Nostitzstrasse, and he pointed down the road without speaking. I walked a long way,

---

* This may also read 'reflection'.

always finding someone to direct me when the road that I was on came to an end.

I walked along wide alleys lined with plane or linden trees, down dirty cobbled lanes, I crossed rivers and parks. In my pocket, my watch beat like the heart of a wild animal, echoing between the stone faces of the buildings and shaking the leaves of the trees. I was afraid of the noise disturbing the inhabitants of those silent streets, so I took out the watch and wrapped it in my handkerchief to dull the sound, but this made no difference. From time to time I took Anja's letter from my pocket and looked at the address again, even though I already knew it by heart.

I crossed a small bridge and then I saw the sign for Nostitzstrasse, which stretched out ahead of me. I stood and looked down it. There were only a few lighted windows in the houses, on the upper floors, and as I walked along the houses slowly fanned past.

Number 70 had heavy double street doors and the list of names next to the bells did not include Anja's. I chose a name at random and rang the bell. I could hear its chime sound on the floor above, but just then I saw that the street door was ajar and I went in. The entrance hall was dusty and littered with dead leaves and the tiles were cracked and broken. It seemed unthinkable that I would find Anja in a place such as this. There was no light, and I began to ascend the staircase, stopping at each door to peer at the nameplate, but I reached the top of the house without finding Anja's.

As I walked back down, I passed a door from beyond which came a familiar sound. It was difficult to hear anything with the monstrous beat of my watch constantly in my ears, so I stood close to the door and pressed my ear against it.

The sound was a scratching scuffle, like small animals burrowing in the dry undergrowth, and it stopped and resumed at IRREGULAR* intervals.

I wondered if it might be MICE, or some burrowing insect in the wooden panels of the door, before I recalled the many times I had stood outside our hotel room at Karlsbad, listening to that same sound as Franz's pen scratched across the paper inside the room. The memory immediately brought with it a wave of the sulphurous air of that town. As I had used to do with the hotel-room door, my fingers slowly reached out for the door handle, gently settled upon it and then steadily gripped it with increasing firmness to silently slide the door's mechanism into itself to open it.

The door was not locked, and a yellow-lighted slit appeared next to my hand, slowly widening to reveal the very small entrance hall of the apartment. I put my hand in my pocket to muffle the sound of the watch and then I stepped inside. The scratching sound that I could hear from outside the apartment was much louder inside and had no clear point of origin; it seemed to come from the WALLS themselves, or up through the uneven floorboards.

There were two closed doors leading off the hall and I approached each in turn and listened. It was difficult to determine where the sound was louder, so in the end I chose the left-hand door at random. I opened it with less care than I had the front door. Inside I found a small bedsitting room. The scrabbling sound echoed around the room and formed a musical pattern with the watch, which was like a metronome, keeping time. The room was empty.

---

* This may also read 'regular'.

Along one wall was a narrow bed, with a heap of bedclothes piled on it. In the corner was a small writing table strewn with papers and books, and a chair pushed back, as though someone had just risen from it. Next to this was a rail on which some clothing hung. I recognised FRANZ's hat. The shirts and jackets were moulded STILL in the shape of the wearer, the elbows slightly bent, the holes for the neck hanging open like round mouths.* There was no sign of Anja.

The scratching paused and was replaced by a softer rustling, and then the pile of bedclothes shifted. I crossed the small room in one stride and looked down into the bed. The bedclothes and pillows were pressed in around a small, shrunken figure and littered with sheets of paper and flecked with spots of blue ink.

Loose sheets of writing paper spilled off the bed and onto the floorboards around it. I looked down and saw some of the crumpled pages underneath my shoes, dirty and torn. The smudged lines of blue ink looked familiar to me. I thought it looked like my own handwriting. I stooped down to pick up one of the crumpled pages, and it looked like the story I had written that night so long ago. I read a few lines, but the words had changed and I could no longer remember what I had written before. The figure in the bed sighed and shifted. It leaned its head back onto the pillows to look up at me.

I knew that it was Franz, but it was difficult to find any feature that anchored him to this identity. The bones of his face pushed

---

* The description of the room is an addition to the text given in the margins. The ink is the same as that used throughout the text.

218

out painfully like the blades of knives against the inside of the skin and his face seemed to have widened and flattened. His eyes were DARK animals hiding in shrunken hollows, his hair a mass of dirty cobwebs spread over the skull. His hands were crowded with large bones, too heavy for his bird-like limbs, and they lay abandoned on the bedclothes. He smelled of death, of earth and mould and dark silence.

I was conscious of the sound of the watch in my pocket. I was still holding my hand curled around it, afraid to let go and release the deafening sound into the room. I asked him where Anja was, and my voice trumpeted out of me and hurt my head. He did not respond—perhaps he did not hear me—but only sank further back onto the pillows and closed his eyes.

It seemed impossible that Anja could be in any of the rooms of that dingy apartment. I remembered suddenly the other door that opened off the entrance hall. I imaged Anja inside, sitting silently, or tied up, gagged, being kept PRISONER. I went to it and threw the door open so hard that it bounced off the wall behind it. I was faced with a MAN* standing on the other side of the room, watching me. I froze, but then saw that it was only my reflection in the black window. The room was completely bare, empty of furniture, with the naked glass of the window like a great eye looking in. The sound of the watch bounced from the hard surfaces into my face like physical shocks.

I went back to FRANZ's† room and shouted at him to tell me where Anja was. My mouth stretched with crude savageries and

---

* This may read 'myself'.

† 'The other' is crossed out, and 'F's' is written in the space above it.

my hot breath hissed against my teeth. I leaned over him, into the fog of pestilent air that hung about the bed. But Franz looked completely unaffected by my outburst, and his only reaction was to stretch his white lips over his teeth in a caricature of a smile. Slowly, he raised one of his limp hands from the bedclothes and pointed across the room. His dry voice was in my ears; it hissed and sighed like a sibilant Eastern language, it rustled like paper, and I could not understand his words. The beats that came from the watch fell onto his words and sliced them into pieces of animal noise.

He began to speak and gesture more insistently, and I could see that he was pointing at the writing table. I went towards it and looked down at the sheets of paper covered with his spiked writing. I remembered the letter from Anja that I had found in Karlsbad and the letter in my pocket. Had he written these to lure me to him? Or was Anja somewhere here, behind one of the closed doors on the landing? I leafed through the papers on the table with one hand and read a few phrases here and there. I opened the drawers of the writing table at random and scooped the contents out onto the floor. My fingers found a tightly bound stack of folded paper. I pulled out a sheet and saw that it was covered with my own handwriting. It was a page from one of my letters to Anja, my outpourings of love for her, which I had written all those months ago in Karlsbad.* There was a pain in my stomach like a wound. I opened another sheet from the stack, and it was the same. The

---

* 'Anja, Anja, Anja' is repeated here for four lines in Brod's writing. This had been omitted in the interest of fluency and coherence.

whole drawer was full of these little folded parcels, a stockpile, a mausoleum of my useless affection.

It did not occur to me to wonder how they had come to be here. My eyes were swollen with the weight of hundreds of uncried tears, and I could see again every image of Anja I had ever witnessed, every scene I had enacted with her. They moved past me one after the other like pictures in a gallery. Her face was as clear to me as though it were projected onto the blank wall above the writing table.

I stuffed the folded papers back into the drawer and sat down in the chair. The papers on the desk swam together under a film of tears and I ran my hand over them as if over the surface of the ocean. A patch of cream PAPER stood out against the sea of white and I pulled it out and held it before my eyes. 'My darling Franz, my love.' I closed my eyes against it, the sheet of Anja's writing.* I could feel the tears pushing against my eyelashes as though they were grains of salt, hard little stones. A coldness rolled down through my body and filled me with ice.

So Franz had won in the end. And it was the end. He had used me like a parasite. He had wormed his way into my life, into my love, and had eaten them hollow, leaving only a calcified, empty shell. Even my writing† had been sapped by him in some mysterious way. I was like a mother who gives birth in the bloom of youth, unwillingly, and is left haggard and exhausted, having passed the energetic spark of her life on to her child. For in some ways Franz was like my child. An unwanted one.

---

* This line has been crossed out with several strokes, but is still easily legible.
† 'Body' appears underneath the word 'writing', but is clearly legible.

And what was left to me now? A book I had sweated and toiled over, certain at the outset that it would be a masterpiece, which had been a complete failure. Anja was lost to me. I was nothing more now than a crippled worker at the Prague post office. Anja, Anja. Fresh tears pressed in my throat at the thought of her. Now I was left with only Uta. *Uta.* Her coarse face leered at me and the muscles in my ears clenched at the thought of her voice of affected childishness.

The sound of the watch was now so loud that it was shaking the room, as though the walls of the building were being struck by a battering ram. The legs of the furniture jumped and scratched over the floor. Loose sheets of paper snowed from the bed and the writing table and the clothes on the rail began to jerk their arms and legs in a phantom dance. I still had my hand wrapped around the watch, but with each beat it was becoming more and more painful to hold, and I was afraid that if I let it go I would be deafened in an instant. I waited for the space between two beats and then took the watch out, still wrapped in the useless handkerchief, and flung it onto the floor. It spun on its back like a golden beetle and I brought my foot down upon it with all my force. I felt its hard form resist painfully under my heel. The beat slowed and I seized a chair and smashed it down again and again onto the tiny metal object, until its innards, miniature wheels and cogs, all spilled out onto the floorboards in a small golden pool. In the spreading silence I could hear the tinkling music of these tiny mechanical components rolling away into cracks in the floorboards.

I went back to the bed. Franz's whole BODY was still and lay there among the bedclothes like the discarded skin of a reptile. All the life that he yet contained had become distilled in his quivering eyes and eyelids. He was whispering something to me, the same phrase again and again, but his dry lips were two rigid straps and he could not form the words. I leaned closer and held my breath, afraid to inhale his contagion.

'It was me she loved.'*

His stale breath dampened my face as he spoke, and he said it again and again. I hissed at him to be quiet, to hold his tongue. I leaned further over him and took one of the pillows from beside his head. His eyes were closed with the effort of speaking his phrase and I hugged the pillow to my chest and let myself fall onto him, into him, the pillow between my chest and his FACE. I could feel his lips still mouthing through the layer of feathers and cloth. I leaned harder. I thought that I would crush his BONES with my weight; I could feel them rising from the mattress like a fragile construction built of twigs and paper. I closed my eyes and held my breath, and then there was nothing but darkness.†

---

* This sentence has been crossed out and then written again beside the crossing-out.

† This section is followed by several pages of illegible text: heavily crossed-out writing with some pages torn and missing.

25.

*THE NEXT THING I REMEMBER IS WAKING TO THE SONG OF A BIRD
and light pressing on my closed eyes, illuminating the dense
network of pink veins that threaded through the insides of my
eyelids. I could hear soft rustling sounds and breathing, which
seemed to come from close by. There was, too, a nagging feeling
that something was missing, or that I had forgotten something.
I opened my eyes and the light from the window flooded the whole
room with whiteness. When the features of the room came to me,
I saw that I was in a completely white room, lying in a narrow
bed. There was a small table next to the bed and a picture on the
wall opposite of a boy holding a dog in his arms. The soft sounds
came again and attached themselves to a woman, who I noticed
was hunched over in one corner of the room. As I looked at her she
slowly began shuffling along sideways with her face to the wall and

---

* The following sections are written in a smaller notebook, which has some water
  damage, but the text is still legible.

her back to me. This animal scuttling motion of hers frightened me and made me nauseous, until I realised that she held a cloth in one hand and was cleaning the dust from a kind of picture rail that ran along the wall. She turned swiftly and when she saw me looking at her hurried out of the room.

There were several other beds in the room, all empty, and I recognised it as a hospital ward. I realised that I must have been injured; perhaps I had been in some kind of accident. I scanned my body for areas of pain, but could find none. I looked down at my arms and lifted them up in front of my face. I turned my hands this way and that, I tested my legs and the motion of my neck, but all seemed to be in order. From the bed I cast my eyes about, but nowhere in the room was there any machinery that might be used to straighten my back, which was the next explanation that came to mind. I even sat up in the bed and looked at the headboard for some traction device that might be located there, but all I could see was a small white card with a name on it that was not mine. I must have been put in the wrong bed by mistake, I thought. Although I knew it was just an administrative error, I couldn't help feeling uneasy, as if I were being mocked.

I swung my legs out from under the bedclothes and hoisted myself to sit on the edge of the bed, preparing to get up. I noticed that my clothes had gone and I was wearing only a white night-gown. It was an effort to stand. I made my way slowly around the room looking at the labels on the other beds, in case I would find my name on one of these, but the spaces to hold the cards were all blank. I stood looking at the mislabelled bed. 'Certainly an administrative error,' I told myself.

The room, on closer inspection, was very bare. Nowhere was there any medical equipment to measure my vital signs, no charts to record them nor medicine to treat any illness. I had begun to shiver with cold, and turned back to the bed, but the idea of getting into that bed, which after all was labelled as not my own, was suddenly loathsome to me; like wearing another man's clothes. I was still standing there, shivering and hesitating, when I heard steps approach the door, causing me to jump with alarm. I leaped into the bed, forgetting its irksomeness, and pulled the cover up over my insubstantial gown.

The door opened and a tall man in a suit came in, followed by a woman dressed as a nurse. I asked the man if I could speak with a doctor, and he smiled and introduced himself as Professor Pick. He had a perfectly neat triangular beard and heavy-lidded eyes, like a country vicar or a school principal.

'Professor Pick,' I said, 'there has been a mistake. To begin with, I am not Brod; my name is Kafka. Your administrative staff have made an error.'

I gestured behind me to the label on the bed. I waited for Professor Pick to respond, but he only dropped his heavy lids over his eyes and wearily raised them a few times before saying, 'Mmm,' which hung in the air ominously.

Something about the man disturbed me, and the skin on my scalp began to contract in fear. I went on, a little uncertainly now, 'Secondly, I have not the slightest thing wrong with me.' I pushed the bedclothes off and sat on the edge of the bed in order to demonstrate my healthfulness. 'My body, I know, appears to be weak, but

I am just coming now out of a long illness, but really I can manage perfectly well.'

I looked down and was suddenly ashamed of the exposure of my naked legs, which struck me as obscenely thin and white, to this well-dressed man. I twitched the edge of the nightgown down as far as it would go to cover them.

'Herr Brod,' Pick said, stepping closer to me and putting one spread hand in the middle of my chest.

I wondered if the man was deaf.

'Kafka,' I corrected him. 'Kafka.' I spoke loudly and slowly and indicated myself with my hand pointed to my face. Should I spell it for him?

He pressed me rudely back into the bed. 'I assure you, Herr Brod, that the error is yours.'

He pulled a notebook from his pocket and scrawled something in it and then left the room, trailed by the nurse. They shut the door behind them and I could hear their footsteps echoing for a long time after they'd left.

My encounter with Pick left me feeling unsettled and in the strangely empty room this quickly mounted to panic. I needed to leave the hospital immediately. I made a more thorough search of the room for my clothes, but they had disappeared. There was not even a locked cupboard or box or wardrobe that might contain them. As I much I disliked the idea, I resigned myself to going out in my nightgown.

I had expected the door to the room to be locked, but I found that it opened easily. Outside was an empty corridor. I felt very self-conscious in my bare feet and legs and the draughty nightgown and my first intention was to locate my clothing. I knew that my identification papers were in my pocketbook in my jacket, and these would surely put an end to the whole farcical situation. The corridor was long and stretched away in either direction in a perfect mirror image of itself: just rows of closed doors and blank walls. I stood, hesitating. The wall opposite was set with long windows, which looked out onto a grassed area.

Being without my clothing made me feel like a fugitive and my heart soon began to race with anxiety. I turned left and ran lightly along the corridor, the skin of my bare feet making soft kisses on the floorboards. There was no clear exit, although I could see a closed door at the end of the corridor ahead of me, still quite far away. I tried to remind myself that I was not a prisoner and there was actually no reason to be running in such an undignified manner. With an effort, I forced myself to slow to a walk. I tried swinging my arms to give the appearance, if only to myself, of nonchalance. I would have liked to hum a tune, but I could not think of one.

At that moment the door ahead of me opened and two men dressed as orderlies came out into the corridor. I tensed, ready to bound away back down the corridor. I looked wildly about me and had the mad idea of opening one of the windows and jumping out of it and running away across the lawn, but I saw that the windows were overlaid with light grilles of metal. The men came silently on and my instincts told me that, as with facing an unknown dog, I should not show any fear. I stopped walking and raised my hand loosely in greeting.

'Good morning, gentlemen,' I said. 'I wonder if you could direct me to the central administration area? There seems to be an error with my identity.'

They ignored my request and continued to walk towards me.

'Or perhaps you could assist me in locating my clothing, or at least my pocketbook . . .' My voice trailed off. The men still advanced as if I had not spoken. Had I in fact spoken aloud? Somehow I was not certain. They were both large men, broad and muscular, but at that moment this did not bother me as much as the fact that they were clothed and I was not. Their clothing transformed them into a different and far superior type of animal. The leather capsules of their shoes enclosed their feet and the hard soles tapped along the boards in a unified percussive beat, like hooves. Their clothing fit exactly around their limbs and torsos. I felt like an urchin with my flimsy gown flapping around my white legs and my feet spreading out their cold toes along the floor, sticking slightly to it with each step.

The men came one on each side of me, took me by the elbows and propelled me back down the corridor. As we dashed along, my questioning voice trailed away behind us like a fluttering ribbon. The faces of the men were as fixed and blank as the faces of the stone gargoyles that look out over the roofs of the city. When we arrived back in the room, the nurse who had accompanied Professor Pick earlier was waiting. The men pushed me towards the bed and stood side by side just inside the door, watching me.

Again I had the feeling of revulsion towards that bed. The bedclothes and mattress lay like a heap of rags and seemed to me to be diseased. My skin shrank from contact with the bed and the thought of climbing into it was now as repulsive being asked to enter the bed of a leper. I protested that the bed was not mine, and that the owner of the bed was a murderer; he had killed me in Berlin, or tried to kill me. I frowned. There was something wrong with the order of my thoughts, but I had no time to consider it. My words flew out of my mouth and circled the room, not finding the ears of anyone present. I repeated my name, shouting it, but it felt like I was swimming upriver in a strong current and making no headway.

The men began to advance towards me and I shuffled backwards until the edge of the mattress grazed the back of my naked knees. One of the men now stood in front of me with a tired expression on his flat face. He began to lean towards me, about to push me into the bed. I could see there was nothing that I could do, so I inched myself down onto the edge of the bed of my own accord rather than give in to the further humiliation of being pushed there by the silent man. I pulled the bedclothes over my legs, holding them with two fingers only, with my teeth clenched and my face screwed up in disgust.

The nurse came forward holding a small cup, which she offered to me. I struck it out of her hand, furious and afraid. The men came towards me and held me down, and the nurse, unperturbed, turned away and then turned back again with another, identical cup. I began thrashing around in the bed with all my strength, certain that the cup contained some poison. I thrust my head from left to right, until it was seized by one of the men. I clamped my lips shut, but they were forced open and the contents of the cup were poured into me. The men held me for a few moments more, until I ceased my struggle.

My body became soft and light and the perimeter of it seemed to become elastic and merge with the objects in the room. I lost my name for myself, even the name for the idea of myself, my 'I'. It sounds alarming, but I felt nothing more than a great sense of relief. My existence in the hospital bed became unimportant and I forgot about the whereabouts of my clothing, my urgency to leave the hospital, the problem of the names. I came to live in the fog brought by the medicine. My thoughts floated around in my head like leaves blown by the wind. I watched them from a distance, sweeping past me in long arcs, and never bothered to try to catch hold of any one.

Scenes of my life before—writing, and going to work every day, and my family and Anja—were like sequences in a novel read long ago. They were suspended at a pleasant distance, only minimally interesting and amusing, and not at all important or particularly connected to me.

Words lost their definition and drifted away from the objects to which they were usually attached. Language became a kind of alchemy, an impossible marvel: to make a sound, an arrangement with one's lips and tongue and breath, which would conjure up the image of a thing, a hard object, in the mind of another. It was like a magician's trick. I would hear the words of others coming at me through the air, and perhaps I sometimes sent out words of my own, sounds, also. Words became meaningless; I lived in the surer world—to me it seemed surer—of the senses, of hot and cold, of colours, and feelings pleasant or not.

Now and then Professor Pick would appear, although I did not recognise him at the time, and dictate notes to an assistant. At

231

other times he would arrive with a group of young people, who I realise now must have been medical students, and who examined and measured me and asked me condescending questions. They crowded around to discuss the notes in Pick's little book. I watched the whole proceeding as if from a vantage point outside myself, detached from the action.

I floated in this state for some time—weeks, months—and then one day something changed. There was a sensation of movement and changing lights and I became aware of being transported out of the room to a different place. Here I experienced an all-encompassing coldness, and then the air surrounding me seemed to thicken and bring warmth and lightness. My arms began to float upwards and I could feel a hard surface below me. It took me a long time to identify myself as being in a bath. The word 'bathtub' came to me, four-square, pleasantly solid, standing on little hooks of feet, exactly like the object. It floated before my eyes, a flag waving in the air, but after a moment it disintegrated and became only another shape to be made with the lips, a string of coloured beads to play with. I felt the sides of the bath with my hands and gripped the curled lip of the rim, trying and trying to remember. I looked blankly down at my unfamiliar body as it lay there, pink and naked, in the porcelain shell.

In the following days and weeks I was subjected to an endless number of baths of varying temperature, duration and method. I had water dribbled over me gently, like rain; I was wrapped in wet towels, like a package of meat to be transported; I was sprayed with a hose like a horse and rubbed dry by one of the battalion of silent nurses who populated the hospital corridors. The baths must have elicited from me some kind of physiological response, because it was they alone that stood out from the swirling mass of days in the hospital.

In the bath I could remember the things that had been nagging at me. I would rise up out of the water, like a drowning swimmer, shouting, waving my arms, gasping for breath. Words came to me and I called for help, the word 'help' like the alarm cry of a bird dashed against the hard white tiles. I would call other words, my own name, that important word, again and again as though another self would appear and spirit me away from that place.

Instead, the only people who came were the two orderlies, twinned in their muscular silence. They would hold on to my slippery arms, ignoring my wet skin and hair, which left damp patches on the fronts of their uniforms. Their dry, flat palms would push expertly onto my mouth, neatly holding my jaw together, covering my nose and making it difficult to breathe until the nurse arrived with her little cup. There seemed an endless supply of this medicine: no matter how many times I spat it out, sprayed it into the faces of the men, of the nurse, there came always another cup. Cup followed cup like an undefeatable army; it was useless to fight. I would allow the medicine into my mouth and from there it would slip inch by inch down my throat and everything would unravel again and I would slide down once more into that swirling, elastic world.

I began to learn that, when I surfaced, I must sit quietly in the bath and not draw attention to myself in any way. I learned to come up slowly, to creep into my own body and peer out through my eyes like a burglar creeping into a darkened house. I would look around the room moving my eyes only, and as I looked the words would begin to reattach themselves to the world. I wanted to shout with joy the moment when I had sat and looked, with my eyes turned down towards the bathwater, at the ten pink excrescences that were partly in, partly out of the water, and I discovered that I could move them at will, and their name came to me. Fingers. I would whisper the word to myself when I wanted to shout it: *fingers*. My fingers. I would move my lips a millimetre, feeling the way the muscles moved to shape the word and beaming with joy.

Then my eyes would move stealthily to the next object in the room and I would wait for the word to fly at me. I held all the words together in my head, shielding them, but as they gathered it became more and more difficult to keep them hidden silently within me. Eventually the name of some object in the room, or an emotion I was feeling, would come shouted out of my mouth.

I began to surface at other times too: in my bed, or walking across the lawns with the two silent orderlies. Slowly, I also became aware again of the hospital and my life before it. Anja, in particular, came back to me. I began to dream of her as I slept.

My awareness expanded to include the other people of the hospital; I began to recognise the nurses, the orderlies and Professor Pick. One day I woke to hear an echo of my breathing in the room and I realised that there was someone in one of the other beds. I hoisted myself up and saw that it was an old man with a large beard that covered the lower half of his face. The beard would have been white, but it lay on top of the bedclothes, whose bleached industrial whiteness turned the hair an unpleasant shade of yellow. We looked at each other silently for a long time.

Somehow, in that place, the usual daily social conventions lost their meaning, or, in any case, they seemed as unfamiliar and strange to me as the customs of a foreign culture. The words *good morning* materialised in my mind but seemed somehow wrong. I lay there and the stranger and I blinked at each other across the room. Eventually I realised that I could get out of bed and shake hands with him by way of greeting. As I got out of my bed, he did the same, and we met in the middle of the room, facing each other between the rows of empty beds.

I put out my hand, and so did the man. He was very tall and his body seemed to fit into his robe differently from mine: the fabric fell in sculptural folds from his wide shoulders like Roman drapery, and this, together with his beard, gave him the look of some prophet or ancient philosopher.

'Promoli,' he said to me, like a pronouncement. His voice was sonorous and the word had exactly the same intonation as the opening chords of the final movement from Beethoven's String Quartet No. 16: the difficult decision. My head unexpectedly filled with this tune as our clasped hands pumped up and down through the air. *Promoli*. This was a word I had not heard before. Its syllables rolled through my head like a wave. I liked the word immediately; its shape and rocking-horse rhythm.

'Promoli,' I repeated, tasting the word, careful to use the same intonation that the man had used.

'Promoli,' he said again, but this time it was the beginning of a question: Beethoven's 'must it be?' He frowned at me, waiting for an answer. His fingers let go of mine and drifted up to land on his chest.

I panicked as I felt the world slide away again from the language that anchors it and began to sweat as though I were standing before a professor in an oral examination. The man towered over me. Promoli, I thought to myself. Promoli. What is the reply? I stared at the man's massive fingers where they brushed against his robe, level with my eyes. They were like carved objects, hewn from stone. Promoli. What was the meaning? I tried to attach it to a thing in the world, but it just hung like a loose string.

I had been silent too long and I said again, desperately, 'Promoli,' though I knew it was the wrong answer. My head dropped in shame and I looked down at my bare feet. I caught at the name for my two feet with relief and began to run through as many words for things as I could in order to anchor myself. I closed my eyes.

'My friend,' the man's voice rumbled at me, 'Promoli is my name. Your name is not that. At least, I have never yet met another Promoli, and I have lived a long time. Your name is . . .'

I still had my eyes closed and could feel the air shift as he stepped past me towards my bed to peer at the little white card. I held my breath as I waited for him to tell me my name, like waiting for a doctor's diagnosis.

'Brod,' came his voice, through the dark of my lowered lids.

The word was familiar to me, but carried with it an unpleasant, musty odour of discomfort, of lack. I disliked its squareness, the way that the sound plopped from the lips straight to the floor, like a tasteless mouthful of food; chewed at slightly and then rejected. Another word scuttled about behind a screen in my mind; another, better name. I could not quite catch hold of it. It was a sharp one,

236

mysterious, one that could take flight with clicks in the back of the throat.

And besides, *brod*: bread. Had I heard him correctly? I wanted to go and look at the card myself, but I was too ashamed. To be named after a food, the blandest, most basic food. It seemed an insult.

'Brod,' I said, watching him through my eyelashes, testing to see if it was right.

'A good name.' His face had a kindly expression and he nodded.

'But Promoli, this is your name only, and not the name for any other thing in the world?'

'I am the only Promoli.'

'But *brod*. To eat?' I mimed eating, moving my fingers to my lips, in case he did not understand. The other name came to me in a rush at that moment, it was the name too of a thing; of the jackdaw, *kavka*, Kafka. The k's clicked like closing beaks, I saw it printed on a white page, the word took flight and became a bird in the tree outside, its whirring call. Kafka. A thief of a bird.

Brod and *kavka* are names for more than one thing in the world. My thoughts moved slowly, feeling their way. And I; I am a thing in the world connected to more than one name. There was no connection between bread and jackdaws except myself and some ink marks made on paper. I felt dizzy and sat on the edge of the nearest bed.

'Yes, of course. Forgive me: Brod. I have been in this room for such a long time alone.'

Brod. Kafka. I let Kafka fly away. I offered Promoli my hand again, and he took it in both of his and held it for a long time.

26.

PROMOLI BECAME MY GUIDE IN THE HOSPITAL. HE SEEMED TO know and be liked by everyone. He showed me around and introduced me everywhere, to people I had seen a hundred times: the nurses; the silent guards whose stony faces Promoli transformed as if by magic into smiling ones; and also to other patients in rooms behind that row of closed doors in the corridor.

Promoli was on close terms with Professor Pick and claimed to be his assistant, which I did not quite believe. Yet from time to time I would see him from the long windows walking out on the lawns with Pick, their heads bent together in conversation. And at other times I saw him standing with the little group of medical students as they discussed something with Pick. It seemed inconceivable that he could be doing these things and at the same time be here in the ward with me, wearing a robe and being ordered about by the nurses.

I started to become suspicious of Promoli, worried that he was a spy of Pick's, sent to observe the patients when Pick himself was not in the ward and then report back to him. What else would they be discussing on their rambles over the grounds? But I felt guilty about these suspicious thoughts; despite the grain of mistrust, I had immediately felt a strong sense of kinship with Promoli. Nevertheless, I observed Promoli closely for signs of illness, but could never discern any. He was always happy and energetic and never lay all day silent in the bed, brooding, as I still sometimes did.

What was he doing here in the hospital if he was not ill? I considered challenging him about it, and intended to do so many times, but at the last moment my resolve always failed me; it seemed rude and ungrateful. I had learned that the code of politeness of that place dictated that prying into the illnesses of others was taboo, and it was a topic only discussed when first raised by the sufferer himself.

There was a vast array of illness to be found in the hospital, which seemed to be populated only by men. There were those who were mute and watchful, who had retreated behind their eyes and hid themselves from you, deep in their bodies. There was a man known as The Owl, whose every second word was a hoot. Other men laughed and sang, or there were those who gave off an electrical charge of violence. There were also among the patients several holy men, who tolerated each other benevolently in their various holinesses, even those who were, or claimed to be, the same man.

There was a man who believed himself to be Saint Methodius, and was called this by other patients. When I first met him, he bowed down before me and insisted on walking backwards around me, facing me all the time as though I were a pagan king. Promoli explained to me that Methodius could see into the future and was living out his two years of imprisonment in Ellwangen, waiting for the arrival of the bishop whom he knew was coming to free him under orders of the pope.

Methodius was convinced that I was the bishop, and it took me a long time to prove to his satisfaction that I was not. I later saw him doing the same with each new arrival at the hospital and I tried to explain to him that the bishop, when he came, would not be dressed like we patients; surely he would be instantly recognisable in his robes.

'Well of course the bishop must travel in disguise, to protect himself from his enemies,' Methodius said. He then pulled me aside and whispered, 'Just like I am in disguise here as a patient in a madhouse. How did you recognise me?'

One night, a commotion in the ward filtered through the heavy veil of my sleep and became absorbed into my dreams. When I woke in the morning, I looked over and saw that Promoli's bed was empty. The bedclothes were stripped away and the mattress and pillows were folded and stacked neatly. The name-card was gone from the little holder on the bedframe. I asked the nurses about it, and the patients in the other wards, but no one could tell me. Some of the patients told me, with grisly relish, tales about experiments or operations done on the patients. Methodius gave dark hints about certain orders given by the pope, to which only he was privy. I decided to wait for Pick's next visit and ask him about it, but days passed and he never appeared.

Without Promoli I was alone a lot more during the days; alone with my thoughts. The last few months before I had been admitted were a confusing mass of time for me. There were many things from those months that were lost from my memory, and I knew that something dark was buried there, something that caused a wild, guilty grief to rise up in my breast. I tried not to think too much about it—it was too painful—but at night-time this half-memory would appear to me unbidden, but only for a moment, like a bolt of lightning, long enough to illuminate the sleek, dark shape of the thing, but too short for me to grasp at the details.

I also had other worries. I often thought that I might have fabricated Anja, that she had sprung into the world from a fragment of myself, a form of parthenogenesis, and that she was an illusion only I could see. I feared that when I returned home I would find no trace of her. On my walks I began to favour the slope that looked out towards Prague and I would prowl along it for hours, my gaze trained on the smudged mass of the distant city. My eyes searched for landmarks that would allow me to orient myself towards the position of Anja's house. This was an easier task in the evening, when the lamps were lit and winked out at me, and then I would tell myself that one particularly bright or friendly-looking pinpoint of light was coming from her house, from her room, or the lamp in the street outside her window. I knew that this was a fairy tale I told myself, but it comforted me all the same.

27.

I WAS STILL REQUIRED TO FOLLOW A BATHING REGIMEN, AND ONE day I was interrupted during a bath by an orderly.

'Hurry up and get dressed,' he said. 'You have a visitor.' He reached down to pull out the plug from the bath while I still sat there. 'Move,' he said.

The water began to shriek down the drain. I clambered out of the bath and hurriedly dried and dressed. It was a strange thing for the bathing schedule to be disrupted. This had never happened before. I felt nervous. I had had visitors before of course—my mother, Sophie and Kurt—but they were required to keep to the strict visiting hours of Sunday afternoons, between two and five. This was a Wednesday morning. It could only be bad news, I decided: a death in the family, maybe, or a serious illness. Perhaps my mother. The half-remembered sinister memory that haunted me at night appeared again, and I felt the chill of fear, the source of which I still could not identify. I hurried down the corridor in my bare feet, my gown flapping about my still-damp legs, anxious now and my heart pounding through me.

Visitors were received in an elegant little parlour at the front of the hospital, which was kept locked except during visiting hours. The orderly was waiting for me at the door with his ring of keys ready in his hand.

'Who is it?' I asked him, but he just ignored me, as I had known he would. He unlocked the door and pushed me through into the parlour. It felt strange to be there at such an unaccustomed hour, sacrilegious almost. I heard the door close and lock behind me. The room was very beautiful and I still remember it vividly today. It was a calm island, sequestered from all the pain and confusion that the asylum building housed. It had high ceilings and two bow windows that looked out onto a little wild park. The windows faced east, and on this morning I could see none of the view, owing to the strength of the early sun that came blazing into the room, dazzling me.

'Hello, Max,' said a vaguely familiar voice. I could make out the dark shape of a man outlined against the window, but I could not place the voice. The shape moved over to sit on one of the small sofas. The details of the room were still taking shape as my eyes adjusted to the light. I came around to sit on the other sofa and saw a bald man in a suit: Theodor. My heart gave a jolt. I had not given Theodor a single thought for months. I felt pleased to see him and my mind flooded with happy memories of my first publication, which seemed so long ago.

'Theodor,' I said, extending my hand to him. We shook hands, but at his touch that familiar foreboding feeling came over me again, a guilty stain that seeped into my heart. It occurred to me to wonder why he was here at this irregular time. Then all at once everything came rushing back to me: Alexandr and Gustav, and the cheque, and Franz's dead-looking eyes staring up at me from that room in Berlin. All the blood dropped out of my face and my arms hung limp at my sides.

Franz. What had I done? I wondered why the police had not come for me before now, and my eyes darted around the room in case they were standing hidden in the corners, unseen, ready to leap out and arrest me. And then there was Theodor, dear Theodor, whom I had deceived and stolen from.

'Look, Max . . .' said Theodor.

I knew what he was going to say. I wanted to apologise to him, but I found that I could not speak.

'Max, I know you're not well,' said Theodor. 'I've spoken to your doctors, to Professor Pick.'

I opened my mouth, but only some stammering noises came out.

Theodor silenced me with an upraised hand. 'No, don't try to explain. I wanted to come and tell you what I know.'

'Theodor,' I managed to get out. 'Theodor, I'm sorry. The last months were . . . I don't know what happened. I lost myself somehow. I'm sorry for the harm I did you.' Perhaps the police were waiting outside, I thought.

He was looking at me uncomprehendingly.

'No,' said Theodor. 'It is I who am sorry. I knew something was wrong, but I did nothing to help you.'

'Help me? Why would you help me? I was deceiving you.' I spoke in spite of myself. It was surely better for me to remain silent and admit nothing.

'I knew it was you,' said Theodor. 'I knew you were Franz.' His words made no sense, and for a confused moment I was thrown back to my first week in hospital, when I too had thought I was Franz. It occurred to me that this interview might be a kind of test devised by Pick.

'No,' I said firmly, as though Pick were listening, 'I am Max. Max Brod.'

'Yes, yes.' Theodor waved a hand impatiently. 'I know that. And I know too, or at least I think I understand, why you needed Franz. You had me fooled for a while, but after that party I smelled a rat. That fellow you hired—Gustav? Not a very good double, my friend. And then there was that matter of the cheque, that little test I arranged for you. You failed that test, Max. It was most unlike you to steal money from a fellow writer. So then I had Franz investigated, and everything kept leading back to you.'

'Investigated?'

'I hired a detective,' he said. Detectives. Now I knew that the police were a certainty. I stood up, thinking they must be outside. I saw no point in delaying the inevitable. I rushed to the door leading back to the wards, but it was locked. The police would in any case be more likely be waiting in the entrance hall, I reasoned. I crossed the room and tried that door, but it too was locked.

'Where are they?' I asked, rattling at the handle. 'Do you have the key, or do they?'

'Who?'

'The police. I'm ready to go now, if I am to go.' I banged on the door with the flat of my hand. 'You can come in now,' I called through the door.

Theodor gave a little laugh. 'Police? Of course there are no police. Over a couple of hundred crowns?' He laughed again. He stood and came over to me, and pulled me away from the door and back to the sofa.

'No, no. Not because of the money. Of course I'll pay you that. You can ask my father; he will give it to you immediately. No, because of Franz. In Berlin.' I did not know how to put that night into words. I tried to get up again, but Theodor took both of my hands in his, and kept me sitting.

'Max . . .' He stared into my eyes. 'Listen to me. There is no Franz. You are Franz. It was you. You wrote those stories. You just became ill.'

'I am Franz? No.' I had recovered from that delusion! I had to show that I had learned my lesson.

'Yes, Max. You are. You are Franz. It's alright. I can understand it.' Theodor sounded very certain, and as much as I tried to deny it to myself, something in what he said rang true.

'You mean,' I said slowly, 'that *I* am Franz?' I hardly dared to say it aloud. 'But then that night in Berlin . . .' The memory of it had come back in extreme detail, and I shrank from it.

'In Berlin? Yes, I heard from Pick that you had some kind of fit at a house in Berlin. Someone brought you here.'

I crouched on the sofa in horror, waiting for him to go on, to speak of murder, of death. I was too afraid to ask him.

'Was there nothing else in Berlin?' I asked in a whisper. 'At—at the scene of the crime?'

'Crime? Well, yes, I believe you broke into the house where you were discovered, but clearly you were at that time a sick man in need of help.'

246

Could I have dreamed it? The more I thought of that night, the more it did seem like a dream. I could see my fury, and my pain in that room in Berlin, but perhaps that was the most sinister thing that the room contained. Theodor's words had calmed the deep agitation that had been there all the time.

'I see now,' I said, and I did see. I knew that Theodor was right, that it was true. And I too had been right. I was Franz. Now the picture was clear to me. It shifted into focus and a new landscape opened out before me. I had needed Franz to hide behind, to speak for me. But I had allowed him to become too real, too strong.

'So now I'm coming to you with a proposition,' Theodor said. 'And I don't want to hurt you by saying this, but Franz—I mean to say, you as Franz—is a success of a kind never seen before. I mean a once-in-a-generation success. I never even dreamed I could be part of something like this. What I wish to ask is this: when you come out of here, which I trust will be soon, will you keep writing as Franz?'

'But Franz is dead,' I said. And this was also true.

'He is only dead if you want him to be.'

'I do want him to be.'

Although Theodor's words had flattered me, it was true: I was relieved to be rid of Franz. He had exhausted me, burned me up. Without him now I felt light and clean. And yet there was some hesitation. Theodor's words had awakened in me that old desire for fame, for adulation. Even as I sat and declared Franz dead, as I felt the lightness of his absence, I could feel that little flame flickering, and I could almost taste the success that waited for me, so very close. All that I had ever wanted. Almost all.

'But what do we do about the problem of the body?' I asked. 'I mean, I was paying for Gustav by the hour; it costs a fortune. And someone will find out sooner or later.'

Theodor was silent with concentration.

'That's easy,' he said after a long pause. 'You wanted Franz dead? Fine, we agree that Franz is dead. Tuberculosis. He was sent to a sanatorium, but tragically it was too late. That leaves the coast clear for you to be appointed his literary executor.'

'Does anyone else know about this?' I asked. 'About me, I mean?'

'Only you and I, my friend.'

Already I could feel the strength of that hunger growing, filling me with a fierce energy. I was strong and tall, made of burnished steel, hard, shining.

'I need some time to consider,' I said, but I had already decided, and I think he knew it.

28.

*SOON AFTER THEODOR'S VISIT I WAS DISCHARGED. LEAVING THE asylum at last, my thoughts were fixed on Anja. I allowed myself the luxury of dreams. I pictured a life with her, the two of us in her house in the Martinsgasse or some other place—in the country, perhaps. I would work and write; there would be children; she would be a kind mother. I knew that these dreams were a dangerous game, sharp-edged, but, heedless, I gorged myself on them.

The same day that I was discharged I went to Anja's house. I had made the journey so many times in my imagination that when it came to actually walking down the Martinsgasse it was like being in a dream. The curtains were still drawn over the windows, even though it was late morning, and for a moment I felt as if I had travelled back in time and was reliving one of my many fruitless visits of so long ago.

---

* This section of the manuscript is written on unlined letter paper. The pages were folded and found in the centre of the booklet containing the previous section.

The place was full of memories. As I rang the bell I remembered the concierge, my old enemy, who had refused to open the door to me. Now I almost had a feeling of affection for him, but he did not appear, and instead the door was opened by a strange man who waved me through to the stairs indifferently.

Instead of feeling nervous, as I had expected to, I floated up the staircase, euphoric. But this soon faded. The house was darker than I remembered and an unnerving smell lingered in the air. I arrived at the door; the landing on this floor was even darker than the staircase, surely much darker than it used to be. I could hear muffled footsteps in the apartment. My eye was caught by a dark mass attached to the door and at first I could not decipher what it might be, its shape was so indistinct in the gloom. It looked like one of those large bulbous fungi that grow on the trunks of some forest trees. I reached out to touch it, feeling a wave of revulsion as my fingers approached it, expecting a sticky coolness, a spongy cobweb texture, but my fingers instead found the dark shape to be soft and dry; velvet. Specks of dust had stuck to my fingers when I pulled my hand away. I realised that it was the large velvet bow on a wreath, a funeral wreath. I felt a wave of angry jealousy, as for one mad second I thought that the house was in mourning for Franz, but then an even more terrible thing occurred to me: what if it was Anja? The ground wheeled away from me and I had to steady myself against the wall for a moment before I started hammering at the door. Almost immediately the door was opened and the housemaid stood before me, wearing a black armband.

The housemaid's face was blank and she did not appear to recognise me. She turned immediately to usher me through to the living room, before flitting off.

'Anja?' My voice followed her down the corridor, but she seemed not to hear. I paced around the living room, frantic at the thought that I might have lost Anja. I strained my ears for the sound of her voice, and my heart raced until I thought I might choke with anxiety. I forced myself to sit down and slow my breaths. I looked around the room, trying to distract myself. The apartment was completely different to how I had remembered it. In my memory it had seemed so grand, but now it was close and crowded with furniture, dimly lit by a single lamp. This contraction of size was partly caused by the drawn curtains, and I now saw that the mirrors were also shrouded in dark fabric.

The sight of them instantly reminded me of my brother. He had died when I was very young, too young to remember his death at all, but those covered mirrors remain a strong image of my childhood. While Otto's death had not troubled me, the thought of losing Anja almost struck me down. Flashes of my idle dreams of a life with her came to me like taunts, and I had to fight back my tears.

Then came the sound of footsteps approaching the door: a woman's step, slightly clicking, fast and light. The door opened and I saw a pale hand, and I could not tell if it was hers, though I thought of all the times I had watched Anja's hands fluttering and unfolding like white butterflies. Then came an arm, black-clad, and a shoulder, and then there was Anja, in the room.

Unthinking, I launched myself out of the chair towards her, my arms outspread, the tears unchecked, but tears now of relief. I folded her, little Anja, in my arms, and I thought I would die of pleasure from her warm, small body, the smell of her hair. I smiled while the tears still sprang forth. I held her tight and presently noticed a throbbing in her body: sobs. She pulled away then and covered her face with her hands.

I remembered myself, and that she had suffered a death—her mother's, perhaps.

'Little Anja,' I said. 'I'm so sorry.'

She could not speak at first, and only nodded.

'Every time I come into this room,' she said in a choked voice, 'I expect him still to be here, sitting in his chair.' She looked over at the plush armchair by the fire, where Herr Železný had sat at our first meeting. And it was true that an air of expectancy hung about the chair, like the throne of a king awaiting the heir. And that heir—I could not stop the thought—could be me. My mind filled again with dream pictures of a life with her. I was a different man now to the one she had known; stronger, and worthy at last of her affection. It was hard to keep from laughing with joy at the thought that she could still be mine, and keep my countenance suitable for a house of mourning.

The door opened again and a man entered the room. He looked at me with a wary face.

'Tomáš,' Anja said, 'this is my great friend Herr Brod, of whom you have heard so many stories.'

The man nodded, glaring at me.

'Max, this is Herr Liška.'

My face turned to stone. So this was the man. Liška. Tall, muscular, with a clever face, he was worse than my most paranoid imaginings. I strained to keep my expression under control, to look welcoming and pleasant.

He came towards me with his hand outstretched. We shook hands and I could see him sizing me up, taking my measure, while I tried to place him. Was he here to make a bid for Anja, like me? Or had he already done so? And if that were the case, had he won or lost? We seemed to circle each other like two dogs.

'Brod,' he said. 'I've heard a lot about you.'

I did not say, *And I of you*, but only, 'Yes.'

He began pacing the room, his eyes on me the whole time. I tried to glean his position from Anja's attitude. She seemed to make no overtures towards him, but neither did she seem to spurn him.

'But it is a great shame to meet at such a sad occasion,' he said. He stopped in front of Herr Železný's chair. 'Poor Anja has been out of her mind with grief. It's good for her to have her friends around her at such a time.'

Friends? Did he mean he himself?

Then Liška held out his arm, beckoning, and Anja crossed the room to his side. He enfolded her casually in one arm and lightly kissed the top of her hair, his eyes on me. Then he sat down in Herr Železný's chair, leaned back magisterially and regarded me.

Anja went over to the window and pulled back the curtain a small way to look out. Liška and I locked eyes, and I remembered doing the same with Herr Železný on my first visit here, but this time I did not let my eyes fall. How I hated Liška at that moment. After a few seconds Liška rose, saying, 'I'm sure you two have much to talk over. Anja, I must go out, but I'll be back in an hour.'

He nodded to me and left.

My dreams were nothing but dead things now, yet my mind could not yet accept this. I floundered for words, but Anja broke in. 'Max, tell me of yourself. You have been so unwell, I know. I hope you have made a full recovery.'

I cursed myself for not having prepared a cover story to account for the time I had spent in the asylum.

'Yes, I was ill. Trouble with my leg, you know. It plagues me sometimes. But I am now fully recovered. Indeed, I am much stronger than ever before.'

I knew this was feeble.

Anja made a wry face and came over to where I stood. She took one of my hands. 'Max,' she said, 'you know I was there. In Berlin.'

I could hardly make sense of her words.

'Do you remember that night?' she asked.

The details of the night in Berlin came back again and I could still feel the traces of their savagery pulsing through my body.

'I have memories of it. But I could not say I remember what happened.'

'Well,' Anja said, 'you broke into our apartment—we don't know how you got in—and, well, you had a kind of fit.'

How shameful, I thought, for her to have witnessed this. I tried to pull my hand away from hers, but she held on.

'It was Papa who found you. He could see you were in trouble, and he called the doctors. We were so afraid for you.'

'So you knew where I was this whole time?' I asked. 'Why did you never visit me?'

'But I did visit you. Only you didn't know who I was. You were insensible—drugged, I suppose. And then, after I had seen you, well, I became a coward. I felt so ashamed for having been one of those who put you in that place. It wasn't my intention! I thought it would pass in a day or two. And then when it took so long I thought you could never forgive me.'

'Of course I forgive you! Anja, I love you. That's what I came here to tell you. Forget Liška! I suppose you two are engaged.'

It was an effort for those words to pass my lips, and I had to avert my eyes from her nod of assent.

'But I know I love you more than Liška does. I can give you everything you want. Everything! I will do anything for you. You are my queen.'

I turned my eyes back on her face, hoping, hoping against hope, though I knew all was lost. Her eyes were sad. She took up my other hand and held both of my hands together in both of hers. Her skin was as cool and soft as in my dreams.

'Oh, Max, I love you, I do.'

And so I came to hear those words that I had longed for from the moment I first saw her so long ago. But to hear them like this—hollow, pregnant with rejection—was worse than not hearing them at all. I could hear her 'but' hanging in the air long before it reached my ears.

'But, Max, my love for you is the love for a brother.'

I could not speak, and only nodded. I closed my eyes over the tears and heard her say, 'I know this is not the love you want, and I'm sorry. But perhaps this love I can give you is a greater kind of love than the other.'

Was this true?

I turned from her and left the house without saying anything. There was nothing to say. I walked, I do not know where, with no objective other than to keep moving, to keep my muscles propelling my body forward with the same repetitive motion. The familiar buildings pressed in on me, I could feel them leaning over me, surrounding me. People passed by, someone called my name, and then the river was in front of me and I came to a stop. I looked along it, at the other bridges and the weight of all that water flowing quietly past, and my face there, quivering, on the moving surface.

Editor's afterword

A NUMBER OF PHOTOGRAPHS AND PHOTOGRAPHIC NEGATIVES were also uncovered among the Kafka papers. These have been dated, and range from the years 1908 to 1924. Unfortunately, many of them have been severely damaged and are decayed beyond the point of restoration.

Many of the photographs will be immediately familiar to Kafka scholars and enthusiasts, but some hitherto unseen images were also uncovered. Most of the photographs include Kafka, but there are several individuals who are yet to be identified. One photograph, which has been dated to 1911, is proving particularly challenging. It has sustained some water damage, but the image is still discernible. In the photograph, Brod is easily recognisable, and he is pictured with a group of young men whose names are not noted. A note on the back of the photograph, in Brod's handwriting, is the caption: 'Self-portrait 1910.'

During the processing of the papers, the image was sent to various international Kafka scholars* to ascertain whether Kafka was present among the group. The response has caused some confusion, as various scholars have responded with conflicting identifications of Kafka. Professor Wilhelm Herrmann at Berlin's Humboldt University and Professor Eric Goldbaum from Charles University in Prague have both independently identified all the men surrounding Brod in the photograph as Kafka. The matter has been referred to the forensics team for further investigation. The complete collection of images will be made available online.

---

* Professor Wilhelm Herrmann, Dr Helene Barbere-Flores, Professor Axel Stifter, Professor Eric Goldbaum and Dr Ben Staub.

Acknowledgements

I AM GRATEFUL FOR THE GENEROSITY OF *THE AUSTRALIAN*/VOGEL'S Literary Award and Allen & Unwin. I would especially like to thank Annette Barlow and Christa Munns from Allen & Unwin for their efforts in bringing this novel into the world, and also Ali Lavau for her insightful editing and Sandy Cull for the cover design.

I would also like to thank Michal Hartl for guiding me around Max Brod's Prague and unearthing some interesting historical details. In my research for this novel I drew on Derek Sayer's *Prague, Capital of the Twentieth Century: A Surrealist History*; Gustav Janouch's *Conversations with Kafka*; and Josef Cermak's *Through Franz Kafka's Prague*.

Thank you also Annette Castillo, Brooke Silcox and Colin Harte for carefully reading the early drafts and offering such thoughtful suggestions and advice.

Most of all I am indebted to James R. Fleming. James, thank you for your endless encouragement, support and patience: without you, this novel would never have been written.